Praise for Steve Frech

'I absolutely LOVED this book . . .
An unputdownable page-turner of a read'

'This book just pulls you right in . . . I couldn't put it down!'

'One of the best thrillers I've read this year'

'So gripping I just could not stop reading'

'Like riding a roller coaster . . .
Should be on everyone's reading list'

'I burned through this'

'I was hooked from page one'

T0356673

STEVE FRECH lives in Los Angeles. In addition to writing, he produces and hosts the *Random Awesomeness* podcast, an improv-comedy quiz show that has been performed at Upright Citizens Brigade, The Improv, iO West, and Nerdist.

Also by Steve Frech
Dark Hollows
Nightingale House
Deadly Games

The Detective Somerset Series
Secrets to the Grave
Want You Dead

The Good Husband

STEVE FRECH

ONE PLACE. MANY STORIES

This novel is entirely a work of fiction. The names, characters and incidents portrayed in it are the work of the author's imagination. Any resemblance to actual persons, living or dead, events or localities is entirely coincidental.

HQ
An imprint of HarperCollins*Publishers* Ltd
1 London Bridge Street
London SE1 9GF

www.harpercollins.co.uk

HarperCollins*Publishers*
Macken House, 39/40 Mayor Street Upper,
Dublin 1 D01 C9W8

This paperback edition 2024

24 25 26 27 28 LBC 6 5 4 3 2
First published in Great Britain by
HQ, an imprint of HarperCollins*Publishers* Ltd 2024

Copyright © Steve Frech 2024

Steve Frech asserts the moral right to be
identified as the author of this work.
A catalogue record for this book is
available from the British Library.

ISBN: 9780008598587

Printed and Bound in the United States

All rights reserved. No part of this publication may be reproduced, stored in a retrieval system, or transmitted, in any form or by any means, electronic, mechanical, photocopying, recording or otherwise, without the prior permission of the publishers.

This book is sold subject to the condition that it shall not, by way of trade or otherwise, be lent, re-sold, hired out or otherwise circulated without the publisher's prior consent in any form of binding or cover other than that in which it is published and without a similar condition including this condition being imposed on the subsequent purchaser.

For Barb & Steve
7/25/75

Prologue

"Mr. Burcham?"

"Yes?"

"It's Detective Harper. How are you holding up?" His tone is pensive and full of dread.

"Okay, I guess."

"We have the preliminary results of the autopsy," Detective Harper continues.

"Already?" I ask.

That was quick.

"The coroner had some time and took care of it," Detective Harper answers. "If you would like some more time before we discuss our findings, that's understandable."

"No. I want to know what happened."

"Okay," he says, clearly wishing I had taken his suggestion. "But you might want to sit down."

"I am sitting down."

"All right . . . our initial findings suggest that your wife died from an accidental overdose. The lab results came back positive for cocaine."

My heart stops.

In my head, I see Amy's body lying on that table, the necklace resting on her chest, and one question flashes through my mind: Why are the police lying to me about my dead wife?

Chapter 1

"Amy. It's me again. Starting to really worry, here." I have to pause because there's a plane that looks like it's about to land on top of my car. Mercifully, it continues on. "I'm waiting in the parking lot and the website says you landed over an hour ago . . . So . . . just, uh . . . yeah . . . I'm starting to really worry. Call me."

I hang up and stare out over the massive parking lot, watching people drag their luggage to the designated stands so that they can be picked up by one of the prowling buses that will take them to the main terminal.

Come on, Amy. Where are you?

She called me on Friday evening to let me know that she had arrived safely in Boston and that she had checked in to her hotel. She's been to Boston a couple times these past few months. During our call, we said our "good nights" and "I love yous," which is the routine that we've established over twenty years of marriage. Whenever she goes on a business trip, we call each other every evening, if only for a few minutes, just to see how the other's day was, tell each other "I love you," and say "good night."

But that call on Friday was the last I heard from her.

It's now Sunday afternoon.

She didn't call me last night, and she didn't answer her phone

3

when I tried to reach her. It wasn't a big deal, or at least, I didn't think so at the time. She's in a different time zone. The meeting with the potential client could have run long and I know it's causing her a lot of stress. She's on edge, has been for months, but she said she was getting close. So, I assumed that she had simply fallen asleep last night. I left her a message, wishing her a good night, telling her I loved her, and to call me in the morning when she woke up to confirm her flight.

But I didn't hear from her this morning.

There was no call letting me know she had fallen asleep. No call to let me know that she was on her way to the airport. No call to let me know that she had landed and that I should head to the terminal to pick her up.

My thumb nervously taps the steering wheel as another plane roars overhead.

I need to get home— No. Correction: *Amy* and I need to get home.

Tatum, our seventeen-year-old daughter, and Aiden, her nineteen-year-old boyfriend, are hanging out tonight, and there is a standing rule that they are not to be alone in the house together.

I check my phone again and sigh.

She had to have missed her flight, but why wouldn't she message me?

What's going on, Amy?

A few hours of radio silence is one thing. Phones die, people get busy, but this doesn't feel like that.

Something's up.

I pull up the contacts on my phone and scroll down to the number for Malcolm Davis, Amy's boss at Fortis Capital, the hedge fund where she's in charge of recruiting new accounts. Amy gave me his number three years ago when she got the job but was adamant that it was to be used for emergency purposes only. I've never dialed it until now.

Malcolm answers on the third ring.

4

"Hello?"

"Malcolm. Hi. It's Mark Burcham."

"Mark. Hello," he answers in genuine surprise. "It's been a while."

"Yeah. It has."

Malcolm and I have met a few times at holiday parties and functions here and there. He's in his early sixties but has the energy of someone in their thirties. He's athletic and sociable, and has become somewhat of a paternal figure to Amy.

"I'm glad you called," he says, before I can say more. "Have you heard from Amy? She didn't show up for dinner last night."

I blink. Amy didn't say anything about Malcolm going on the trip with her.

"You're in Boston?" I ask.

There's a pause.

"Boston? What would I be doing in Boston?"

"I thought you maybe went with Amy to talk with that potential client."

"A client? What client?"

"The one in Boston. The one Amy's been trying to recruit for—"

"Whoa, whoa, whoa. Hold on, Mark. Maybe we should start over." He takes a breath and employs a calm, controlled manner. "Now, what's going on with Amy? Where is she?"

"She's— She went to Boston again to meet with that client you wanted her to bring in." I attempt to match his calmness, but I can't help speaking faster as I try to explain. "I was wondering if you had spoken to her because I haven't heard from her since Friday night. I'm at the airport, waiting to pick her up. Her plane landed over an hour ago and I still haven't heard anything—"

"Mark," he interjects. There's now a crack in his calming tone. "I have no idea what you're talking about. Amy was supposed to meet with the team last night for dinner here in Los Angeles to discuss new strategies, but she never showed. I don't know of any potential client in Boston."

There's a sudden ball of lead filling my stomach.

"What? No. Malcolm— She's been going to Boston. She said . . . you've been sending her to meet with this guy."

"Did she mention the potential client's name?"

"No. She said it was confidential. She's been there a couple times these past few months. You had to have noticed that she was gone."

He hesitates.

"Malcolm?"

"She has taken some time off," he says, choosing his words carefully. "But she said she was spending time with you and Tatum."

The ball of lead crashes to my feet.

Amy lied to Malcolm? And she lied to me? No. That can't be right. Amy would never do that. Why would she lie? This has to be some sort of misunderstanding. Malcolm has to be confused because this doesn't make any sense. Why would Amy tell me that Malcolm was sending her to Boston and tell Malcolm she was taking time off to spend with me and Tatum? Where would she—?

"Mark?" Malcolm asks, bringing my swirling thoughts to a temporary halt. "Is everything okay?"

". . . I don't know."

There's a long silence, punctuated by the rumble of another incoming plane.

"Did Amy say anything before she left?" he asks. "Was she acting differently in any way?"

"I, uh . . . I'm sorry, Malcolm. I don't know."

"Well, will you please call me the moment you hear from her?"

"Sure," I respond, my voice drifting.

I hang up the phone.

Amy. What's going on?

Chapter 2

"Thank you for calling The Viceroy Hotel. My name is Chris. How may I help you?"

"Hi, Chris. My name is Mark Burcham. My wife had a reservation at your hotel this weekend. She checked in on Friday. I just wanted to make sure she checked out this morning. Her name is Amy Burcham," I say, keeping my eyes on the road to navigate the stop-and-go traffic on my way back to Sherman Oaks.

"Is your name also on the reservation?"

"No. It would have been through her . . . her company, Fortis Capital." Knowing what I know now, I can't help the hesitation. "But her name will be on the reservation," I quickly add.

"I'm sorry, sir, but I can't give out that information."

"Okay, but could you tell me if there is a reservation for Fortis Capital?"

"No. Again, I'm sorry."

"Listen, uh, Curt?"

"It's Chris."

"Chris. Sorry about that, but look, you won't get in any trouble. I promise. I'm just trying to find my wife . . . She's missing."

Speaking the words aloud is terrifying, but she is missing . . .

isn't she? It's been over thirty-six hours since I've heard from her, and I have no idea where she is.

"I'm truly sorry, sir, but I can't give out any sort of information regarding reservations. It's against company policy."

"No. I understand," I say with a sigh. "Thank you."

I hit the button on the steering wheel to end the call while rolling to a stop behind a pickup truck. Lanes of idling cars stretch out before me into the Sepulveda Pass on the 405.

Do I call the cops? What would I say?

"My wife is missing."

"When was the last time you saw her?" the cop will ask, taking notes with a pen and a notepad, I assume.

"I dropped her off at the airport. She told me that she was going to Boston on a business trip, but she told her boss that she was taking time off work to spend more time with me and our daughter."

The cop will stop writing and look up at me. "So, she lied to you and your boss about where she was going?"

". . . Yes," I will have to answer.

The cop will take a second to chew on the end of the pen before replying, "Well, technically, it doesn't sound like she's missing. It sounds like she doesn't want to be found."

I don't know if that's what the cop would say. The truth is that there is no cop. I'm the one who pointed out to myself that it sounds like Amy might not want to be found.

The Amy I know would never do that, but it's the only explanation I can think of.

My brain runs laps inside my head for the entire hour-plus drive back into the valley, without arriving at any other conclusions.

Eventually, I pull into the driveway of our house. It's white with a black roof and trim. The technical term for the style is "industrial farmhouse." I hate that label but love how it looks.

I hit the clicker to open the garage door and pull inside. Taking a moment to collect myself before exiting the car, I glance in the rearview mirror at the Mustang parked in the street as the garage door closes. Normally, that would be a huge problem, but right now, it's the least of my concerns.

I finally get out of the car and walk slowly to the door. Twisting the knob, I enter the kitchen, which opens up to the living room on my right.

There, on the couch, Tatum is reclining against Aiden. The Bad Boy. The Rebel (even though his parents were the ones who bought him the Mustang that's sitting in the street). Aiden, with his dark eyes and disheveled hair. He's every father's worst nightmare, and he's cuddling with my daughter, whom I will forever see as my little girl. The little girl who used to crawl into bed with Amy and me when she was really upset. She would curl up into a ball next to me and I would stroke her hair until she fell asleep.

As you can tell, I'm having a hard time accepting that my little girl isn't a little girl anymore.

"Hey, Dad," Tatum calls over her shoulder without taking her eyes off the show she and Aiden are watching on the television.

"Guys," I say, tossing my keys onto the counter and taking a few steps toward the living room. "You know the rule about being in the house alone."

Aiden's little smirk nearly sets me off before Tatum turns toward me.

"You were supposed to be back two hours ago. Should we have waited outside or something?" She stops and looks behind me. "Where's Mom?"

"She had to stay another night in Boston," I lie. "Last-minute thing."

Tatum considers it for a split second before shrugging, turning back to the TV and resettling against Aiden.

"Hey, we still need to talk about you two being alone in the—"

Tatum groans. "Ugh. Fine. Next time we'll wait. Okay?"

Any other time, I'd point out to them that that rule is there for a reason. A few months ago, Amy and I caught Aiden sneaking out of Tatum's room in the middle of the night. I was ready to tell them that their relationship was over right then and there, especially when Aiden tried to play it off like it was no big deal. Then, Amy pulled me aside and explained that my way would only make things worse. As evidence, she brought up her own father's aversion to me when we started dating, and how it only made me hotter in her eyes. I countered that Aiden didn't need my help in that department but took her point. In the end, Amy and I decided that there were going to be some new rules; first and foremost was that Tatum and Aiden were never to be alone together at our house or Aiden's. Parents always had to be present, and if anything like that were to happen again, we were going to do things my way. Tatum responded with a pouty "Fine." Aiden mumbled, "Whatever," which once again almost caused me to go nuclear, but Amy defused me by placing her hand on my knee.

"Dad," Tatum says from the couch, snapping me out of it. "I said that we'll wait next time."

She's misinterpreting my hesitation as a desire to keep arguing when they want to be alone.

"Okay. Good. I'll, uh . . . I'll be in the den," I mutter. I don't know what I'm going to do in there, but I need to think. I move through the kitchen, but before passing back into the hall, I call out over my shoulder, "Ten o'clock."

"Yes, Dad," Tatum answers.

I can practically hear her eyes roll.

Stepping into the den, I close the door behind me, slide into the chair behind the computer desk . . . and just sit.

I don't like lying to my daughter about her mother, but if I tell Tatum that Amy didn't show up at the airport, she's going to freak out. She'll ask me a ton of questions that I won't have the answers to. I can rationalize lying to her to buy a little time, but what am I going to tell her if I don't hear from Amy soon?

I swivel the chair to look out the window. The sun has dipped

10

below the horizon. Its rays have set the underside of the clouds on fire.

Maybe I should call Liz.

That would certainly be crossing a line. Amy hasn't spoken to her sister in over two years. I doubt she knows where Amy is, but maybe . . .

I take out my phone and pull up Liz's number, but instead of dialing, I only stare at it.

If I call Liz, one of two things will happen: either she'll blow me off and hang up, or she'll freak out and, like Tatum, she'll ask a lot of questions I can't answer.

I quickly stuff my phone back in my pocket.

I'm not calling Liz. Not yet, anyway.

I return my gaze to the window and decide on a simple plan.

If I haven't heard from Amy by the time the sun comes up, I'm calling the cops.

I hope it doesn't come to that. I don't think it will, but having a plan, even a basic one, gives me a little comfort.

I'm sure she'll call.

This is all one big misunderstanding.

It has to be.

Chapter 3

It's two hours later, and I haven't moved from this chair.

The sky outside the window has gone completely dark.

I've checked my phone at least a hundred times and left over a dozen messages on Amy's phone.

The only progress I've made is the realization that I'm in denial, maybe even shock. I thought it was odd when I didn't hear from Amy this morning. That "oddness" changed to worry as I waited in the parking lot at LAX, but there was still a possibility that there was a simple explanation, a dead phone or that Amy was so overwhelmed that she forgot to check in. It was an absurd possibility but one I clung to because I couldn't process the alternative.

The call to Malcolm obliterated that possibility.

Something is definitely wrong.

Amy lied to Malcolm, and she lied to me.

I'm not angry. More than anything, I'm confused.

Amy and I are partners. We're best friends, and lovers. I can't imagine my life without her. We wrote our own vows for our wedding. I told Amy that I didn't know what I was living for, and then we met, and I told her, "It was always you." She said she fell in love with me all over again, right then and there. We've built a life together. We've raised an amazing daughter. Of course, like any other couple, we have our ups and downs, but we worked on how to deal with the downs. When we fight, it's never about winning. It's about helping the other understand your point of view, even if they don't agree. That requires trust and there is no one in this world I trust more than Amy. It's the only reason we've gotten this far.

Which is why there has to be a reason she told me one thing and Malcolm another.

But the shock and numbness of denial are being taken over by the fear and dread at the realization that something is horribly wrong.

Another check of my phone lets me know that Amy hasn't texted or called and that it's ten past ten.

I push myself out of the chair and head to the door to announce that it's time for Aiden to go home, but stop when I hear voices in the kitchen and then footsteps proceeding down the hall to the front door. A moment later, the door opens and then closes.

At least I don't have to play the curfew police, tonight.

I step out of the den and into the hall to begin my nightly ritual of closing up the house for the night. I check to make sure that the windows are locked and the lights are off. I turn off the TV in the living room, which they left on. After locking the back door, I go to the fireplace and make sure that the gas is off. The pilot light broke last week, so I've added it to my nightly routine. As I double-check to make sure the gas is all the way off, there is the roar of Aiden's Mustang in the street. My jaw involuntarily clenches. The neighbors have assured me that it's a sound they *love* at ten in the evening. The growl of the Mustang is still audible as the front door opens and closes once again, and I hear Tatum's footsteps climb the stairs to her bedroom.

I finish my rounds and arrive at the front door. I enter the code on the security panel and it replies with the three sustained beeps to let me know that the system is armed.

13

My hand goes to turn the deadbolt but stops.

There's something unnatural about this, as though I'm closing the castle gates and leaving Amy outside to fend for herself with whatever is happening.

The fear and anxiety are speeding up. It feels like that moment when you realize you're having a nightmare and begin frantically to tell yourself to wake up.

I try to shake it off as I head upstairs. Walking down the hall to our room, I stop outside the closed door to Tatum's bedroom.

For a moment, I contemplate telling her everything, but I once again imagine how upset she'd be and the questions she'll ask that I can't answer. No good comes from telling her right now.

"Good night, Tatum," is all I can manage.

"Good night, Dad," she answers through the door in the same tone and cadence that she always uses.

I continue on to the bedroom.

My brain is on autopilot as I change and brush my teeth.

There's a faint voice in my head.

Mark, what are you doing? You need to wake up.

Getting into bed hammers it home even more. I had no problem sleeping alone in this bed last night, but now, Amy's supposed to be here.

Mark . . .

Staring up at the ceiling, my mind is spinning in circles.

That voice in my head is growing louder, trying to break through the last of the shock and numbness.

Mark, you have to wake up.

My mind is in such a fog that it's another hour of staring at the ceiling before I realize I've forgotten to turn off the bedroom light. I get up, flip the switch, and get back into bed, but an hour passes, and my eyes are still wide open.

Wake up!

I begin sweating. The fear and anxiety are front and center. The numbness is gone.

Mark! Wake up, right now!

Something snaps. I'm awake, not just physically but mentally.

I need to act. Something is clearly wrong. Amy could be in danger.

I have to call the cops.

Throwing off the covers, I sit up and snap on the bedside lamp.

As I reach for the phone, it begins to glow and vibrate against the table.

I grab it and stare at the caller ID.

I don't recognize the number but hit the answer button. "Hello?"

"Mr. Burcham?" a man's voice asks.

"Yes?"

"I'm Detective Jeff Harper with the Los Angeles Police Department. I'm sorry to call so late, but—"

"Is it Amy? Is she okay?" I ask, breathlessly. My hands are shaking so bad, I almost drop the phone.

"I'm afraid we need you to come downtown. I'm going to send a car to pick you up."

"No. Tell me where she is."

Chapter 4

After pressing the green plastic button with a crack running through it, the machine buzzes and spits out a ticket. I pull it from the dispenser slot and the arm of the parking gate rises.

There are plenty of open spaces on the first level, but the signs say that they are reserved for staff. I wind my way up to the second level, which is nearly empty. I pull into a spot near the stairwell and walk back down.

Emerging onto the street, I'm struck by a cold breeze. I forgot my jacket. It was all I could do to pull on a pair of jeans.

I didn't wake Tatum. Instead, I left her a hastily written note on the kitchen table, saying I had to go out. I hope she doesn't read it. I hope she's still asleep.

Even at three in the morning, the sound of the traffic on the 5 freeway, which is only a block away, is a steady drone of hissing tires, punctuated by the occasional high-pitched whine of a motorcycle.

I begin walking, keeping my gaze on the sidewalk to avoid the eyes that peer out at me from the handful of filthy, ramshackle tents that are pressed up against the rusted chain-link fence to my right.

"You lookin' for something?" a woman asks, standing next to a shelter consisting of a tarp and two shopping carts. She has to be in her fifties with cropped, matted hair. She nods to an opening in the tarp that serves as the entrance. "I got it."

I return my stare to the sidewalk and continue on to the brick-and-concrete building. It's a discordant mix of architecture that I can't pin down, but a lighted plastic sign above its fence is clear.

County of Los Angeles
Department of
Medical Examiner/Coroner
Law and Science Serving the Community

I'm only vaguely aware of my feet carrying me down a walkway and up the steps to a large wooden door.

Through the glass panes, I spot a uniformed police officer scrolling through his phone behind a plexiglass shield in a booth just inside the lobby. He looks up, sees me, leans forward, and presses a button on the desk.

A battered speaker mounted next to the door comes to life.

"We're closed," he says, his words fuzzy and crackling.

I get it. It's cold and I'm wearing this old T-shirt that I planned on sleeping in. I don't look too different from the people I just passed on the sidewalk.

I press the button below the speaker and hold it down as I reply.

"I'm Mark Burcham. Detective Harper called and said I needed to—"

The officer nods, picks up the phone from the cradle on the desk, speaks a few words into it, hangs up, and then hits another button.

The door buzzes so loudly, I inadvertently take a step back. There's the sound of a lock being thrown back and the officer beckons me to enter.

I pull the handle, causing the heavy door to swing outward, and step inside.

The lobby is warm and there's the faint whiff of antiseptic.

The officer in the booth motions to a wooden bench built into the wall.

"Have a seat. Detective Harper will be up in a minute."

I mutter something between "thanks" and "okay."

As I go to sit, I notice the parking validation machine on a wooden shelf next to the booth and make a mental note to get my ticket stamped before I leave.

Oh my God.

What the hell is wrong with me? Why am I thinking about parking validation at a time like this?

I shake my head and sit.

The bench is too narrow, forcing me to keep my back ramrod straight.

The officer has already gone back to his phone, seemingly forgetting about my presence.

This place has the feel of a high school mixed with touches of art deco you see in old noir films, but the illusion is ruined by the harsh fluorescent lights overhead. Faint echoes reach the lobby from the halls that branch off to the left and right, but I don't see anyone, as if the building is haunted, which makes a perverse sort of sense.

An elevator chimes from the hallway to my right. Moments later, a man emerges into the lobby. He's about my age, maybe a little older, tall, well-built, and with a buzzcut to match. The officer nods to me and the man turns as I stand.

"Mr. Burcham?" the man asks.

"Yeah."

He steps over and solemnly shakes my hand. "I'm Detective Harper." His grip is hard, but his features are compassionate. "Follow me, please," he says, motioning back toward the hall from which he emerged.

18

I follow his lead as he guides me to the elevator, which is still waiting from his arrival. We step inside.

The interior is large and there are doors at the front and back, like the kind you would find at a hospital.

"Any trouble finding the place?" he asks in an attempt at small talk as he hits the button for the level below.

"No," I answer, mechanically.

"Any trouble from our 'neighbors'?"

I shake my head.

"Good, but all the same, I'm going to have Officer Garland accompany you to your car when we're done. He's the guy in the lobby."

"Okay."

The elevator comes to a stop and opens to a hallway lined with doors. There are more fluorescent lights overhead that reflect off the black-and-white linoleum floor.

"Right this way," Detective Harper says, stepping out of the elevator.

I fall in behind him and steal glances into some of the rooms as we pass. Most are dark, but the ones that are illuminated have the look of old high-school science labs.

I continue following Detective Harper as he turns down a side hall and stops outside a door marked "Viewing 4."

He turns to me.

"Listen, Mr. Burcham, we don't necessarily have to do it this way."

I blink. "What do you mean? I thought I had to—"

"Well, yes. I'm sorry. I should have been clearer. We do need you to do this, but we don't have to necessarily do it *this* way. We can show you a photo if you would prefer."

It takes a moment to process what he's saying.

"No," I answer. "I need to see."

"You're sure?"

I nod.

"Okay," he says with obvious reluctance. "Now, this isn't going to be easy. It never is. There's no way around that. The best thing to do is to get this first part over with. One question. That's all, and we'll take it from there. Understand?"

I nod again, but none of this is real.

It can't be.

"In here," Detective Harper says, opening the door for me.

I step inside.

The room is small, narrow, and dark. Most of the light is coming through the large window that takes up most of a wall. Through the window is a nearly identical room to the one that I'm standing in, except that it holds a gurney with a familiar shape resting upon it, covered by a sheet. A man in his late twenties, wearing a lab coat, waits at the head of the gurney.

Detective Harper enters the room and stands at my side.

"One last time," he says, gently. "Are you sure?"

My knees are starting to give, and my pulse is erratic but I'm able to whisper, "Yes."

Detective Harper looks at the guy through the window and makes a subtle motion with his hand.

The man in the other room lifts the sheet and slowly pulls it back.

Lying on the table is the body of a woman.

Her face is serene, as if she's sleeping, except for the lips, which have turned a darkish-blue.

"Mr. Burcham," Detective Harper says. "Do you recognize this woman?"

It's the most surreal question I've ever been asked.

I know every inch of this woman. Her hair, her neck, her shoulders, her breasts, her arms, her hands, even the wedding ring on her finger. There's even the necklace. The necklace with the small rose pendant. She wore it often, even though it made her incredibly sad.

Yes. I recognize this woman.

20

What I don't recognize is what she's wearing, which is why I'm seeing most of her body: a scarlet lace bra, matching underwear and stockings, and black stiletto heels.

"Mr. Burcham?"

"That's Amy . . . That's my wife."

Chapter 5

"She was found in an alley on Skid Row. It appears she had been there for a day or two. Someone found her and flagged down a cop."

Detective Harper and I are sitting in a small office a few doors down from the viewing room.

"Skid Row? What was she doing on Skid Row?" I ask. "And whose clothes are those?"

"That's what she was wearing when we found her," he replies after taking a moment to bite his lower lip. He then consults his notes. "We also found her purse, but it was picked clean, which isn't a surprise for where she was found. The only thing they left was her ID. That's how we knew to contact you."

"They left her ID?"

"I've seen it before. The ID is worthless to anyone who found the body and took her things. All the ID would do is prove that they were there, if they were caught with it."

"But why wouldn't they take her ring? Or her necklace?"

He bites his lip, again, and shrugs. "I have no idea. The ring may have been too hard to get off. As far as the necklace, who knows? It may have fallen behind her and they didn't see it. The chain is pretty thin. We might not ever know."

I nod and look down at the floor.

Amy, what are you doing here? What's going on? Why are you—?

"—time you saw your wife?"

"What?" I ask, snapping back to the present.

"When was the last time you saw your wife?" Detective Harper repeats, jotting in his notes.

"Uh . . . Friday. Around noon. I dropped her off at the airport. She was flying to Boston for a work thing."

"What line of work was she in?"

Was.

His use of the past tense feels wrong, but it isn't. After all, I've just seen Amy lying dead on that table.

"Mr. Burcham?" he asks, looking up from his notepad.

"She works— worked at a hedge fund."

"What did she do there?"

"She was in charge of bringing in new accounts."

He nods, scribbles, and continues. "And yourself?"

"Me?"

"Yes. Line of work?"

"Oh. I'm— I'm a stay-at-home dad. We have a daughter. Tatum. She's graduating high school this year."

God, I hope that Tatum is still asleep. What am I going to say to her? How am I going to tell her that her mother is g—?

"—with your wife?"

Again, I'm snapped back to the present.

"I'm sorry, detective. What did you ask me?"

He dismisses my apology with a sympathetic wave of his hand. "It's okay. This is a lot to take in. I was asking if that was the last time you spoke with your wife."

"No. She called me Friday night to let me know that she had checked in to her hotel."

"In Boston?"

My automatic response of yes catches in my chest. She called

23

me from her cell phone, but after speaking with Malcolm, I realize that I don't know where she was. I assumed that she was in Boston because I had dropped her off at the airport and that's what she told me, but maybe she was already back in Los Angeles. And for some reason, I'm not telling Detective Harper that Amy was lying to me and her boss.

My bewilderment gets the better of me.

"I don't understand," I say, pressing a hand against my forehead, attempting to stave off a growing migraine. "You said that she had been in the alley for at least a day?"

He nods.

"So, why would she get on a plane Friday only to come back the next day?"

It's a question more for myself, but Detective Harper obviously has a thought because he stops writing and chews on the end of the pen.

"What?" I ask.

He's about to answer but stops.

"Detective?"

"Look, Mr. Burcham, it's no use speculating at this point—"

"Tell me," I insist, unable to keep my voice from rising.

He sighs. "Mr. Burcham, it's more likely that your wife never left Los Angeles."

"What?" I ask, almost laughing in disbelief. "No. She was on American Airlines, flight four-thirty-nine, nonstop to Boston. I dropped her off at the airport."

"Did you see her get on the plane?"

"Of course not."

There's that lip bite, again.

The migraine notches upward.

I know that Amy lied to me about the potential client in Boston, but for some reason, it never occurred to me that she didn't get on a plane.

Of course, Detective Harper is right.

Amy's lie has just become much deeper.
She not only lied to me about meeting a client.
She lied about going anywhere, at all.

Chapter 6

"Are you sure you're okay to drive?" Detective Harper asks as we step into the lobby. "You can leave your car here overnight and pick it up tomorrow."

"I'm okay," I reply.

I'm not sure if I am, but it feels like that's what I should say. I need to get home before Tatum wakes up. I need to be there for our daughter.

Detective Harper had some more questions. They were general in nature, and I answered them as best as I could. I thought that I was starting to feel calm, clear-headed, and in control enough to drive, but that was thirty minutes ago, and the nausea and shakiness are coming in cycles.

"You're *sure*?" Detective Harper asks, again.

"Yeah."

"And you don't want Officer Garland to escort you to your car?"

From his booth, Officer Garland gives a look that says he'll do what Detective Harper orders, but he would rather continue scrolling through his phone.

"I'm okay," I respond.

Detective Harper nods. "All right. Get home safe and, like I said, if you or your daughter need to speak to someone, we can put you in touch with excellent counselors."

"Thank you," I answer numbly, still thinking about the image of Amy on that table when suddenly, I'm hit by a thought. "Can I please have her ring? And the necklace?"

Detective Harper grimaces. "I'm sorry, but we need to hold on to both of them for a few days. They might have evidence, like fingerprints. I'll make sure to get them back to you as soon as we're done with the tests and the autopsy results. In the meantime, if you think of anything else, you give me a call."

He hands me a card.

"I will," I say with a nod and stuff the card in my pocket. "Thank you, detective."

He shakes my hand, turns, and heads back to the elevator, leaving me standing in the lobby.

Autopsy.

They're going to cut Amy open and take her apart.

As if finding her nearly naked in an alley wasn't enough, Detective Harper is going to slice her up.

And for that, I just *thanked* him?

A wave of nausea rips through me.

Thank you, detective. Thank you for desecrating my wife's body. Thank you for making all of this worse.

Are they going to open her skull?

In my head, I see Amy lying on the table with that serene face staring upwards while the whirling blade slowly inches toward her forehead. Those eyes. Those blue lips. Those lips that I kissed on Friday, while we stood on the curb outside LAX. That kiss, which is now the last of a thousand kisses.

Amy's gone.

A million images race through my brain. A million memories. Twenty years of marriage. Of milestones and frustrations and the greatest moments of our lives that we navigated together. The memories crest and crash against those two words: Amy's gone.

Amy can't be gone.

In a few hours, she's going to call me and explain that her

phone died. She'll tell me that the meeting with the potential client went great and that she can't wait to be home and to sit down to dinner with Tatum and me, where the three of us will—

A horn blasts behind me.

I'm sitting in my car at the exit to the parking garage. The grime-flecked display on the terminal outside my window is asking for my ticket.

How did I get here?

I don't remember walking to my car. I don't remember getting in and starting the engine, and I don't remember driving down to the lower level to arrive here.

The rusty van in my rearview mirror lays on the horn again and a voice calls out from the open driver's-side window.

"Fucking go!"

The voice echoes off the concrete floor, ceiling, and pillars.

After waving a sheepish apology, I fish out my parking ticket.

I forgot the validation.

I feed the ticket into the machine. It informs me that I owe twelve dollars. I fumble with my credit card, insert it into the blinking slot, and wait.

Suddenly, I'm no longer worried about the guy behind me. I'm worried about the fact that I can't remember exiting the building and arriving here.

The terminal spits out my card. I grab it and toss it onto the passenger seat.

The arm on the parking gate rises, and I wait for two cars to pass before—

Tap-tap-tap.

I nearly scream.

"Can you help me out?" a man with a filthy beard and drawn face asks, as he stands outside my window.

I shift my eyes forward, press my foot on the gas, and pull out onto the street.

Chapter 7

There it is.

The sound I've been dreading: footsteps in the upstairs hall. Tatum's awake.

Somehow, I made the drive home. I don't remember much about it, just like I don't know how I navigated the parking garage. The last thing that I can recall was parking in the driveway, coming inside, and sitting in the dark at the kitchen table.

Outside, the sky has gone from black to purple to pink and now light blue.

I thought about waking Tatum but decided against it. I want her to have one more sleep, maybe one more dream about her mother that won't devastate her upon waking.

I still don't know what to tell her. Where Amy was found? What she was wearing? That she lied to me? To us?

I don't even know how Amy died.

So, I've been sitting here for what feels like an eternity that has somehow passed in the blink of an eye. More than once I've told myself that I'm dreaming, that I need to open my eyes so that I can find myself in our bed upstairs with Amy asleep by my side. I'll wake her up and tell her all about my nightmare so that we can laugh about it and then fall back to sleep.

But I'm awake. This is real.

And now, Tatum is awake, and I have to tell her that her mother is gone. That will seal it; this isn't a dream.

It's a nightmare.

I remain motionless, listening to Tatum getting ready for school; the water runs through the pipes in the wall to the shower upstairs. There's the quiet as she stands in front of the mirror, putting on the makeup that I am not a fan of. Then, the footsteps back to her room as she goes to get dressed. I've listened to this routine so many times, I know at what point in the process I should start making breakfast, because if I don't, she's going to grab some junk food from the pantry, but my legs won't move and my thoughts are too heavy to stand.

There is the rapid *thud-thud-thud* as she descends the stairs. Tatum hops off the landing and onto the hardwood floor of the foyer.

She emerges into the kitchen, tapping away on her phone. She's the spitting image of Amy with her blue eyes, raven hair, upswept nose, and strong jawline.

She doesn't see me at first. She's too focused on the screen. She takes a few steps toward the pantry before she finally notices me sitting at the table, which brings her to a stop.

"Dad?"

I nod to the chair across the table. "I need you to sit down, sweetheart."

She rolls her eyes. "Dad, if this is about Aiden and me being alone in the house, I said that we won't—"

"Tatum . . ." I nod, again.

She slowly makes her way to the table, keeping her eyes on me as she lowers herself into the chair.

I open my mouth to speak but nothing happens. The moment's arrived and I still don't know what to say.

"Dad?" she asks, her voice tight, sensing that whatever is wrong is way bigger than Aiden.

I can't do this. I can't tell her. It's not even real to me yet, so how can I tell my little girl that—

"Dad? What's wro—?"

"Mom's gone," I hear myself say.

The world changes in an instant.

There was our life before this moment and there will be our life after, and the two will be totally different.

Tatum's forehead creases and her eyes narrow.

"Yeah. I know. You said that she had to stay another night in Boston or something."

"No, sweetheart. She didn't. Last night, I got a call from the police. They found her body downtown. I had to go the coroner and identify her."

That's all I'm going to tell her. Everything else can wait until I know more.

Tatum blinks. "What are you—? . . . This is a joke, right?"

"No. I'm sorry. It's not."

Tatum waits for some sort of punchline that isn't coming. Over the span of a few seconds, her expression goes from waiting to pleading. "No . . . Come on, Dad . . . You're messing with me."

My refusal to answer proves I'm not.

The horror sets in and her eyes begin to well with tears.

". . . Dad? . . . Please . . ."

"I'm sorry, Tatum."

Her mouth hangs open. She begins looking around, unsure of what to focus on. Her face contorts in pain and her body begins to tremble.

I'm already out of my chair.

I move around the kitchen table and wrap my arms around her as she begins to wail uncontrollably.

31

Chapter 8

Tatum is asleep upstairs in her room.

There was no way to calm her down and I didn't really try.

I simply held her while we both sobbed.

She alternated between anger, confusion, and disbelief. She begged me to tell her that I was joking. She promised that she wouldn't be mad, but I had to stop saying that her mother was dead.

"How are they sure it was Mom?" she frantically asked. "I mean, did you call—?"

"Tatum," I said, firmly but gently. "It was her. She was wearing her wedding ring . . . and her necklace."

The fact that she was wearing the necklace has the same effect on Tatum that it had on me. It was the confirmation that Amy was gone.

It set off another round of Tatum crying while I held her.

She kept insisting that it wasn't Mom. She kept insisting that I was lying to her and I needed to stop. When I calmly explained once again that I wasn't lying, it set off a flash of rage. She shoved me away and ran upstairs. She slammed her bedroom door and locked it. We've had a standing rule since she was six that, with the exception of the bathroom, we do not lock doors in the house.

"Tatum, open the door," I said, standing in the hallway.

She only continued to cry.

I insisted a few more times but received no response.

"Tatum," I finally said. "I'm not going to come in. All I ask is that you keep it unlocked, okay?"

There was a pause, a shuffling of feet, and then, the click of the lock.

"Thank you," I said.

Through the door, I could hear her hiccup, sigh, and move away.

True to my word, I made no attempt to open the door. I sat on the floor in the hallway, my back to the wall, listening to Tatum sob. Eventually her sobs became a whimper, and finally the heavy breath of sleep. That's when I somewhat went back on my promise and poked my head inside.

She was asleep on the bed, her arms wrapped around the pillow, and her makeup streaked from tears.

I closed the door, went downstairs, sat on the couch, and looked around, absorbing the life Amy and I had built.

We bought this house ten years ago for $1.75 million. Never did I think I'd live in a million-dollar home, but Amy's hedge fund was knocking almost every deal out of the park and her star was on the rise.

We both loved the house, but I balked at the price tag.

"Mark," she told me, "this is what it's all been for."

She was right, of course.

Amy is the go-getter, the risk-taker. I think raising Tatum as a stay-at-home dad has made me a little more conservative and, together, Amy and I make the perfect team. I can't count the number of times over the years I had stopped myself to marvel at how lucky I've been. The fact that Amy and I found each other seems impossible. It couldn't have been chance.

And here I am, referring to her as if she's still here. I have to get used to using terms like "*was* the go-getter" and "*made* the perfect team."

33

I absent-mindedly wipe at the tears that have started rolling down my cheeks.

Part of me wants to do something normal, to grasp onto some sliver of mundane. I need to go to the store to get something to make dinner. I need to replace the solar-powered lanterns in the walkway. They're way too weak. I need to fix the pilot light in the fireplace. Amy said that the house was going to blow up. It was a joke I didn't appreciate.

But as much as I'd like to pretend nothing has changed, I have to acknowledge what's happened. Putting everything off is only going to make things worse.

I should be making phone calls. The only one I've made was to Tatum's school, after I came back downstairs, to let them know she wouldn't be coming in for a while. I didn't say why.

I have to call Liz and let her know that any attempt at a reconciliation is now gone forever.

How do I start that conversation? Where do I begin?

Maybe I shouldn't call her just yet. Maybe I should wait until I know a little bit more.

Until then, I'm just going to sit here.

An hour later and my phone rings.

"Mr. Burcham?"

"Yes?"

"It's Detective Harper. How are you holding up?" His tone is pensive and full of dread.

"Okay, I guess."

Okay, I guess?

No, I'm not "okay." Why am I lying to somehow make this easier for *him*?

"We have the preliminary results of the autopsy," Detective Harper continues.

"Already?" I ask.

They only found her a few hours ago. How in the hell did they—?

"The coroner had some time and took care of it," Detective Harper answers. "If you would like some more time before we discuss our findings, that's understandable."

"No. I want to know what happened."

"Okay," he says, clearly wishing I had taken his suggestion. "But you might want to sit down."

"I am sitting down."

"All right . . ." There's a pause, and I imagine he's doing that thing where he bites his lip just before he gives bad news. "Our initial findings suggest that your wife died from an accidental overdose. The lab results came back positive for cocaine."

My heart stops.

In my head, I see Amy's body lying on that table, the necklace resting on her chest, and one question flashes through my mind: Why are the police lying to me about my dead wife?

"Bullshit," I say, barely above a whisper.

There's a pause.

"Listen, Mr. Burcham," he says, a little rattled by my interjection. "I know that it can be hard to process information like this when it's someone we—"

"And I'm telling you that information is bullshit. Amy would *never* use cocaine."

"Well, as I said, the tests may show that it was some other substance that—"

"You are not listening to me, detective."

"Please, Mr. Burcham. I need you to settle down. You're upset and that's completely understandable. When someone hears something like this, the initial reaction is always disbelief and sometimes, even anger."

"Detective Harper, my wife didn't die of a drug overdose—"

"Mr. Burcham, I am only stating what we believe based on the evidence we have—"

"—and I'm telling you you're wrong because she was wearing that goddamn necklace!"

". . . I beg your pardon?"

"That necklace. The one you found on my wife. Back in college, Amy had a friend. Her name was Colleen Gardner. Colleen was shy and my wife was the extrovert." I've heard this story so many times from Amy, that it rolls out of me as if it were my own. "At the beginning of their sophomore year, they went to a frat party and the two of them got split up. Colleen was trying to come out of her shell. Some guys offered her cocaine. She wanted to fit in, so she tried it, but it had been laced with methamphetamines. She and the three other guys were taken to the hospital. The guys pulled through, but Colleen had a heart attack and died. Amy never got over that. She blamed herself for not staying with Colleen at the party. That necklace? That was Colleen's necklace. She was wearing it the night she died. Amy asked Colleen's parents if she could have it. So, I'm telling you, there's no way on God's green earth that my wife overdosed on anything."

Every time Amy told that story, I tried to get her to see that Colleen's death wasn't her fault. She wouldn't listen. She also told the story to Tatum to warn her of the dangers of drugs. Amy smoked cigarettes for a time, and she occasionally drank, but anything beyond that was a massive red line she wouldn't go near. Over the years, she told the story less and less, but still wore the necklace, and I knew that she remembered, because I knew my Amy. There is no way she overdosed while wearing Colleen's necklace.

"Mr. Burcham," Detective Harper says, after a long pause. "I understand your skepticism, but I'm merely telling you what is on the toxicology report that I'm holding in my hand."

"Run it again."

"We did. It's standard procedure that when there is enough evidence, we'll run the test twice. It confirms that at the time of your wife's death, there were high levels of cocaine in her system."

"Utter bullshit," I scoff.

"I'm sorry to have to be the one to tell you, but—"

"Oh yeah?" I interrupt. "What else do your tests say?"

Silence.

The realization hits me.

There's something more and whatever it is, is worse than the cocaine.

"Detective?"

"Mr. Burcham, maybe we should wait until you've had some more time to process everything."

"What else did you find?" I ask, no longer scoffing.

"There are indications that . . ."

His voice trails off.

"Detective Harper?"

"This really can wait until you've—"

"No. It can't," I snap.

He sighs. "Mr. Burcham, did you and your wife have sex before you dropped her off at the airport?"

"No. We didn't. We hadn't had sex since . . ."

I try to remember the last time Amy and I had sex. I think it was last week. We couldn't sleep. It was three in the morning, so we decided to have a little fun, but we had to be quiet because we didn't want to wake Tatum . . . but he's not asking when was the last time Amy and I had sex. He's asking if we had sex before I dropped her off at the airport.

"Why are you asking me that?" I ask.

There's another pause that could be measured with a calendar.

"There is evidence that your wife had sex with someone shortly before she died."

Chapter 9

"The 405, the bane of our existence," I said, lifting my foot off the brake to allow the BMW to slowly roll forward.

The Sepulveda Pass was its usual congested self.

I stole a sideways glance at Amy.

She was staring out the window at the hillsides, her mind a world away.

"Hey. You okay?" I asked.

She turned to me as though she had forgotten that I was in the car with her.

"What?"

I smiled. "Hi. Welcome back."

"I'm sorry. I'm out of it."

"The trip?"

"Yeah." She sighed, running a hand through her hair.

"Surprised these still weigh so much on your mind. You've done enough of them."

"Malcolm really wants me to land this guy. It could be a ton of money for the company," she said. "I'm hoping this will be the last trip."

I reached over and put a hand on her thigh. "It'll be over before you know it and we can get back to planning that trip."

She smiled at me. "You still thinking Italy?"

"Damn right."

"Four-star hotels?"

"Mostly four stars, but we'll find a Fairfield Motel, just to stay humble."

"Hmmm," she mused before turning back to the window.

It wasn't my greatest joke, but I thought it was a little funnier than a "hmmm."

Our twenty-third anniversary was approaching. We took occasional weekend trips to Napa, but it had been too long since we had escaped for any substantial period of time. Amy had been going nonstop for three years, ever since she had gotten the job as head of new investment development at Fortis Capital. She was working her ass off, and while Amy thrived under pressure, I could see the burnout creeping in. The last two years had been exceptionally brutal on her. We were dealing with it, constantly checking in to see what the other needed and I came to the conclusion that what we needed was a vacation. We were going to take a few weeks, maybe even a month, away from everything. Once Tatum went off to college, we were on a plane to Italy to celebrate the raising of our daughter and the life we created for ourselves.

"Dammit," Amy suddenly hissed.

"What's up?"

"I forgot to pack that green sundress."

"A sundress? For Boston at this time of year?"

She shrugged. "I like that it has a pocket."

I shook my head. "You're weird."

She laughed. "Mmmmmm. Pockets. You should get me another sundress with pockets for Christmas."

"Great. Thanks for the ten-months-in-advance heads-up."

"You're welcome," she said, turning back to the window.

The Getty Museum loomed overhead at the top of the hill.

It's a world-class museum housed in a complex of structures that offers a stunning view of the city to the east and the ocean to the west. Amy and I used to go there often, but I couldn't remember the last time we had been. It was one of those things in Los Angeles that we now took for granted.

I stole another glance at her and hoped, as she said, that this would be her last trip to Boston. I did a mental tally in my head. This would be her fourth in the past month and a half. I had no doubt that she was tired, but I couldn't help feeling there was something more behind those heavy eyes.

"Just promise me something," Amy said, still gazing out at the hills.

"Sure."

"Don't do anything crazy while I'm gone."

"Like what?"

"I don't know. Like get a tattoo or something."

"A tattoo?"

"Yeah."

"I can't promise that. You know how badly I want that butterfly on the small of my back," I replied, attempting to play along with the joke. Amy had to know that I was the last person in the world to get a tattoo.

"What have you got against tattoos?" I asked when she didn't laugh.

She shrugged, again. "I never trust guys with tattoos."

"Okay . . . Good to know."

She continued to stare out the window.

"You sure you're okay?" I asked.

"Yeah," she said with a sigh that hinted otherwise.

I pulled up to the curb outside Terminal 5 at LAX.

The nearby cop who was tasked with keeping the traffic moving was already timing us.

I popped open the trunk and hopped out of the car. I walked

around, pulled out Amy's suitcase, and set it on the curb as she closed the car door behind her.

"Thank you," she said.

We kissed while surrounded by an atonal symphony of blaring horns and squealing brakes. All the while, I could feel the eyes of the traffic cop watching us.

We ended our kiss and looked into each other's eyes, our faces inches apart.

"It was always you," I said, which was our customary send-off.

Amy smiled sadly.

"It was always you . . ." she said.

Her words had a sense of finality, as if she were truly saying good-bye.

"Okay. That did it," I said. "Amy, what's going on?"

"I'm fine," she replied, but she still couldn't shake that sadness.

"Amy, come on. You're really starting to worry m—"

THWEEEEEEEEEP!!!

The shrill blast from the cop's whistle nearly split our eardrums. He motioned for us to wrap it up.

"I'll call you when I land," Amy said, stepping away and grabbing the handle of her suitcase.

"You better."

We shared one last peck before I walked back around the car. I got in the driver's seat and looked over to see her striding toward the entrance to the terminal.

The doors slid open, and she disappeared inside without looking back.

THWEEP! THWEEP! THWEEP!

I faced forward.

The cop was looking right at me, urgently motioning for me to pull through.

Sorry, I mouthed and started the car.

Is that how it happened?

Sitting in traffic on my way to Fortis Capital, I'm replaying the last time I saw Amy alive in my mind.

Did she look that tired? Was she really that distracted? Was she behaving that strangely when I dropped her off? Or am I imagining it, now that I know she was lying to me.

And I have to accept that she was lying.

She never got on that plane.

Detective Harper is right about that, but there is no way that she overdosed on cocaine. Someone either made her take it or the test is wrong.

But that brings me to the bigger issue, which is that Amy slept with someone before she died.

I was sick to my stomach when Detective Harper told me. I couldn't breathe. The absurdity of Amy overdosing was now overshadowed by the suggestion that Amy was having an affair.

And just like the overdose, that's simply not possible.

I would have noticed if something was wrong. Amy used to say that I knew her better than she knew herself. There's no way I wouldn't know that she was having an affair . . . or am I deluding myself?

Am I in denial?

There's evidence. There's *physical* evidence of narcotics in her system, and there's also physical evidence that she slept with someone shortly before she died.

And she lied to me and to her coworkers.

Could I have grown so complacent that I totally missed or maybe even ignored the signs that Amy had met someone else. That she could have—?

A horn blasts behind me.

I look up to see that there's twenty yards of space between me and the car ahead.

I twist in my seat to look out the back at the guy in the Mercedes who is gesturing for me to go.

Staring at him, I remember the van from the parking garage this morning, and yell, "FUCK OFF!"

Chapter 10

The tall woman in the power suit standing next to me in the elevator is pretending that my appearance is completely normal, as though sleep-deprived men with haggard hair and stubble mixing with people wearing thousand-dollar suits in this building is part of her every day.

I don't care.

Nor did I care a few moments ago when I barreled past the receptionist in the lobby. I couldn't remember his name, but I'm pretty sure I saw him at the office holiday party last year.

The tall woman gets out of the elevator on the seventeenth floor. I've got the rest of the building to go.

Amy liked to keep her work and family lives separate. So, I need to know what she said to her coworkers. Was she acting differently? I'm hoping that there's some clue here that will help me figure out what happened.

The elevator eventually stops, and the doors open to the lobby of Fortis Capital. It's a kaleidoscope of black-and-white marble. I'm here so infrequently, I keep forgetting how opulent it is.

What I don't remember is the guy standing next to the door leading to the main offices, nor do I recall the metal detector.

The man is in his mid-forties with dark cropped hair, chiseled face, and a muscle-toned build. He could be mistaken for a movie star with an easygoing smile that belies his commanding presence.

The receptionist, a young woman with another name I can't remember, discreetly, but quickly, presses a button on a panel on the desk.

"He's here," she says quietly and gives me a tight smile.

The man steps forward and offers his hand.

"Mr. Burcham. I'm Henry Vaughn. Head of security for Fortis."

I'm baffled, but out of reflex, I shake his hand and am instantly worried that his grip is going to turn my hand into a diamond. Detective Harper's firm handshake was nothing compared to this.

"How did you know I was coming?" I ask.

"Andrew downstairs let us know you were on your way up."

Andrew. That's the name of the guy in the lobby. He must have also mentioned that I looked out of sorts.

"Everything all right?" he asks.

"No. I need to speak to—"

A door opens behind him and out steps Malcolm Davis, the head manager of Fortis Capital.

He's just as I remember him, older but energetic, assertive, and wearing an immaculate suit.

"Mark?" he asks, stepping closer.

"Hi, Malcolm," I answer, unsure of what else to say.

"I see you've met Mr. Vaughn," he says, giving Henry a quick nod before continuing. "Did you hear from Amy? I've tried calling her at least a dozen times, but she's not—"

"Amy's dead."

They both stare at me with open mouths.

"What?" Malcolm whispers.

"They found her body in an alley on Skid Row this morning."

Malcolm's frozen. "Good God . . ."

Henry is speechless.

"She was lying to me," I sputter, unable to control myself. "She told me you were sending her to Boston to meet that client and I dropped her off at the airport, but she never got on the plane—"

Malcolm puts his hand on my arm.

"Come on. Let's go to my office."

He leads me to the door next to the reception desk, but the metal detector emits a soft, elongated beep as I pass through.

Henry and Malcolm have pained expressions.

"I'm sorry, Mr. Burcham, but we have to ask you to leave your cell phone here with Linda," Vaughn says.

Malcolm is obviously embarrassed. "We're keeping a tight lid around here."

"No. It's okay," I say and hand my phone to Linda.

"If anyone calls, I'll come and get you," she offers.

"Thanks."

"Okay." Malcolm sighs. "We'll be in my office."

Chapter 11

I accept the glass of water from Malcolm's assistant with a shaky hand.

"Thank you, Tess," Malcolm says. "We'll let you know if there's anything else."

She gets the not-subtle hint and walks out, closing the door behind her.

I take a sip of the room-temperature water and glance around.

I'm not a fan of the décor in Malcolm's office. He's got photos of his hunting trips and the "trophies" he's bagged: a grizzly in Alaska, a wild boar in Louisiana, and even a lion he shot on safari in South Africa. Amy told me that it was one of those trips that people pay tens of thousands of dollars for and the money goes to lion preservation. I asked her why not just give the money to wildlife preservation and not shoot the lion at all? But I guess that's how he wants to spend his millions. He fits the profile of someone who sees themselves as an alpha male. I suppose he would have to be to get to where he is, but Amy liked him. She didn't approve of his décor or extracurricular activities either, but he had taken her under his wing.

Malcolm isn't contemplating his photos. He's leaning back against his desk, gazing out the window with a pallid expression at the Los Angeles skyline.

Like Tatum, I've only given him the basics: Amy's dead and the police found her body in an alley this morning. I leave out the lingerie, the evidence of sex, and suspected cocaine.

We turned more than a few heads as we made our way into Malcolm's office. Fortis is a labyrinth of corridors with a mini-trading floor at its heart stuffed with young traders sitting at computers, wearing headsets, and watching fortunes rise and fall on their screens. It's a bit of a madhouse outside the glass wall of his office, but a heavy door has reduced the noise to a low hum.

Malcolm finally turns to me, unsure what to say.

He nods to a corner where there's a table stocked with vodkas, gins, and whiskeys.

"Would you like something stronger?" he asks.

"No, thank you."

". . . Mark, I know there's nothing I can say that would make any of this better. Amy was family to us. If there's anything we can do, please don't hesitate to ask."

"That's why I'm here, actually. I'm trying to figure out what happened, because as I said, I dropped her off at LAX Friday to fly to Boston to meet with a potential client."

"And as I told you, I'm unaware of any potential client in Boston."

"I know. The police think she never left Los Angeles." I stare at the spotless glass of water in my hands. "And she told you she was taking time off to spend with Tatum and me?"

Malcolm nods and then is hit by a thought. He quickly strides around his desk to his open laptop. "When did she go to Boston— I mean, when did she say she was in Boston?"

"Um . . ." If I had my phone, I could look through my texts, but since I left it at the front desk, I'm forced to rely on memory. "She went twice last month. It was over her birthday. She left Wednesday morning and came back on Friday."

Malcolm taps a few keys on the laptop. "Yeah. I've got it here on the calendar, but I remember that." He looks at me and then shakes his head. "She told me she was taking that time off to celebrate her birthday with you."

I have to set the glass down on the black marble coaster on the table in front of me to keep from dropping it.

"And last Friday?" I ask.

"She said she was going to work from home."

A tremor begins to build in my hands. "And she was supposed to meet you for dinner on Saturday, here in Los Angeles?"

Malcolm nods. "And it wasn't just me. She was meeting the whole team. Speaking of which . . ."

He hits a button on the phone set on the desk.

"Yes, Mr. Davis?" Tess asks through the speaker.

"Tess, I need Spencer and Nadine in my office."

"Yes," she answers, hesitantly. "But Spencer is in a meeting with Reynolds and Shaw."

"Now, Tess." Malcolm jabs the button, ending the call, and looks up at me. "I'm sorry, Mark. I need to tell them and Amy may have told them something."

I nod.

There's a strained silence as we wait.

Through the glass wall, we watch as Tess approaches, followed by Nadine Trembly. I met her at Amy's first office holiday party. She's in her fifties. Her facial features are like cut marble, and her hair is pulled into a tight bun.

Tess pushes the door open, allowing the noise from the trading floor to reach our ears as Nadine steps into the office.

"Where's Spencer?" Malcolm asks.

"He's extracting himself from his meeting with Reynolds and Shaw," Tess answers.

"Tell him to hurry it up."

Tess is about to head back out the door but a movement catches our attention.

A figure hustles across the floor toward us. He throws open the door and bursts into Malcolm's office.

49

"I'm here, I'm here." Spencer Harris looks agitated as he enters. He's straight out of the movie *Wall Street*: early-forties, slicked-back hair, fit, attractive, self-assured, and annoyed. "Malcolm, what are you doing, calling me in here while I'm meeting with Reynolds and Shaw? You know how much we need them, and they're this close to dropping—"

Malcolm holds up a hand. For the first time, Spencer and Nadine notice my presence. Tess extracts herself from the office, once more closing the door behind her.

"Nadine, Spencer," Malcolm says. "You know Mark Burcham, Amy's husband?"

They look at me in polite but obvious confusion.

"Have you heard from her?" Nadine asks. "Clients and even the staff have been asking what's going on."

There's a strained silence.

Malcolm clears his throat, considers his words, but then comes right out and says it. "Amy's dead."

This is the third time I've had to watch people react to the news of Amy's death and I'm already sick of it. It's like I'm reliving my own reaction all over again.

"Dead?" Nadine whispers. "How?"

Malcolm struggles to hide his frustration. "First off, I think we all want to express our condolences."

"Of course," Nadine says, grimacing. "I'm so sorry."

"If there's anything we can do," Spencer adds.

"That's why I called you all in here," Malcolm begins. "There seems to be some confusion. Amy was supposed to meet us for dinner Saturday night, but her body was found early this morning in the city, and she told Mark that she was meeting a potential client in Boston this weekend."

"In Boston?" Nadine asks. "Who?"

"There may not have been a client in Boston," I say, no longer able to remain quiet.

"There wasn't," Spencer scoffs, which earns him a look of

reproach from Malcolm. Spencer misses it and continues. "All I know is that she was supposed to meet us for dinner Saturday night at Bourman's to discuss strategy and she never showed, even though she was the one who arranged the dinner."

"Has she been missing any other meetings?" I ask. "Did either of you notice anything different about her recently?"

They exchange glances. There's something they don't want to tell me.

"Please. My wife is dead and I'm trying to figure out what happened. If there was something—"

"A few weeks ago, I came across her in the stairwell," Nadine blurts out. "She was upset about something. I asked her what was wrong." She appeals for help with a look to Spencer and Malcolm, but this is the first time they're hearing of this.

"What did she say?" I ask.

"She— She asked me to forget it and not tell anyone, so I—"

"Nadine," Malcolm interjects. "What did she say?"

Nadine's been trying to avoid it, but finally has to meet my stare.

"She would only say that it was a personal matter."

"Did she say anything else?" I asked, stunned.

Nadine shakes her head. "No. She apologized, said that she shouldn't have said anything, and she asked me to forget it."

"And then?"

"And then . . . she left."

This is her office.

Amy worked so hard to earn this space. She took so much satisfaction in it. There are framed testimonies to Fortis Capital's success on the walls, successes in which Amy had played an integral part. There are also photos of Amy with powerful people: the mayor, the chief of police, and titans of LA's financial industry. I make a cameo in some of them, but Amy is the star. Staring at the photos, a surge of pride for what Amy accomplished flows through me. I know she felt the pressure, but she loved it.

Even on those rare occasions that she vented to me about her job, I knew she reveled in the high stakes.

Malcolm and Vaughn are waiting awkwardly by the door as I slowly turn, taking it all in.

I'm hardly aware of their presence until our eyes meet.

"Could I have a moment?" I ask them.

"Take all the time you need," Malcolm says. "Henry and I will be waiting in my office."

I nod.

Vaughn hesitates for a moment, but then follows Malcolm out of the office.

Through the glass wall, I notice some of the traders trying not to stare.

The door closes, cutting off the sound from outside.

My mind starts reeling.

I came here for answers, but I've only found more questions.

Why would Amy lie to them and to me? What was the "personal matter" that she wouldn't tell Nadine about?

That she was having an affair, stupid.

My pulse skyrockets, and I squeeze my eyes shut.

I can't accept that. It's not possible.

But then how do I explain the physical evidence that she had sex with someone before she died? Doesn't an affair make sense? Doesn't everything—the lying to me and her coworkers, the lingerie, the drugs, the evidence she slept with someone— doesn't it point to the fact that she was with someone, someone she had been seeing for months, at least? Someone who shared her love of adrenaline and got her to forget her guilt over Colleen's death, like I had been trying to do for two decades, and that's who she was with before she died? Why don't I believe everything that's in front of me? Everything that says that Amy was having an affair?

Because I *knew* Amy. I knew her better than anyone and she wouldn't do that. Not to me and not to Tatum.

I slowly open my eyes and see the small framed photo on her desk: of Amy and me on our wedding day. We're laughing during our first dance. A perfect moment captured. It was my gift to her after we got back from our honeymoon. I had the sturdy silver frame custom made with the engraving "It Was Always You."

I pick it up and stare down at the two of us at the start of our life together.

This is the Amy I knew. The Amy I believe. The Amy I have to remember. The Amy I have to hold on to.

I tuck the photo into my back pocket, and leave everything else behind.

Lost inside my head, I walk through the labyrinth of Fortis, back to the lobby, through the door and metal detector, to the waiting elevator doors.

Just as I press the button, I hear the door to the offices open behind me and a voice calls out, "Mr. Burcham!"

I turn to see Henry Vaughn walking toward me. I completely forgot that he and Malcolm were waiting in Malcolm's office.

"Don't want you to forget this," he says, extending his hand, which is holding my phone.

"Oh. Thanks." I put the phone in my side pocket.

"So, um . . . Did you find everything you need?" he asks.

"Nothing to find, really."

There's an awkward pause.

"It's so unreal. She was like family around here," he says with a sympathetic expression, but then freezes at the realization that he's talking to someone who *was* family.

He's not on the hook. It was an innocent mistake.

"Let us know if there's anything we can do," he says.

"I will."

The elevator doors open. I step inside and turn to see him still standing there, staring at me. It has to be my frayed nerves, but that homecoming-king smile feels oddly ominous.

53

"I mean that, Mr. Burcham," he says. "Anything at all."

"Thanks," I reply.

The doors slide close.

"How are you feeling, sweetheart?" I ask, settling into the glacial flow of traffic.

"I'm okay," Tatum wearily answers through the car's speakers.

"I should be home in a little bit. We'll order pizza for dinner."

"Okay . . . Dad?"

"Yeah?"

"Can Aiden come over?"

"Sure."

She sniffles. "Thanks."

"I'll be there in about an hour, okay?"

"Okay. I love you, Dad."

"Love you, too."

She hangs up the phone.

I glance down at the photo resting on the passenger seat.

Amy would want me to do everything I can to help our daughter, now.

Having Aiden over for dinner will be a small price to pay if it'll help Tatum.

Chapter 12

"Hello, Aiden."

"Hey, Mr. Burcham."

There's a strained silence. I've met Aiden at this door dozens of times, but never under circumstances like this and to my surprise, not only are the circumstances different, but so is he. There's none of that cool defiance or smugness.

"Is Tatum here?" he asks, apprehensively.

There are footsteps behind me and Tatum dashes by. She throws her arms around Aiden, buries her face in his shoulder, and starts to cry. He puts his arms around her and to my amazement, Aiden starts to cry with her.

I don't know what to say. I've always been suspicious of Aiden's intentions with Tatum. What father wouldn't? But watching them, seeing him share her pain, leaves me speechless.

Quietly, I go back down the hall to the kitchen to order the pizzas and give them some space.

A little over three hours later, we are all in food comas in the living room, while *Dirty Dancing* plays on the television.

Aiden and Tatum are half asleep on the opposite couch. His arms are over her shoulders as she leans into him while

Patrick Swayze informs Jerry Orbach that "nobody puts Baby in a corner."

I'm half-watching the movie, half-watching my phone. I've been doing this all day, waiting for Detective Harper to tell me more shocking info about Amy, but by the time the movie ends, my phone has remained silent and Aiden and Tatum are passed out.

The credits finish and the Blu-ray disc goes back to the menu screen. I stretch and groan, pick myself off the couch, walk across the carpet, and gently nudge Tatum's shoulder.

"Hey, you two . . ."

They blink their eyes awake.

"It's late. Time to call it a night," I say.

They go through a similar cycle of stretches and groans. As they do, I head to the kitchen, grab a glass from the cabinet, half fill it with water from the faucet, and start closing up the house. I leave them alone to say good night when Tatum stops me near the stairs.

"Dad?" she whispers.

"Yeah?"

"Can Aiden stay the night?"

"Tatum—"

"Please. Just for tonight. He can sleep in the guest room."

I feel the sadness in her voice, I really do, but I've got enough going on in my head. Even though there appears to have been a change in Aiden, I can't spend the night worrying about him sneaking into her room.

"Maybe another time, sweetheart."

"Dad, please—"

"It's okay," Aiden says, appearing behind her. "Your dad's right."

She turns to him, clearly as surprised as I am.

This is a new sensation. This one act of respect and understanding is so different than anything he's ever shown me, like the time he called me Mark. Once again, it had been Amy who kept me from going off.

But if I had been surprised before, imagine my shock when Aiden holds out his hand to shake mine.

"Thank you for dinner, Mr. Burcham."

Stunned, I shake his hand, and before I realize what I'm doing, I pull him in for a hug, which he returns.

"Thank you for coming, Aiden," I say, and I mean it. He's had a calming effect on Tatum. For a few hours, he's taken her mind off the death of her mother, and for that, I'm grateful.

"Get home safe," I tell him as we separate.

"I will."

"I'll walk you out," Tatum says, taking his hand and guiding him toward the door. "I'll get the alarm, Dad."

"Okay," I reply.

Once they're outside and the front door closes, the magnitude of what just transpired hits me.

This is a different Aiden.

Maybe under that "bad boy" exterior, he's more mature than I've given him credit for. Maybe he does understand the horror of what's happened. Even in the short amount of time I've had to process Amy's death, I knew that Tatum was going to lean on him, and I worried that Aiden would be "too cool" to cope with it, but if tonight is any indication, and I can't believe I'm saying this, I want him around for Tatum.

Why couldn't you have been here to see this, Amy?

The amount by which my world has changed is too much to take in. My head is swimming and exhaustion is rearing its ugly head.

I do my nightly round of closing up the house, checking the windows and the fireplace, and head upstairs to our— my bedroom.

I don't want to turn on the lights.

There's something about seeing the bed and knowing Amy and I will never share it again that prevents me from doing so.

If I had the energy, I would collapse onto it and weep, but I'm too tired. The emotional breakdown will have to wait for tomorrow.

I move to the window and peer down to the driveway.

Tatum and Aiden are embracing next to his Mustang.

It's a good thing I didn't turn on the light. I don't want them to see me up here, watching them.

Aiden kisses her one last time and they separate. He gets in the car. The engine starts with a roar and the headlights spark. Aiden pulls away from the curb and drives off down the street.

Tatum watches him go.

I follow her gaze.

As Aiden drives away, he passes a parked black SUV. There are always cars parked on our street, but this SUV catches my eye, due to the arm sticking out of the window. By the glow of the streetlight, I can see a cigarette clamped between two fingers. Curls of smoke rise from the darkened cabin.

Once Aiden turns at the intersection, Tatum begins walking back toward the house.

I go to the bed and lie on top of the covers.

There's the sound of the front door opening and closing, and then the soft beeps as Tatum arms the security system. As she climbs the stairs, I can hear her muffled crying, which is cut off by the closing of her bedroom door.

I want to go and comfort her, but I can't. I'm struck again by the fact that I'll never spend another night with Amy. If I go to Tatum, I'm going to lose it and I don't want her to see me like that. Hot tears flash in my eyes. I clench my jaw, willing them back, but they spill out and run down the sides of my face.

I can't hold them back. Why should I? Amy is gone and I—

Just before I'm about to bury my face in the pillow to allow the sobs to overtake me, there's a sound in the hall.

A moment later, my bedroom door opens.

I can barely make out the shape of Tatum standing there, her arms clutched around herself, but I can hear her sniffling and stunted breaths.

Without a word, she walks to the bed, lies down next to me, nestles into the crook of my arm, curls into a ball, and begins to quietly cry.

The sobs I've been holding in check vanish. The worry that Tatum would see me utterly broken is gone.

My daughter needs me.

It's just us, now.

I gently stroke her hair until she falls asleep.

Chapter 13

It's eleven in the morning and Tatum is still asleep upstairs.

After getting almost no sleep myself, I decided to come downstairs and start planning for Amy's viewing before Tatum wakes up. While in the process of finding a coordinator, I'm interrupted by a call from Detective Harper.

"How are you holding up?" he asks for the second day in a row.

"I have no idea. I'm arranging for the viewing. I've been numb, but now, I have to start telling people that Amy's gone . . . I think I prefer being numb."

"If I may be honest?" he asks.

"Please."

"I've worked plenty of cases like this, too many in fact, and what you're going through is completely normal. I don't say that to diminish you or your daughter's suffering. I only say it because it's a process and you will get through it. Nothing will be the same, but it will get better from here."

"Thank you, detective."

It feels weird talking about my emotions to someone who is barely more than a total stranger, especially after the abrupt ending to our conversation yesterday, but I don't have many people to talk to. Both Amy's parents and mine are gone. Her father died when she was young and her mother passed a few years ago. My father died three years ago and my mother left us after a slow, agonizing decline into Alzheimer's.

"Of course," Detective Harper says. "And if it's any consolation, we're close to wrapping things up."

I'm suddenly alert.

"What do you mean, you're 'wrapping things up'? Are you saying you know who killed her?"

"Mr. Burcham," he says, treading lightly. "This doesn't appear to be a murder."

"What?! What are you talking about? My wife was found dead in an alley. She was almost naked and according to you, she was full of cocaine and just had sex with someone, and you're telling me she wasn't murdered?"

There's a sound through the phone, like light chewing. He's biting his lip, again.

"As I explained before, Mr. Burcham," he says, slowly and calmly. "We're basing our conclusions on the evidence we have. There are no signs of foul play. There's nothing to suggest that she was attacked, nor that she was forced to ingest cocaine. There's also no evidence of anyone else being in that alley. Again, I understand your skepticism and I know that this is difficult to hear, but your wife died of an accidental overdose."

I start pacing the kitchen in impotent rage. "No. No, no, no. You're saying that my wife lied to me, and after I dropped her off at the airport, she met somebody, here in LA, had sex with him, overdosed on cocaine, and wandered down that alley wearing next to nothing to die alone?"

"I know it sounds very unlikely to you, Mr. Burcham, but we're working off the facts in our possession, and as incredible as it may sound to you, there is simply no evidence that this was a crime."

My balance is suddenly gone. I stumble and then guide myself into a chair at the kitchen table.

I can't take this. I believed that the police were at the start of a process to find whoever was with Amy that night, but it turns out they're not interested in finding him, because apparently, he did nothing wrong.

I want to scream at the top of my lungs. I turn my head and see the photo of Amy and myself that I took from her office, which is sitting on the end table next to the couch, and a thought crystalizes.

When Detective Harper told me that Amy died of an overdose, my initial reaction was that he was lying or the test was wrong, but that was dulled by the suggestion that Amy had sex with someone, but now, putting it all together, the ridiculousness that she overdosed, that she was sleeping with someone, the rapidity with which he's trying to wrap up Amy's death, and his constant dismissal of my suspicions leads me to one conclusion: the police are hiding something from me.

"Mr. Burcham? Are you still there?"

"Detective Harper," I reply, my voice trembling. "My wife wasn't having an affair and she didn't overdose on cocaine. I don't care what your tests say. I will never believe that. She would n—"

There's a sound to my right.

I glance toward the hallway.

Tatum.

She's standing in the entranceway to the kitchen with an indescribable expression of horror on her face.

Oh God.

She's heard everything.

Chapter 14

Tatum runs back down the hall and up the stairs.

"Tatum!"

Dropping the phone and forgetting about Detective Harper, I race after her, pleading for her to stop, but she gets to her room, slams the door, and locks it seconds before I get there.

Standing outside her door, I hang my head and silently curse.

I didn't know how to tell her, but it sure as hell wasn't going to be like this.

"Tatum?" I call out. "You know the rule. Unlock the door."

Silence.

"Tatum?"

I try twisting the knob, but it holds.

"Tatum, we have to talk."

There's no sound from inside but I'm not going anywhere. This isn't like yesterday. She needs to understand that what she just heard isn't what happened.

"Open the door, Tatum. Right now."

There's a burst of motion from inside her room and the door flies open. Tatum stares at me with wide, frantic eyes.

"Mom was sleeping with someone?!"

"No. She wasn't."

"I just heard you say it! She lied to you about going to Boston and she had sex with someone."

"Listen, the police are wrong. You know how your mother felt about drugs."

"Then why would the police say that?!"

"Because they're lying!"

She blinks in confusion. "Why would they lie about that?"

"I—I don't know," I stammer.

"Was Mom lying about going to Boston?"

"I don't know," I repeat, but this time, it's an obvious lie.

"Dad," she says, her anger growing because I just tried to lie to her. "Did the police do tests for drugs?"

"Yes, but the tests are wrong."

"And did they do another test that showed Mom was fucking someone else?"

A sudden fury swells within me. "Watch your mouth, young lady!"

Her mouth hangs open in disbelief.

"The cops think she might have slept with someone," I state as calmly as I can. "But they're wrong."

"Then why would they say it?"

I don't have an answer for her.

"And the drugs?" she continues.

"They're wrong," I insist. "You know how your mom felt about—"

"Oh my God! Listen to yourself, Dad. You're trying to make yourself believe—"

"They're lying!" I snap.

Tatum stares at me. Her look of disbelief morphs into something I've never seen from her: pity.

She finally closes the door, leaving me alone in the hall.

Chapter 15

That's it.

I can't avoid it any longer. Now that Tatum knows, I have to start telling people, starting with Liz. Not only because she was Amy's sister, but because there is a possibility that she has answers I need.

Amy never told me what ended their relationship. I tried countless times to get her to explain what happened between them, but she refused.

I find Liz's number in my contacts. When I pull it up, it shows me the last time that I called her, which was over two years ago.

I stare at the screen a good thirty seconds before hitting the call button, but as soon as I do, I'm already reconsidering.

I know what I've been told, but it's different from what I believe. How do I explain that to her?

There's still time. It's only ringing. I can hang up and wait until—

Click.

"Mark?"

Her voice stops me in my tracks. It's eerily similar to Amy's and I can tell by her tone that she already knows something's wrong. Of course, she does. Why else would I be calling her out of the blue after two years of silence?

"Mark? Is that you?"

I can't seem to form the words.

"Mark? . . . Are you there?"

"Hi, Liz," a voice I recognize as my own says.

"Is everything okay?" she asks.

"Amy's . . . um . . . She's . . ."

"Mark? What's going on?"

"Amy's dead."

Silence.

"What?" she asks.

"Amy's dead," I repeat.

"Mark . . . What are you talking about?"

"They found her early yesterday morning in an alley on Skid Row. She was supposed to be in Boston on a business trip. I dropped her off at the airport, but she didn't get on the plane. She lied to me. She lied to people at work. The police think she died of an overdose, and they also think that she was—" I stop myself, not wanting to finish the sentence. "Liz . . . Amy's dead."

There's a sharp pop and clatter. I think she dropped the phone.

"Liz?"

There's a gagging sound from the other end of the line and then hurried footsteps moving away from the phone. Seconds later, I can faintly hear her retching, again and again. A tap runs and there's the sound of her spitting. The water stops, the footsteps return, and she picks up the phone.

"Liz? Are you okay?"

"Yeah," she says in between a series of deep breaths. "How did she die?"

"The police say she overdosed on cocaine."

"Overdosed?" she asks, incredulously.

"I know. She was found downtown. She was supposed to be in Boston for a work thing. At least that's what she told me. She told her coworkers that she was going to meet them for dinner on Saturday, but she never showed. She had been lying to me about

66

going to Boston these past few months." The words are coming faster, now. "She also lied to her coworkers and said that she was taking time off work to be with Tatum and me. They found her in an alley on Skid Row. The toxicology report found cocaine in her system, but you know how Amy felt about cocaine. She was even wearing Colleen's necklace. She was also wearing lingerie and the police . . . They told me that there's evidence that Amy had sex with someone just before she died."

Liz gasps.

"Mark," she says, her voice shaking. "I don't—"

"Listen, I know the two of you hadn't spoken in a while."

She's about to say something but lets out a staccato burp instead. "Excuse me." She takes another breath. "No, we hadn't, but that's not important right now."

"It might be."

She pauses. I feel her tense through the phone.

"Liz, when was the last time you spoke to Amy?"

She takes her time before answering. "Two years ago, when we had our . . . thing. She tried once or twice to reach out, but . . . I didn't answer."

"Amy never told me what happened between the two of you. I'm sorry that I never reached out, but now, you have to tell me; what did the two of you fight about?"

She sighs, takes a couple of breaths, and finally says, "It's not important."

"Please, tell me."

She stops.

"Mark . . . tell me again exactly what happened."

"I dropped her off at LAX for a business trip to Boston, but she never got on the plane. Yesterday morning, around two o'clock, they found her body in an alley on Skid Row. They think she had been there since Saturday. She was wearing lingerie and they told me the toxicology report shows that she died of a cocaine overdose and the police said that she recently had sex . . . It wasn't with me."

I wait for her reply but there's total silence until I hear her whisper, "Oh my God . . ."

"They're lying, Liz. I don't know why, but I need to know what you two fought about."

She doesn't say a thing. For a moment, I worry that the call has dropped.

"Mark?" she says, her voice suddenly forged in steel.

"Yeah?"

"I have to call you back."

"What? Wait. No. Liz, I need to—"

The line goes dead.

Chapter 16

Tatum's gone.

She came downstairs a few hours ago and declared that she was going to Aiden's.

"I'll be back by ten," she said, grabbing her keys from the kitchen table.

"You can stay out later if you want."

She paused. "Really?"

"Aiden's parents are home, right?"

"Yeah."

"Then you can stay out until eleven if they're okay with you being there."

I've met Aiden's parents and I was certain that they'd be fine with it.

"Okay," she said, a mixture of pleasant surprise and confusion. "Drive safe."

"I will."

With that, she was gone.

My "leniency" serves two purposes. Tatum needs Aiden right now, and if this new, respectful, and caring Aiden is sticking around, then I'm okay with giving them some more time together.

I also want the house to myself. My suspicions were first aroused by the call with Detective Harper, and that call with Liz has me convinced there's something more to Amy's death. Liz knows something but wouldn't answer her phone when I tried to call her back, nor has she returned any of my dozen or so text messages. She's not going to tell me what's happening, and I didn't get any answers from Amy's coworkers. If I'm going to find out the truth, I have to do it myself. I need to think, and to that end, I've been sitting at the kitchen table, listening to the house breathe around me. There are sounds that I've never noticed before: the motor in the fridge quietly kicking on and off, the gentle breath of the air-conditioning, the occasional breeze against the side of the house. It's like being inside a dormant living being as I try to think.

While I've been sitting here, still and silent, I can't shake that look of pity Tatum gave me. I'll just say it; she looked at me like I was stupid. Maybe I am, but I still can't believe that Amy was having an affair.

Nothing of what Detective Harper has told me regarding Amy's death makes any sense and it sounds like they have no interest in investigating further. I also can't wait for Liz to help.

If I truly believe that there is something more to Amy's death, I'm going to have to work this out on my own, starting with the official story.

A cocaine overdose? Amy? Ridiculous.

Amy got her thrills from high-stake situations like business deals and jumping out of a plane every now and again. Even though it was over twenty years ago, Colleen's death still haunted her, even more so as Tatum grew older. Amy lived in mortal fear that Tatum would get into drugs when she went to college.

A cocaine overdose doesn't fit.

But I also have to play devil's advocate and admit that it *was* over twenty years ago. Is it possible that Amy actually did get over Colleen's death and met someone who convinced her to give it a try? Picturing Amy trying cocaine is so absurd that I almost laugh. That's not the woman I knew, but maybe I only thought I knew Amy.

So, does that mean the police are lying? I understand Tatum's disbelief. Why would they lie? They say they're basing their findings on evidence, while I'm going on my gut.

I'll put a pin in it.

The bigger issue is the supposed affair.

I keep telling myself that there's no way Amy could have hidden that from me. I would have known. I would have seen the change in her. We were in love. We were a team. We had been for over twenty years. I would have noticed.

But the voice of the devil's advocate in my head suddenly grows loud.

Isn't this exactly what someone would delude themselves into thinking to avoid the truth? the voice counters. *She was lying to you about the trips to Boston. She was lying to her coworkers about being with you. Doesn't all of that point to the fact that she was having an affair with someone here in Los Angeles. She spent Friday and most of Saturday with them. She was supposed to meet the others from Fortis on Saturday night for dinner but before that, after having sex with this guy, they went to Skid Row to score more drugs and she accidentally overdosed in the alley. The mystery man freaked out and ran away, leaving her there. It adds up, and let's not forget, the cops are saying that there's physical evidence to back it up.*

All right. Just for the sake of argument, I'll consider it.

Was there a change in Amy that I missed? Had I become so oblivious that I was taking our marriage for granted?

I don't think so but isn't denial the first step?

It's only been forty-eight hours. Maybe it hasn't settled in yet and once it does, the lights will come on. I'll remember little things here and there, clues that went unnoticed that she was seeing someone else, and I'll feel like a fool. So, how can I hold on to this ridiculous fantasy that Amy wasn't having an affair?

And I repeat, the devil's advocate confidently states. *Just like the cocaine, there's physical evidence that she had sex with someone else.*

I shake my head in frustration and my gaze finds the photo I took from her office, which is sitting on the end table, and I come back to the same answer: I can't believe it because I *knew* Amy.

The devil's advocate throws up his hands. *Then why did she lie to you and her coworkers? She didn't want them to know what she was doing and she used you and your daughter as part of that lie. And it wasn't one time. She was lying to everybody for months.*

That's true.

Amy lied every time I dropped her off at the airport. She lied every time I helped her pack. She lied with every phone call to say that she had made it to the hotel and every time we called to say good night.

Was there something that I missed?

I don't know. I can't trust my memories. I might be adding details that have been artificially inserted because of what's happened.

The only time that she was lying and I suspected something was off was during that last drive to the airport. The sadness in her eyes. The odd comments.

What was different? Why did I catch it that time and not the others?

The answer is obvious; it's because something *was* different about that time. Something was about to happen and she knew it was coming.

Did Amy know that she was about to die?

Not possible. If Amy knew that she was about to die, she would have asked for help. She wouldn't walk away knowing we would never see each other again, nor would she ever leave Tatum without a mother.

But she knew *something.*

Something was weighing on her mind.

Remembering her face as we said good-bye outside the airport makes that clear, but that wasn't where her odd behavior started.

It started in the car.

It started with her far-off stares out the window and the comments about getting a tattoo. I thought it was a joke that fell flat, but now, everything potentially has another meaning. There was also that odd comment about forgetting to pack the sundress and that remark about getting her one for Christmas. If she knew that something was about to happen, that there was the possibility that she might die, why would she use our last conversation to bring up tattoos and a sundress, her favorite feature of which wasn't the color or the cut, but the fact that it had—

I bolt for the stairs.

I hit the switch by the door and the overhead light fills the walk-in closet of our bedroom.

Hanging from the racks, arranged in perfect order, are Amy's suits, blouses, and occasional dresses.

I step over and begin sliding her clothes one by one across the rod. The hangers make a hissing sound as I push them out of the way, searching for the green sundress.

I send a yellow blouse to the other side of the rod and there it is.

Seeing it hanging here, I'm suddenly awash in doubt.

This is ridiculous. *I'm* being ridiculous. This whole exercise has been a plunge down the rabbit hole because I'm unable to cope with the fact that Amy's gone.

I start mentally preparing myself for disappointment.

Taking the dress off the hanger, I begin moving my fingers around the fabric, searching for the pocket.

This is it.

If there's nothing here, I'll have to accept everything that Detective Harper has told me: that Amy was having an affair and that I was so clueless, I didn't catch it, and that Amy had a whole other life she was keeping from m—

My heart stops.

There's something here.

My hands are shaking, which interferes with my frantic attempts to find the opening to the pocket, but I manage to finally locate it.

My fingers reach inside and close around something cold and metallic.

I lift the object out and hold it up to the light.

A key.

A black metal key. There's a number engraved on it: 4487. Above the number is a strange, intricate logo of elegant loops and swirls, like calligraphy.

I stare at the key in shock.

I was truly expecting to find nothing. Part of me was ready to accept the official story, but this key confirms everything.

There is more to Amy's death than I'm being told. The police are lying to me and most of all, Amy is trying to tell me what really happened.

The light in the closet faintly changes as headlights sweep the front of the house and find their way through the bedroom window and open closet door.

Tatum's home.

Stuffing the key into my pocket, I exit the closet, move through the room, step into the hall, and close the bedroom door behind me. I hurry downstairs and arrive at the landing as Tatum opens the front door.

"Hey, sweetheart," I say, trying to control my breathing.

"Hey . . ." she replies, suddenly brimming with suspicion.

My attempt to play it cool has failed spectacularly.

"How was Aiden's?"

"It was fine . . . Thanks for letting me stay out an extra hour."

"Sure."

She studies me while I try to maintain a reassuring smile.

"You okay, Dad?"

"Yep."

I'm fine, sweetheart, just this key burning a hole in my pocket.

"Well . . . I'm going to go to bed," she says.

"Okay."

I move out of the way so she can go up the stairs. She gives me a curious side-eye as she passes.

My brain starts overreacting, searching for some way to defuse her suspicions. It's not until she's climbed the stairs that I realize she's forgotten to close the front door. I'm about to make a lame dad joke about paying to air-condition the neighborhood, but thankfully stop myself. She's already weary and I shouldn't engage in more conversation.

I step off the landing to close the door and inadvertently glance outside.

Parked on the street, nearly hidden in the shadows, is a black SUV. I can't see the face of the driver, but I can just make out the glowing tip of the cigarette in the hand that's dangling out the driver's window.

I close the door but stay rooted to the spot.

Is that the same SUV as last night? It has to be. What are the odds that two black SUVs with two different drivers who smoke cigarettes would be parked outside the house two nights in a row?

I lock the door but instead of doing my nightly ritual of locking up the house, I begin climbing the stairs. I want to run, but that might alert Tatum, who just closed her bedroom door.

As quickly as I will allow myself, I head down the hall to my bedroom. Once inside, I turn off the light, hastily move to the window, and look down into the street.

The SUV is gone.

I immediately put the SUV out of my mind. Maybe it was the same one, maybe it isn't. Either way, I've got more important things to worry about.

I head back downstairs, close up the house, grab my laptop, go upstairs, say good night to Tatum through her bedroom door, walk to my room, shut the door, and fire up the laptop.

What are you trying to tell me, Amy? What does this key open?

Chapter 17

Around, up, back down, through, and done.

I slide the knot up to my Adam's apple and check the length of the tie in the bathroom mirror. It's comically short.

I curse and pull the knot loose.

No. I don't wear a suit to an office every day, but I can tie a tie. I simply don't have the mental capacity for it at the moment.

When I haven't been arranging for the viewing this afternoon, every other second of the past few days has been spent attempting to decipher the logo on this key, which I've added to my key ring.

That first night, I fell asleep next to my laptop just as the sun was coming up and I was no closer to finding out what this key goes to than when I started.

The logo might be letters. They sort of look like Js or Es or Ls, but the design is so intricate, I can't be sure.

If they are letters, are they the initials to a business? A person? I've been scouring the internet, using only the vaguest of search terms: JE key, JJ storage, EJ business, JL garage. I've tried different variations, but my imprecise terms only cause Google to vomit page after page of meaningless results, while constantly asking me questions like, "Did you mean E&J Brandy?" When I tried adding "black key," the only new information I got was about a band I've never heard of.

Somewhere between the Google searches and managing to keep it a secret, I visited our attorney to settle Amy's affairs. Everything goes to me, which is no surprise. Amy also had life insurance, but our lawyer thinks it might be a bumpy road. The insurance company can lean on the police report to say her death wasn't murder. They might even argue that Amy committed suicide, which they won't cover. I can fight it, but it could drag on in the courts for years. Thankfully, I don't have to make a decision right now. I'll get a job, which was always the plan after Tatum went off to college, anyway. Amy and I had it worked out that we'd sell the house, move east where we could find something comparable for half the price, and add the difference to our savings. Tatum and I will be fine.

I've got enough to worry about at present.

Arranging the viewing has been pretty straightforward. We had everything spelled out in our wills if the unthinkable happened. We did it shortly after our parents died, but it was under the assumption that it wouldn't come into play until after Tatum was grown, we became grandparents, and enjoyed our retirement . . . but now, the unthinkable has happened.

I found a good funeral coordinator and explained the situation. She expressed her sorrow for our loss, asked a few delicate questions, and gently informed me that she would take it from there.

Back in the bathroom, my hands begin fumbling with the tie in preparation for my fourth or fifth attempt.

Liz finally got back to me. I left a lot of messages and was successful in convincing her that I wasn't asking about their falling out. I wanted to know if we could hold the reception at her bungalow in Pasadena. Tradition would have us hold it here at the house, but my sanity is maxed out and there's no way I could play host. Liz mercifully agreed to have the reception at her place, but that was the extent of our conversation.

My hands continue struggling with the tie, but I'm concentrating on those sunken, tired eyes in the mirror. I've aged a decade in a matter of days. I'll probably age another decade by the end of the evening, because in addition to the words I've hastily thrown together on a piece of paper, I don't know what I'm going to tell everyone about the circumstances of Amy's death.

I can't tell anyone how she was found.

I can't tell anyone about the indications that she was having an affair.

I can't tell anyone about the cocaine or that the police are lying about it.

I can't tell anyone that she was lying to me.

I pull the fabric through the knot.

I can't tell anyone that I keep seeing some guy in an SUV parked outside our house.

I can't tell anyone about this key.

I slide the knot toward my throat.

And what does this key open, Amy?

My frustration physically manifests itself as I inadvertently slam the knot against my windpipe. I curse, loosen it a fraction of an inch, and check the length in the mirror, again.

Close enough.

"Dad?"

In the mirror, I can see Tatum standing in the doorway behind me.

"Yeah, sweetheart?" I ask.

"We need to go."

Chapter 18

Forest Lawn Memorial Park sits on the northern hillside of the Santa Monica Mountains, overlooking the San Fernando Valley. I slowly navigate the car up one of the winding roads to a small parking lot next to a flat area that's been carved into the gentle slope.

Once we've parked, Tatum and I are greeted by the funeral coordinator, Candice Costinez. She's polite, gentle, sympathetic; all the things you would expect from someone in her position. She makes pleasant small talk as she leads us from the parking lot to the viewing area. Judging by her tone and rehearsed questions, she's done this many, many times.

A ring of perfectly manicured bushes and trees surrounds the viewing area. Within the enclosure, rows of wooden benches face a section of wall that provides some shade. In the shade, on a pedestal draped in black cloth, is an open casket with Amy's body resting inside.

Tatum sniffles at my side. I put an arm around her shoulder and look to Candice.

"Take all the time you need," she says.

Tatum and I walk down the center aisle between the rows of benches and stand before the casket. Amy's expression is peaceful and serene, just as I remember it. She's wearing a simple black dress that I provided from her wardrobe. Her hands are clasped below her breasts. The makeup gives her skin a waxy, pale sheen and causes the rouge on her cheeks to stand out.

This is the Amy I loved, the woman I was going to spend the rest of my life with. Not the Amy I saw through the glass in the morgue.

Unable to shake that image of her lying on the table, I turn my head to scan the surroundings. It really is beautiful up here. The valley is laid out below with only the slightest whisper of cars on the 134 freeway reaching our ears. The sky overhead is a brilliant blue. The grass is a perfect green with darkened alternating strips from the mower. There's also a refreshment table with water and sodas set up off to the side of the benches.

Tatum begins to tremble.

A horrible realization dawns on me; this is the first time she's seen her mother since the morning she said good-bye as we left for the airport, and this is the last time Tatum is going to see her ever again.

I haven't prepared her for this.

I've been so caught up in trying to unravel Amy's secret life, I haven't been there for my daughter.

I place my arm around Tatum's shoulders to give her a comforting squeeze, but to my surprise, she shrugs it off.

"I'm okay," she says in an indecipherable tone.

It's a mixture of sadness and resentment. She's looking down at Amy as if she's . . . angry. Another thought occurs to me: she believes it. She believes that Amy was having an affair. I don't believe it because I knew Amy. I knew Amy better than Tatum knew her. It's impossible to explain to your child that you and your spouse had a life before them. That there was a time when it was just the two of you against the world, and when you're raising a child together, you really find out a lot about your partner. That's why I don't believe that Amy was having an affair, but I can never explain that to Tatum.

80

A pang of guilt rips through me.

I *really* didn't prepare her for this. On the drive over, I told her that we shouldn't tell people too much about what happened and that we shouldn't say anything at all about the police report. Those are the issues I was focusing on, not how she was feeling.

"Mr. Burcham?"

Candice is standing next to me.

"Yes?"

"The guests are arriving."

The top brass from Fortis, minus Henry Vaughn, are some of the first to arrive.

Malcolm is here solo. His wife passed away some time ago. He's quickly followed by Nadine and Spencer. Their expressions are appropriately somber. They smile sadly as they approach Tatum and me, shaking our hands and telling us what a wonderful person Amy was.

More people arrive.

I hardly recognize many of them, but Malcolm and the rest of the Fortis brigade know who they are. They begin glad-handing, speaking in low tones, and visiting the refreshment table. It feels wrong, seeing these people that I've never met at Amy's funeral, but her job brought her in contact with a lot of people. It's not her fault that I don't know who they are.

There's a definite split between Amy's business mourners and the handful of neighbors and parents who know Tatum and me.

Tatum is visibly uncomfortable. She thanks those who offer their sympathies, but she keeps her eyes down in an attempt to become invisible. When Aiden arrives, dressed in black pants and button-down shirt, she goes straight to him. They embrace, become fused at the hip, and move to a stone bench on the perimeter of the viewing area. She leans into him and he puts an arm over her shoulder. The two stare silently at the open casket across the rows of benches while Aiden strokes her arm with his thumb.

I'm once again thankful that he's here for her.

My world is very different from where it was a week ago.

The past half hour has been a blur.

Strangers have offered me their condolences and praised Amy as an amazing person. Thankfully, as everything got started, only a few asked what happened to her. They tried to be subtle, but it was obvious. One of them was a guy with black hair and a dark blue suit. I kept it simple. She was on business. It was sudden. We still don't know specifics and are awaiting tests. I was appreciative that he was there, but had no problem lying to him. After he walked away, I watched him out of the corner of my eye as he relayed the information to two women by the refreshment table. Moments later, the trio split up to make the rounds, and I could practically see the news spread through the gathering like a hushed wildfire.

After that, no one else asked.

Aiden and Tatum haven't moved from their bench. I'm content to let them stay there. They're by themselves and I don't want her to have to join in my lies about the circumstances of Amy's death. I also don't know how much she's told Aiden.

Across the seating area, Malcolm detaches himself from a small knot of people and approaches.

"Fortis isn't the same without her," he says.

"She loved that place. She was incredibly proud of her job."

"As she should have been," he says, before shifting gears. "I wanted to ask you; did you get everything you wanted from her office? I noticed that there were still a lot of photos on the wall."

"Thanks, but I got everything I needed."

He looks flummoxed, begins to speak, but then stops to rephrase. "I hate to ask but our legal department insisted; you didn't happen to take any papers, did you?"

"No. Why? Is something missing?"

"No. No, no, no. They're just covering the company's ass."

Seemingly out of nowhere, Tess, Malcolm's assistant, steps up to his side. "I'm terribly sorry to interrupt, gentlemen, but Mr. Davis, Mr. Reynolds is here and wishes to speak to you."

Malcolm smiles at me. "Please excuse me, Mark. I have to take care of some business, but I'll be here when the service begins."

"Sure," I answer, but he and Tess have already turned and are walking away.

I watch them go, but in my periphery vision, I notice one head turn, and then another, and another. While it's been quiet in this mini-courtyard, it now goes utterly silent.

I must admit; part of me has been waiting for this and I take a strange pleasure in watching everyone's reaction. There's even a gasp or two, which is not uncalled for, I guess.

The ghost of Amy is slowly walking down the aisle.

She stops in front of the casket and gazes down at herself. The image is flawless; the upswept nose and the brunette hair, which unlike the Amy in the casket, is cropped in a bob cut. I can see the other differences, as well, such as the softer features.

Stillness reigns over the small assembly.

I assume that many people here probably knew that Amy had a sister, but I'm guessing a good portion of them didn't know she was a twin. After all, Amy and Liz hadn't spoken in years.

I shouldn't be enjoying this as much as I am, but I think even Amy would have gotten a kick out of it. It's like watching someone haunt their own funeral.

My enjoyment abruptly ends as I notice Liz's shoulders begin to sag and tremble.

I immediately go to join her, feeling like an ass for letting her stand there alone.

"Hi, Liz," I softly say.

She turns to me.

If I hadn't seen the wedding ring on Amy's finger or Colleen's necklace around her neck as she lay dead on that table in the morgue, I might think that Amy is standing in front of me, but I can't do that. I will drive myself insane.

Despite the two-year absence, Liz looks the same.

Liz looks up at me with shimmering eyes. Then, she suddenly throws her arms over my shoulders and grips me in a fierce embrace.

Just as she wasn't ready to see her sister lying dead in a casket, I wasn't ready to be looking at a facsimile of Amy's face.

We merely stand there, holding each other as we cry.

Chapter 19

It's almost time.

People are starting to find their seats. Tatum and Aiden have left their bench and joined Liz and me in the front row.

Tatum slightly leans toward me.

"Hey, Dad?" she asks, quietly.

"Yeah?"

"Is it okay if Aiden and I skip the reception?"

"Skip the reception? What are you going to do?"

"We were gonna go get ice cream."

My knee-jerk reaction is to say no, but she's kept her end of the deal by not saying anything to anyone about how Amy was found. She's also clearly miserable. There's no reason to prolong her suffering.

"Sure," I answer.

"Can I have your keys? I need to get my purse out of the car."

I get them out of my pocket and hand them over.

"Hurry back."

"We will."

She and Aiden stand and walk back toward the small parking lot, which is adjacent to the viewing area.

Panic grips me as I worry that she's going to spot the black key on my key ring, but she's so wrapped up in Aiden, she doesn't notice.

I watch them walk away before turning my attention back to Liz.

"You okay?" I ask. "If you need to step away for a minute—"

"I'm fine," she responds, staring straight ahead.

There are a million questions I need to ask her, but we have to get through the viewing, first. It'll be different at the reception. She's going to have to tell me everything.

Tatum and Aiden return to their seats just as Candice walks around the benches and stops in front of us.

"We'll begin in another minute or two, Mr. Burcham."

"Thank you."

She walks away.

"Are you sure you don't want to say anything?" I ask Liz.

"I don't think I can," she replies, her eyes firmly locked on the casket.

Candice weaves her way through the courtyard, informing the last of the stragglers around the refreshment table that we're about to begin.

Once everyone is seated, she stands by the casket and addresses the crowd of forty or so, seated on the benches.

"On behalf of Mark, Tatum, and Liz, we'd like to thank everyone for coming. It would have meant a lot to Amy. Mark is going to say a few words and then we'll pay our respects."

She nods to me and I stand.

Pulling a folded piece of paper from my pocket, I make my way to the casket. Candice steps off to the side and discreetly moves to the back of the viewing area. I finish unfolding the piece of paper upon which are the words I hastily threw together this morning and face the small crowd, but it's too much. I have to keep my eyes on the paper.

"First of all," I begin, "like Candice said, I want to thank you all for coming today. It truly means a lot to Tatum and myself . . .

If you had told me a few days ago that I would be standing in front of you, speaking at Amy's funeral, I wouldn't have believed you. I've spent the last few days still trying not to believe it, trying to convince myself that Amy's at work, or on her way home, and that at any minute, she's going to walk through the door, or call me to tell me she's running a few minutes late. I was even trying to convince myself of that this morning as I wrote this. So, please forgive me if these words miss their mark. You could have given me a year to prepare this speech and I still wouldn't have been able to say what I'm feeling. There's no way to express what you're feeling when the person you loved, your best friend, the person you planned on spending the rest of your life with suddenly isn't there anymore . . ." I slightly turn toward the figure of Amy, lying in the casket next to me. "I love you, Amy . . . and I wish I could have gotten to know you better . . . I wish I could have gotten to know you as a grandmother. I wish I could have known you as someone who went to Italy. I wish I could have known you as a retired businesswoman, sitting next to me on the couch as we grew old. I wish I could have known you as someone who was celebrating their fiftieth wedding anniversary . . . I wish I could have known you better." I take a breath. ". . . Good-bye, Amy . . . I love you. I've always loved you . . . It was always you."

I look up from my paper.

There are sad smiles and a few tears. Liz is staring straight ahead. Her face is stone.

To avoid any more eye contact, I look past the benches and up the gentle slope of a hill to one of the roads that winds through the cemetery.

My body goes rigid.

A black SUV is parked there on the side of the road, looking down on us. The driver's tinted window is rolled down an inch or two. As I stare transfixed, a plume of cigarette smoke crawls out of the opening and climbs into the air.

He's here.

Whoever this is, he's been watching us. He's been watching the house, and now, he's here at Amy's funeral.

I fold the paper and tuck it back into my jacket pocket. I begin calmly walking back to my seat, but I'm preparing myself. My pulse is racing. Adrenaline courses through my veins.

Once I hit the aisle, I'm going to sprint. There's no way I can catch him, but I don't need to. All I need is a license plate.

I'm mapping out a path through the gravestones but suddenly, the SUV begins to pull forward.

My leg muscles explode as I lunge forward, prepared to charge, but gasps and surprised mumbles from the gathering cause me to immediately abandon my plan.

There's no way I'm going to get close enough to see his license plate and if I run, people are going to ask questions. I quickly bring my legs to a stop and play it off as if I've tripped. I sell it further by looking back and pretending to search for the crack or raised section of pavement that sent me forward.

"Really need to look where I'm going," I say with a light, embarrassed laugh.

People sigh with relief and politely smile.

I look back up the hill.

The road is empty.

Chapter 20

All right. Enough of this.

About half the people who came to the viewing are here at Liz's Craftsman bungalow in Pasadena for the reception. They've all been very nice and sincere, and for that, I'm very appreciative.

My problem is with Liz.

She's pretending to be so busy playing host that she doesn't have time to speak to me.

I've been patient. I've kept my distance as she's spoken to people, obsessively checked the finger foods, and restocked the wines on the counter and in the fridge. Her sister is dead, and she did me a favor by having the reception here, but I can't wait any longer. The reception is a little over an hour old but I don't care. It's been a surreal couple of days and her unwillingness to share what she knows has got me fuming. The glasses of wine I've downed are also adding to that fire as I've waited for my chance to speak to her.

I finally catch her alone in the kitchen, pulling another bottle of chardonnay from the fridge to put in the large bowl of ice next to the wine glasses on the counter.

"Liz?"

She tenses with her back to me.

"We have to talk," I say.

She hangs her head in resignation and then turns to me but avoids eye contact. She tucks the bottle of chardonnay under her arm and picks up an empty wine glass from the row on the counter.

"I suppose we do," she answers, walks across the kitchen, and goes out the door to the backyard.

I follow.

Liz continues walking to the sitting area underneath a sprawling oak tree in the far corner of the yard, where strands of lights hang in the branches, casting a soft, even glow.

She sits in one of the side-by-side Adirondack chairs that face the house. I sit in the other and wait while she unscrews the cap on the chardonnay. She's about to pour it into her glass but stops.

"Fuck it."

She puts the glass down and takes a long, multi-gulp pull directly from the bottle. Once she finishes, she wipes her lips with back of her hand, and offers the wine to me, while still refusing to look me in the eye.

"No, thanks," I tell her. "I've had enough."

She shrugs and sets the bottle on the ground. She then reaches into her pocket and pulls out a pack of Marlboros and a cheap red lighter. She extracts a cigarette, clamps it between her lips, and drops the box next to the bottle of wine.

"When did you start smoking, again?" I ask as she flicks the lighter and kisses the flame to the tip of the cigarette.

She inhales deeply and leans back in the chair.

"About ten minutes after you called," she replies with an exhale of smoke that drifts up into the lights.

Amy and Liz started smoking when they were teens. They would sneak cigarettes from their father. They stopped her freshman year, but then Amy picked it back up after Colleen's death. She said it was because of the guilt. She was still smoking

90

when we met. She knew I didn't like it, but her career was stressful, and she never smoked inside. When she told me we were pregnant, I went through the house and collected every cigarette, even the secret stashes she thought I didn't know about, and tossed them in the garbage.

"That's that," I had told her and she agreed.

Liz continues to stare upward with her head back in the chair. She takes another drag and I can see her eyes start to glisten.

I wait for her to speak, but it becomes clear she's not going to.

"I need to know, Liz. I need to know what happened between you and Amy."

She doesn't say a word and continues to stare upwards into the lights overhead.

"Liz?"

She shakes her head. "It was stupid."

"I don't care."

"First off, you have to promise me—"

"No. I'm not promising you anything until you tell me what hap—"

"Mark, you're not going to like it and you have to understand—"

"Dammit, Amy! Just tell me what happened!"

Liz's eyes finally snap to mine.

I abruptly stand up from my chair, press my hands against my eyes, and start pacing.

It was a slip brought on by stress, exhaustion, grief, and alcohol, but one that I had been fighting. While they were twins and were incredibly close growing up, Liz and Amy each had their own individual styles. I never found it that hard to tell them apart but they were still twins, and seeing Liz for the first time in two years, after not having enough time to process the loss of Amy, has my mind playing tricks on me.

I lower my hands from my eyes.

Liz is still staring at me, tears rolling down her face.

"Liz, I'm . . . I'm sorry. I meant to say— I mean—"

She waits for some sort of explanation, but I don't have one.

"You're right," I growl. "Fuck it."

I lean over, snatch the bottle of chardonnay from the ground next to her, bring it to my lips, and take long, deep gulps. The liquid pools in my stomach, adding to the wine that's already there. I keep drinking until the rest of the wine is gone. Out of breath, I toss the bottle to the ground and sink into the chair. I lean back and stare up at the lights, which are still wrapped in the haze of Liz's cigarette smoke. The chilled wine has already begun to warm my limbs. I haven't eaten anything since this morning and the wine is going to start hitting me qui—

"She was having an affair," Liz says.

I pull my gaze away from the lights to look at her.

She's staring in the direction of the house but her focus is a million miles away.

"What?" I ask.

"Amy was having an affair," Liz repeats. "That's what we fought about. That's why we weren't talking."

A pit opens in my stomach and everything falls through.

I've been fighting against it, despite all the evidence to the contrary. I've been putting my faith in Amy, but this is different. Hearing Liz say it, and knowing that's the reason that she and Amy haven't spoken in more than two years, holds more weight than any police report ever could.

Neither of us speaks.

I'm too stunned. I really had been oblivious. I had missed it. I thought it was the stress of her job. I never considered that she wasn't content, because I was so sure of our marriage. I believed it possible of other couples, but thought Amy and I weren't "other couples."

I finally find use of my tongue to ask the most basic question.

"With who?"

"She wouldn't tell me."

"When did you find out?"

"A little over two years ago. I saw her change. She was growing paranoid. I suspected it, and then finally flat-out called her on it . . . She admitted it. I kept trying to get her to tell me who it was, but she wouldn't say. I asked her how she could do this to you and to Tatum, but she wouldn't answer me." As she recounts her story, every muscle in Liz's body locks up, as though the effort is causing her physical pain. "Finally, I gave her an ultimatum; either she had to tell you, or I would. She begged me to stay quiet, but I gave her three months. Three months to tell you or I would. I was certain that she would do it, but three months passed, and she hadn't . . . That's when we stopped talking."

In addition to the alcohol beginning to slow my responses, I'm also suddenly nauseous. I had seen the change in Amy right around the same time Liz is talking about. I quickly run through all the memories I can, searching for the detail I missed, but the alcohol is getting in the way. I sit up and shake my head to counteract the growing effect of the wine.

No . . . No. I didn't miss something.

Looking back on my life with Amy, all I see are the adventures, the laughs, the late-night talks, the sacrifices we made for each other, and how we supported one another.

And there's still this key. Amy's trying to tell me what really happened. The door that allowed the first hints of doubt to creep in that had only opened a moment ago slams shut.

Maybe I'm being stupid. Maybe I'm being naïve, but until I figure out what she was trying to tell me with this key, I still have to trust Amy.

"I don't believe you, Liz."

She stares at me in shock.

"I'm sorry, Mark, but it's true."

"Then why didn't you tell me?"

She takes another drag from her cigarette before answering. "Because after I got over my disbelief that she wouldn't tell you,

93

I wasn't sure *how* to tell you. Eventually, it was just easier to stay out of it."

"So, you knew it was a big deal, but it was easier for you to let her go on lying to me?"

She shakes her head. "I was a coward, okay? I was angry with her, but she was still my sister. I worried about what it would do to you and Tatum. It became easier to cut her out of my life."

In addition to the disorientation, I can now distinctly feel a knife in my back. Liz is lying or she's not, and her actions in either case are unacceptable.

"You're really going to go with that as your excuse, Liz?"

She wilts under my stare and finally throws up her hands. "Yes, Mark. I was selfish. Okay? I kept hoping that Amy would do the right thing."

"And did you ever stop to think that if *you* had done the right thing, Amy might still be alive?" I ask, continuing to glare at her.

Liz glares right back, her shame morphing into anger. "Are you seriously suggesting that Amy's death is my fault?"

"No," I answer, pulling back a little. "Amy was a grown woman. She made her own choices."

"Then what are you suggesting?"

I stumble for an alternate explanation but there isn't one. It's exactly what I was suggesting and I'm not wrong, but for some reason, I'm still worried about other people's feelings.

"I'm suggesting that maybe things would have been different if you had told me," I feebly offer.

"How is that any different than saying it's my fault?"

I snap. "Because maybe it is your fault, Amy! . . . I mean *Liz* . . . I—Fuck!" I take a second to catch my breath before leaning forward, cupping my head in my hands. "I'm sorry, Liz. I didn't mean it."

"Yes, you did," she says, quietly.

I raise my head to look at her. "Yeah. I did."

There's no point denying it.

Her eyes burn me to the ground as her mind races.

I'm pretty drunk, on my way to being very drunk, and she knew for two years without telling me. My concern for her feelings is waning fast.

"You should have told me, Liz. Amy might still be alive. I might still have a wife. Tatum might still have a mother, and you might still have a sister."

"Get out of my house," she seethes.

"First, I want you to look me in the eyes and tell me that—"

She suddenly grabs the wine glass by her feet. "Get the fuck out of my house!" she screams and hurls the glass at me. It hits the wooden armrest of the chair and shatters. Bits of glass fly at my chest and face. I bring my arms up but I'm too late and a shard grazes my jaw.

Liz and I stare at each other, unblinking.

The faint sounds of conversation coming from the house have stopped. I glance across the lawn to see the windows on the bottom floor are filled with the silhouettes of people watching us.

I turn back to Liz. Her expression hasn't changed.

"Get out," she whispers.

I stand, retrace my steps across the lawn, and go through the door to the kitchen.

The house is stone silent. Every face is watching me. In the hall, Nadine and Spencer move to the side to let me pass.

Without a word to anyone, I walk out the front door to my car, which is parked in the street.

The only thought I have as I start the engine is, *Thank God Tatum wasn't here to see this.*

Chapter 21

My overwhelming paranoia on the drive home is warranted. There's easily a bottle and a half of wine swimming through me. It was a stupid decision to get behind the wheel, so I keep it five miles below the speed limit on the freeway, I don't rush to make any yellow lights, and I take a few extra seconds at every stop sign. Thankfully, the roads are quiet.

I finally pull into the driveway of the house without incident and just sit in the car.

Tatum texted me to let me know that she and Aiden were still having ice cream, and since I left the reception so unceremoniously early, I'll have the place to myself for the next few hours. I need to sober up as much as I can before she gets home.

I'll apologize to Liz tomorrow. I stand by my opinion that she should have told me, but of course Amy's death wasn't her fault. I'll tell her I'm sorry and see what else she remembers. *If* Amy was sleeping with someone like Liz said, then she may have some sort of clue or detail that can help me find this mystery man.

In all the drama and the wine, I forgot to ask her about the key but I don't think that's possible. If I ask her and she doesn't know anything about it, she's going to ask where I found it and why I think it has something to do with Amy.

I'm getting ahead of myself. I need to get inside and start chugging water, but as I pulled into the driveway, I noticed the flap on the mailbox is partially open. I haven't collected the mail since the day I dropped Amy off at the airport.

The cool evening air feels good as I exit the car and walk down the drive. I absent-mindedly grab the mail, close the flap, return to the car, and hit the clicker to open the garage door.

Once I've pulled into my spot, I hit the clicker again and the garage door rumbles to a close behind me. My balance is not all there as I walk to the door leading to the kitchen, carrying the mail in my hand. I fumble with my keys and have to look down to get it into the lock, which causes me to see the small padded envelope amongst the bills and credit card offers.

I'm finally successful in unlocking the door and step inside.

I toss the mail and my keys onto the kitchen table but hold on to the padded envelope. I drop into a chair, slide my finger under the flap to open it, and hold it upside down.

A small plastic bag drops into my hand.

My throat catches.

Inside the bag are Amy's ring and necklace.

I take a closer look at the envelope and see the return address: County of Los Angeles Medical Examiner.

My vision goes blurry as stinging tears fill my eyes and my nose is instantly filled with snot.

Why? Why did this have to arrive today? It feels so cruel to be holding them in my hand on the day of Amy's funeral and after being told that she was having an affair. To have Amy's wedding ring and necklace sent back by mail, in a simple plastic Ziploc bag is a kick to the stomach and I can't choke back the sobs. Some of it is the wine, but only some.

This goes on for a couple of minutes until I remind myself that Tatum will be home in a few hours. I have to sober up and pull myself together.

I stand, walk over to the counter, grab a glass from the cabinet next to the sink, fill it from the tap, and gulp it down. I catch my breath, refill the glass, shut off the tap, and tilt my head back to drink but pause, the rim of the glass touching my lips.

What the hell was that?

I stand perfectly still, waiting for a repeat of the sound I just heard . . .

But the house is quiet.

Wait. Hold on.

The house shouldn't be quiet.

I look back at the alarm panel by the garage door.

The display blinks. "DISARMED: SYSTEM READY."

I didn't disarm it when I came inside—I was too busy focusing on the envelope—which means it wasn't armed. Did I really forget to arm the security system before leaving this afternoon?

That's extremely unlikely. Arming the security system before I leave is something that has become automatic. It feels odd if I don't do it, like not wearing a seatbelt.

On the other hand, I was leaving for my wife's funeral. My mind, to put it mildly, was occupied.

I must have forgotten. It's the only explanation.

It's not that big of a deal.

Right now, I've got to sober up as much as I can.

I go to take another drink but suddenly try to stop mid-gulp. Too late.

I cough and hack as water enters my lungs.

I tried to stop because I heard that sound, again: footsteps in the upstairs hall.

A realization claws its way up my spine. I didn't forget to set the alarm.

There's someone here.

I slowly set the glass on the counter and take out my phone. I slide off my stiff, hard-soled shoes, and silently move across the kitchen to the hall. I briefly look down at my phone and type "9-1-1" on the keypad but I don't hit send. Even in the brief time it's taken me to go from the kitchen to the bottom of the stairs, I'm starting to wonder if I really heard them.

I wait on the landing, staring into the darkness above.

Maybe I am still being paranoid from the drive home. Maybe it's my nerves. Maybe it's the wine.

The tiniest creak from the stairs sounds like thunder as I begin climbing.

By the time I reach the upstairs hall, I'm holding my breath. The phone is still in my hand, "9-1-1" is still typed in, and my thumb still hovers over the call button. The guest room to my right is dark and silent. There's just enough light that I can see that my bedroom door is open at the end of the hall.

Did I leave it like that?

I don't remember but it's enough for me to hit "call" on my phone.

"Nine-one-one, what is the nature of your emergency?" a male voice asks.

"My name is Mark Burcham. I'm at 3355 Sierra Vista Lane in Sherman Oaks. I think there's someone in my house," I say loud enough for someone in my bedroom to hear. I snap on the hallway light and brace myself . . .

For nothing.

I don't know what I was expecting, maybe that the intruder would panic and reveal themselves, but it's quiet.

"Did I hear you correctly?" the operator asks. "There's an intruder in your house?"

I'm still waiting for someone to emerge from my bedroom.

"Sir? Are you there?"

"Yes, there is someone. I mean, maybe . . . I think so," I reply, my certainty fading fast.

"Are you in the house, now?"

"Yes."

"Okay. You need to go outside and wait. I'm sending a police officer, now."

I squint into the dimness to the open bedroom door, searching for any signs of an intruder. Between the lights coming on and the fact that I'm standing here, talking on the phone to 9-1-1, if there was an intruder, they would have made a run for it, right?

But there's no movement from my room, no footsteps, no sounds whatsoever.

The tension flows out of me in an embarrassed sigh.

There's no one here. I'm just being paranoid.

It's the wine. It's the fatigue. It's the fact that my wife's funeral was only a few hours ago and right after that, I was told by her sister that she was having an affair, and then I received her ring and her necklace from the morgue.

"You know what?" I say into the phone, my words mushy. "I'm sorry. I was wrong. It's been a tough couple of days. I was at my wife's funeral this afternoon and I've had a little too much to drink, and then her ring and necklace showed up. There's no one here. I'm just hearing things. I'm sorry to—"

There's a sudden movement in the guest room right behind me.

Before I can turn around, something slams into my back, and I'm sent hurtling down the stairs.

Chapter 22

"So, you weren't able to get a good look at your attacker?"

I wince as I press the bag of ice against the knot on the back of my head as Detective Harper and I sit at the kitchen table.

"No. I told you. He pushed me down the stairs—"

"He? I thought you didn't get a good look."

"He. She. They. Whatever. They pushed me down the stairs and I hit my head on the landing. I was dazed. They stepped over me and ran out the front door."

"Look right here," the EMT hunched in front of me says.

I'm suddenly blinded by his pen light. I squint and turn my head, causing a bolt of pain to rip through my body.

"How is he?" Detective Harper asks.

"He's pretty banged up, but he doesn't appear to have a concussion," the EMT answers. "A day or two of rest, some Tylenol, and he'll be fine."

Detective Harper nods. "Thank you."

The EMT tucks the pen light back into his shirt pocket and picks up his kit. He then heads down the hall and out the door to the ambulance parked in the street, leaving Detective Harper and me alone.

I return the ice pack to the back of my head and lean forward, trying to blink away the pounding in my skull. As I do, I happen to notice the small gun that's tucked into an ankle holster, sticking out of his pant leg.

"Cute backup," I mumble.

"He's right, you know?" Detective Harper says, ignoring my comment. "You need to get some rest."

"Thanks, but I'm more worried about whoever broke into my house. They knew the code to the alarm system."

"And you're certain that you remembered to arm it before you left for your wife's funeral?"

"I'm pretty sure."

My answer isn't as firm as I'd like it to be, and he noticed.

"Mr. Burcham, you've had a hell of a couple of days. Isn't it possible you forgot?"

"Okay. Even if I didn't set the alarm, someone still broke into my house and attacked me."

Detective Harper chews his lip.

"Really?" I ask. "You don't beli—?"

"Dad?!" Tatum yells from the front yard through the open front door. She bursts into the house and runs down the hall into the kitchen.

"It's okay, sweetheart. I'm okay," I say, waving my hand.

She throws her arms around my neck and grips me tightly. It hurts but I'm not going to turn down an embrace from my daughter. Aiden enters the kitchen a few seconds later and stands to the side. I give him a nod to let him know I'm fine.

"What happened?" Tatum asks, releasing me and seeing the ice pack in my hand.

"Someone broke into the house and pushed me down the stairs," I answer.

"What? Who?"

"We don't know. After pushing me down the stairs, he—" I catch Detective Harper's skeptical expression, "*they* ran out the front door."

"Have you found him?" Tatum asks Detective Harper.

He considers her and then addresses me. "Mr. Burcham, maybe you and I should talk in private."

"No!" Tatum yells. "Does this have something to do with my mom?"

"I understand that you're very upset," Detective Harper says. "But it might be best if—"

Tatum has a realization. "Are you the one investigating my mom's murder?"

"Her *death*," Detective Harper corrects her. "Yes."

"What are you doing here?" she asks.

"I called him," I tell her. "I thought that whoever broke into the house might have something to do with your mother, too."

There it is, again. The lip bite. What is this guy's deal?

Despite the pain, I can't keep from shaking my head. "You still don't believe me."

"Mr. Burcham." His tone is almost pleading. "I really think—"

"You can say whatever you're thinking in front of my daughter."

He shrugs in resignation.

"The odds of a burglar being able to disarm your system are very slim," he says.

"Okay. Fine. Maybe I forgot to arm it," I concede. "That still doesn't explain the attack—"

"I spoke to the dispatcher and he played me the audio of your call." He glances at Tatum and Aiden, giving me one last chance before continuing, which I don't take. "You mentioned that you had been drinking?"

Tatum tenses standing next to me.

"Yes," I answer. "I had some wine after the funeral at my wife's sister's house in Pasadena."

"How much wine are we talking?"

". . . I had a glass or two."

"You've had enough that I can still smell it on you," Detective Harper says, pouncing on my obvious lie.

Tatum discreetly inhales through her nose. I glance up at her. She won't look down at me but it's clear that she can smell it, too. Even Aiden is staring uncomfortably at the floor.

"And I assume you drove back to the house?" Detective Harper asks.

I can't believe this. He's playing off Tatum. He's trying to turn her against me.

"Yes, I did but—"

"And in the call, you changed your mind and told him that there was no one in the house. You told him that you had been drinking and were on edge."

"Yes," I hiss. "And that's when someone stepped out of the guest room behind me and shoved me down the stairs."

He glances at Tatum and Aiden, making sure they're hearing this, before returning to me. "Mr. Burcham, isn't it more likely that during what has to have been a very emotional day, you forgot to set the alarm before leaving and that after your wife's funeral, you had too much to drink, and accidentally fell down the stairs? I know it might be embarrassing to admit, but it's understandable."

Over the past few days, I've dealt with grief, anger, bewilderment, and a thousand other emotions. Now, Detective Harper is trying to shame me in front of my daughter and her boyfriend.

"No," I reply, forcefully. "I was attacked. I heard them. They pushed me down the stairs and stepped over me as they went out the front door, but I didn't get a good look at them."

"And why was that?" he asks.

"I hit my head. I was dazed," I respond, holding up the bag of ice in my hand.

Detective Harper's overly sympathetic nod nearly sets me off.

"I know what happened," I reiterate, not caring about the pounding in my head. "There was someone in my house."

"Who?" he asks dismissively.

"I don't know . . . but someone's been watching us. They've been following me."

Detective Harper straightens up, suddenly alert. "What makes you think that?"

"The past few nights, there's been an SUV parked on the street. Someone's been sitting in it, smoking cigarettes and watching us. He was at the funeral today."

"Dad, are you serious?" Tatum asks.

"Did you get a license plate?" Detective Harper asks, ignoring her.

"No."

"Then how do you know it was the same SUV at the funeral today?"

"I saw cigarette smoke coming out of the SUV."

Detective Harper leans back, exasperated.

"Really?" I ask. "You're just not going to believe anything that I say?"

"I believe you saw someone smoking a cigarette while they were sitting in a black SUV parked on your street. I don't believe that means they were watching you. They could have been having a smoke in his car because his wife won't let him smoke in the house."

"And he just happened to be in the cemetery at my wife's funeral today?"

"It's also not difficult to believe that you saw a black SUV at a cemetery. No questions there. I also believe that the person inside may have been smoking a cigarette or vaping. Cemeteries tend to be sad places where people might indulge in a cigarette to cope with grief or they may have simply wanted some nicotine. I believe that you saw one of the thousands of black SUVs in this town and someone was sitting in it, having a smoke. That is way more likely than all these other sinister theories you've dreamed up in your head." Throughout the course of his rant, he's been getting more and more worked up, but now, he notices the concern and fear on Tatum's face. He takes a deep breath and recalculates. "Listen; you two have suffered a terrible loss. The worst kind of loss, and when that happens, we want that loss

105

to be a part of something bigger, because then it would make sense, but that type of thinking only adds to the pain, because there's nothing there. It's that type of thinking that keeps us from getting better. Believe me, I know because I've seen this over and over, again." He finishes with an attempt at a consoling smile. "Please, Mr. Burcham. You need to stop. For your own good."

Tatum is lightly stroking my back.

He's got her. She believes him and despite my conviction that he's lying to me, what's throwing me for a loop is that he does seem genuinely concerned about us.

"I know what happened," I repeat. "There was someone in my house . . . and I never told you that SUV was black."

Detective Harper chews his lip. "Oh for crying out loud. I just guessed it because if there's some shadowy figure watching you, of course their SUV would be black."

"They were in my house! They pushed me down the stairs."

"Fine. If it was a robbery, why didn't they take anything valuable?" Detective Harper gestures to all the expensive items within sight: the TV, the stereo system, etc. "I see about a dozen things here that they could have fenced for thousands of dollars."

"Maybe he was looking for something else," I counter.

"See?" Detective Harper pleads. "This is exactly what I'm talking about, Mr. Burcham. This right here. *If* there was someone in your house and *if* it wasn't a robbery, what could this 'intruder' have possibly been looking for?"

". . . I don't know," I answer, keeping my expression as neutral as possible, but the black key in my pocket is suddenly very heavy.

Chapter 23

"Are you sure, Dad?"

"Yes. It's fine."

"But you said that someone broke into the house last night and attacked you."

No, Tatum. Someone did *break into the house last night and they* did *attack me.*

That's what I want to say, but I hold my fire.

"I'm fine," I tell her with forced reassurance.

Tatum puts her hands on her hips and stares at me. It's a gesture she learned at a young age from watching Amy, who would give me that same look in response to one of my horrible dad-jokes. That look would always get a laugh out of me, which a young Tatum found amusing and would mimic, hoping for the same reaction.

Now, she uses it to express disbelief. She may have a point.

I can't be certain of what last night's intruder was after. I can only assume that it has something to do with the black key in my pocket because there's nothing else to go on, and if this key is that important, they'll try again. That's why I'm perfectly fine with Tatum spending the afternoon at Aiden's, away from the house.

"Aiden's parents are home, right?" I ask.

"Yes," she answers with a roll of her eyes.

"And if you go anywhere else, you'll call me?"

"Yes."

I shrug. "Then, have fun. Tell Aiden I said 'thank you' for coming to the viewing yesterday."

". . . Okay," Tatum replies, infusing an amount of suspicion I would have not thought possible for a two-syllable answer.

Tatum drives away.

It's still hard to watch her drive. The dread you feel when your child starts getting behind the wheel of a three-thousand-pound machine and going seventy miles per hour down a Los Angeles freeway is overwhelming, and it only grew worse last year, when after having her license for only a few months, she put the car into a ditch. She claimed someone cut her off, but I think she may have overreacted to someone drifting into her lane. There was a brief cooling-off period where she could drive only with either Amy or me in the passenger seat, but after a few weeks, we were comfortable enough to let her drive solo, again. That dread never goes away but just as the night that I found the key, I want the place to myself for a little while.

I wait until she disappears around the corner and then fly to the kitchen table, open my laptop, pull my keys from my pocket, and set them on the table. The black key stands out from my house key and car fob.

There's no way I was going to tell Detective Harper about this key last night. I thought about it when I felt that he was being sincere in his concerns for us, but not after his whole admonition about dreaming this stuff up. Not after his refusal to look for whoever Amy supposedly had sex with and his dismissal of the impossibility that she died of an overdose of cocaine. And certainly not after he refused to believe me about this guy in the SUV or that I was attacked last night. If I had told him about the key, I'd never be able to find what it went to. Initially, I had found him to be comforting, but now, he keeps blowing off my suspicions, as though he wants me to stop searching.

His reluctance to even entertain the idea that there might be more to Amy's death has reinforced the conclusion that I arrived at days ago: if I'm going to find out what happened to Amy, I have to do it myself.

I'm no detective, but my confidence has been bolstered by the fact that I figured out the clue to the sundress. I realized that Amy was trying to tell me something and I need to discover what that is.

So, who broke into the house last night? What were they looking for? And why did they attack me?

The most likely candidate is the guy in the SUV. Who else could it have been? I'm going to call him "The Smoking Man." It's a little dramatic, I admit, but I'm certain that he's been watching me. He's been parked on our street. He was at the cemetery. So he's the obvious answer as to who broke in and attacked me, but I can't ask him if he was the one who shoved me down the stairs. And I can't ask him what he was looking for in the house. And I can't ask him if he killed Amy.

The only thing that makes sense is that he was looking for this key, which makes finding out what it opens that much more important.

The events of last night haven't gotten me closer to an answer, but have made my search more urgent.

I pour a cup of coffee and pop a few Tylenol to blunt the dual hangover from last night's wine and my violent trip down the stairs. Then, I pull up Google on my laptop and I'm off to the races.

Since I haven't cleared my search history from the past few days, I start typing something and Google finishes it for me, which lets me know if I've already gone down a particular road. I scan the results, going a few pages deeper than before to make sure I'm not missing anything, and everything still comes up empty.

Every now and again, I stop and stare at the key, trying to think of new ways to describe it. Then, I use those as new search terms. Black key + swirly logo, black key + calligraphy logo, dark key + cursive logo. Nothing gives me an answer. It's as if the whole point of the key is to remain a mystery.

An hour passes, and then another.

I've had way too much coffee and not enough water. That combined with the eyestrain causes my temples to start thumping. The Tylenol has barely made a dent.

I'm typing terms into the search bar and hitting enter, but I barely scan the results before trying something else.

black key + fancy logo + *enter* = nothing.

dark key + etched writing + *enter* = nothing.

black key + swoopy swirly writing + *enter* = . . .

A thumbnail image pops up in the results that looks like the black key.

Sitting up, I click the link.

The page loads and displays a business that sells novelty diaries aimed at young girls. The diaries have plastic locks that can be opened by a plastic key with a custom engraving. You can order them in any color and personalize the engraving on the key. Very Etsy. The banner at the top of the screen reads "My Secret Diary" and the slogan underneath proclaims, "It Will Never Tell." Below the slogan is a photoshopped picture of a young teenage girl. In one hand, she's clutching a book with a pink plastic lock. In her other hand is a cheap-looking plastic key with the letters B and W engraved on it, which I assume are supposed to be her initials.

"Dammit," I mutter.

I lean back and rub my eyes.

Another dead end.

This black key isn't some cheap toy. It's solid and the engraving is elaborate and intricate. It's designed to give whatever it opens a sense of value, of importance.

Not only am I pissed that I got momentarily excited about

a plastic piece of junk, it also opens up a possibility I haven't considered: What if this black key is custom made? What if it's one of a kind? If that's the case, then all of my searching is meaningless because there's no record of this key and there are no others like it.

A renewed sense of hopelessness sets in as I push myself away from the table and stand. I go to the sink, pour myself a glass of water, and shake out two more Tylenol from the bottle on the counter.

Was it only last night that I stood here, doing almost the exact same thing, when I heard someone upstairs? It feels like an eternity ago. Has it only been a few days since they found Amy? How can it seem like it was only five minutes and a lifetime ago, simultaneously? I think again about how much my world has changed in a matter of days. How much will change by the time this is all over? Will it ever be over? Will anything ever be normal, again, or will it—?

There's an old familiar rumbling outside.

"Shit!"

I quickly set the glass on the counter and race toward the door to the garage. I throw it open and slap the plastic button on the wall. As the garage door rumbles upwards, I grab the garbage bin. By the time I've dragged the bin to the rising door, it's open just enough that I can duck through.

Emerging from the garage into the bright sunshine, I already know I'm too late.

The garbage truck is halfway down the block.

To think that I was wondering if anything would ever be the same again; here's my answer. It will still be a chore for me to remember what day the garbage truck comes. It's not a big deal. The bin's not full. We'll be fine until next week. It's a small pain in the ass compared to all the other things I have to worry about.

I'm about to spin around and begin the journey back up the driveway but stop.

It's there, parked up the street, next to the stop sign at the intersection.

The black SUV.

Just as before, a forearm rests on the ledge of the open window and a cigarette is clutched in the dangling hand.

I can see it clear as day and there's not a doubt in my mind; he's watching me.

I let go of the bin and continue to stare.

The hand disappears into the shadow of the SUV's interior. A second later, a cloud of smoke exits the open window and is carried away by the breeze.

I step into the street.

"Hey!" I yell and begin running straight at the SUV. "Who are you?!"

The butt of the cigarette is ejected from the window and falls to the road.

I force my legs to work faster, desperately closing the gap. "Did you kill my wife?!"

The window of the SUV closes.

"Did you kill my wife?!" I scream. "DID YOU KILL MY WIFE?!!!"

The motor of the SUV revs and the tires squeal as it accelerates through the intersection.

I'm flat-out sprinting, but like yesterday, I'm not going to get close enough to see the license plate.

By the time I reach the intersection, the SUV is a speck in the distance.

I bend over and pick up the still smoldering cigarette butt.

A thought freezes me in place.

The SUV was parked as if he had come from the direction of Aiden's parent's house. Detective Harper would call it a coincidence, but I don't believe in coincidences anymore, and if this guy's been watching us, he has to know where Tatum is.

I frantically take out my phone and dial.

112

It rings . . . and rings . . . and rings . . .

"Dammit, Tatum. Pick up the phone . . ."

There's a click.

"Tatum?!"

"Hi, this is Tatum Burcham. I'm unable to take your call right now, but if you—"

I'm already running back to the house.

Chapter 24

"Hi, this is Tatum Burcham. I'm unable to take your—"

I curse and hang up.

In the time it's taken me to get back to the house, grab the keys, and pull out of the drive, I've left three messages. Tatum isn't answering. Keeping one eye on the road, I go to the contacts in my phone and scroll until I come across the number to Aiden's house. I'll be there in less than five minutes, but I don't care. I need to know that Tatum, and even Aiden, are okay. Someone has to answer my calls. I'll take Aiden's parents at this point.

Amy and I met them a few months ago after we caught Aiden sneaking out of Tatum's room in the middle of the night. We decided it would be best for the four of us to have a talk. They invited us over for coffee and we sat around their kitchen table. I expected them to be strict and domineering, which would explain Aiden's rebellious, aloof persona. Instead, Rob and Pam DeSallis were the hippies who never let go. They were well versed in "alternative" forms of parenting, subscribing to the mantra that children had to find their own way, which was essential to the development of their "aura." Their term. Not mine.

I wanted to point out that there was a time and a place for that, and it was called "college." I also had no doubt that they would see things differently if they were raising a daughter instead of a James Dean wannabe. Amy sensed my frustration and gently placed her hand on my knee under the table, which was the signal that I was running hot. She was right in that we were dealing with parents who did things differently. We said our peace and stated that we'd appreciate it if they had a talk with Aiden. They agreed but Amy and I never learned what, if anything, was said.

Rob and Pam DeSallis had read every book on raising children that had an esoteric bent and they believed all of it. They had also subscribed to every holistic-feng-shui-wheatgrass-chakra-garbage way of life that had led to their company, which sold patented cleanses and pills promising customers more energy and focus. After our fruitless conversation, I went on a deep dive and found that their promises weren't backed up by any reputable scientific studies.

This is the research you do when you're a father and someone starts dating your daughter.

Anyway, that was the only time I've been to the DeSallis home until now.

I take the turn way too fast and aim for the driveway of the house at the back of the cul-de-sac. It has the look of a small Mediterranean villa.

I pull in and park behind Tatum's car, which is next to Aiden's Mustang. The open garage is empty.

Horrible scenarios flash through my brain as I leap out and sprint for the porch. The Smoking Man has already been here. That's what he was telling me back at the house. He was coming from Aiden's.

I jab the button for the doorbell, but there's loud music coming from inside. It's so loud, I can't even hear the doorbell, so I began pounding on the door.

"Tatum?! Aiden?! . . . Mr. and Mrs. DeSallis?!!"

It doesn't matter how hard I slam my fist against the door or how loudly I cry out. No one inside will be able to hear anything over the music.

It might be rude or maybe even illegal, but I don't give a shit. I grasp the handle and push.

The door opens.

Stepping inside, I'm assaulted by the thumping bass emanating from the second floor. While the exterior is Mediterranean villa, the interior is all Japanese Zen Buddhism.

"Mr. and Mrs. DeSallis?"

Where the hell are they? And how can Aiden's parents stand this deafening, nauseating music—?

Wait a sec . . .

I saw Tatum's car. I saw Aiden's Mustang.

What I didn't see in the driveway, or the open garage, were Aiden's parents' cars.

They're not here. They can't be. The thumping music would be detrimental to their chi.

And that means only one thing.

I take the marble stairs two at a time to the second floor and storm down the hall to the closed door where the music is coming from. I grab the handle, ready to burst in, but stop.

Yes, I'm going to kill Aiden. That is a given, but the last thing I want is to kick open this door and see what is happening on the other side.

Instead, I pound my fist against the door and scream Tatum's name.

I keep up my steady drum until the music stops.

"Who is it?" Aiden asks, tentatively.

"Open this goddamn door!" I rage.

There's a long beat and then muttered voices.

Finally, the door swings inward.

Aiden is standing there, shirtless, while Tatum, who I assume is naked under the bedsheet she's wrapped in, stares at me in bewilderment.

"Dad?" Tatum asks.

"Get some clothes on and your asses downstairs. *Now*."

Aiden and Tatum cautiously descend the stairs to find me sitting in the overstuffed leather chair that faces the couch across the coffee table. Aiden has thankfully located a shirt to go with his pants. Tatum is wearing the same thing she left the house in earlier.

"Sit down," I instruct them, nodding sternly at the couch.

They step into the living room and settle in across from me, sitting on opposite ends of the couch.

The ticking of some weird antique clock on the mantel fills the silence.

Tatum finally speaks up. "Dad, we can expl—"

I hold up my hand. "No, no, no, sweetheart. I think I can figure this all out on my own. I'm just going to ask Aiden a question or two." I turn my attention to Aiden. "Where are your parents?"

"Dad, it's not all his fault," Tatum pleads.

"I am perfectly aware of that, but I need him to answer my question."

Keeping his focus on the floor, Aiden mumbles a response.

"I'm sorry, Aiden," I say, leaning forward. "I didn't quite catch that."

He raises his face to look at me. The compassionate, mature Aiden of the past few days is gone. The "too cool bad boy" of the past is back.

"They're at a meditation retreat in Arizona."

"A meditation retreat in Arizona? That's great," I sarcastically reply. "How long have they been gone?"

"Uhmnth."

"My hearing must be going, Aiden, because I didn't quite catch that one either."

Aiden squirms. ". . . A month."

"A month? Wow. That sounds like an amazing trip. And when will they be back?"

"In two weeks," he answers with a hint of sarcasm.

I, on the other hand, am done being sarcastic.

For the briefest of moments, I imagine leaping across the coffee table and slugging Aiden in the face. Then, we'll see how much of a rebel he thinks he is when he's up against a father he's been lying to in order to have sex with his daughter.

"So," I say, addressing them both while gripping the armrests to keep myself in place, "these past few days, as all of this has been happening—the death of your mother, Tatum, you pretending to care, Aiden—you both have been lying to me and taking advantage of my trust so that you could come here to have sex."

"Dad, we didn't—" Tatum begins.

"Look, man, it was—" Aiden answers simultaneously.

"That wasn't a question," I bark, cutting them off. I refocus on Tatum. "How long has this been going on?"

She fidgets before answering. "A few months . . ."

I dig my nails further into the armrests. "So, you were not only lying to me. You were lying to your mother?"

A flash of defiance lights up her face. "Mom knew."

The room twists and tilts, like a heavyweight boxer just landed an uppercut on my chin.

A new level of betrayal opens up before me.

It was one thing for Amy to have cheated on me. That was between her and me, but this?

Tatum was our shared responsibility. Every major, and even a lot of the minor, decisions that went into raising her required both of our inputs. To be kept out of this fills me with a rage and frustration I've never felt. Even after everything that's happened over the past few days, I didn't know it was possible to feel this hurt, this angry, this insecure, and this stupid all at the same time.

I want to lash out at everything and everyone, but some last shred of sanity that has been instilled by seventeen years of raising a child, is telling me to get myself and Tatum out of here before I do something stupid.

I stand and walk over to Tatum.

"Let's go."

"Dad, I'm sorry. I—"

"Now!" I seethe, grabbing her wrist and pulling her to her feet.

Aiden stands. "Mr. Burcham—"

I pin him with a stare, letting him know that if he comes anywhere near me, he's going to regret it.

Tatum hangs her head and makes her way toward the open front door. I follow close behind.

Aiden finds the use of his legs and approaches.

"Mr. Burcham? Mr. Burcham, please—"

I turn and get right in his face, causing him to freeze because I will absolutely kick the shit out of this kid if he says another word.

"You listen to me," I fume. "Do not *ever* try to contact my daughter, again. No calls. No texts. Nothing. Do you understand?"

I glare at him, unblinking, making sure he gets the point.

He really wants to say something. Instead, he looks down to the floor.

Satisfied that he's gotten the point, I turn away to follow Tatum out the door and down the path to our cars.

"I'm going to pull out into the street and you're going to drive in front of me," I tell Tatum. "Once we get home, you're going to wait for me before going into the house. Got it?"

She meekly nods and gets in her car.

I get in my car, start the engine, back up into the street, and wait.

Tatum sits behind the wheel of her car and stares back at Aiden, who is watching from the porch.

I slap the horn, causing her to jump.

She starts her car, backs up, pulls in front of me, and heads in the direction of home.

I fall in behind her and give one last look in the rearview mirror and watch as Aiden buries his face in his hands.

Chapter 25

"No! Tatum, what are you doing?! I said 'wait'!"

Of course, she can't hear me because she's already parked in the driveway, walked to the porch, and is opening the front door while I'm only pulling up to the end of the drive.

I lay into the horn, but she doesn't turn around. She only slams the front door behind her.

The tires screech as I hit the brakes, bringing the car to a stop behind hers.

I leap out and race for the door.

Even though I haven't seen the black SUV since it drove off, that doesn't mean the Smoking Man isn't inside, waiting for us. I might open the door and find him holding a gun to her head.

Thankfully, that's not the case and the only thing that greets me is the sound of Tatum's bedroom door slamming shut upstairs.

"Tatum?!"

It's no use waiting for an answer.

My concerns about the Smoking Man evaporate and I'm back to the matter at hand.

I lumber up the stairs, stop outside her bedroom door, and grasp the knob. It's locked.

"Dammit, Tatum, we're not doing this, again. Open the door."

"I don't want to talk to you!" she cries.

"I don't care."

"Then I guess you're going to have to break it down."

"Fine!"

I take a step back, raise my foot, and slam it into the door just below the knob. The frame splinters with a loud *crack* and the door swings inward.

Tatum is sitting on her bed and staring at me in shock.

"I can't believe you did that!" she says, motioning to the remnants of the door. "This is my room!"

"It's my damn house."

Unable to think of a comeback, Tatum crosses her arms and looks away.

"When did your mom find out?" I ask.

She scoffs. "That's what this is about?"

"It's about a lot of things and we're going to talk about all of them; you lying to me, your reckless behavior. I can't believe that you would be so careless that you would—"

"I'm on the pill, Dad."

The air flees my lungs and there's a queasy feeling in my stomach.

"Since when?" I ask, stunned.

"Since I asked Mom. That's when she found out."

"Why didn't you tell me?"

She motions to what's left of her bedroom door. "Gee, Dad. I don't know."

I'm still trying to process this. Shouldn't I feel some sort of relief? Why am I only feeling this sense of anger? Why am I so pissed?

"When did you talk to Mom?" I ask.

"A few months ago. Aiden and I hadn't had sex yet, but we wanted to be safe."

"So, Aiden was pressuring you into having sex with him?"

"No, Dad. We both wanted—"

She abruptly stops. Her eyes widen, her jaw drops, and panic spreads across her face.

"Oh no . . ." she whispers.

The intense anger that occupied every fiber of my body a fraction of a second ago is wiped away by her horrified expression.

"Tatum? What is it?"

She looks around the room, shaking her head, and mumbling. "No . . . no, no, no, no . . ."

"Tatum," I say forcefully, but not in anger. "Sweetheart, what is it?"

"Dad . . ."

Chapter 26

Tatum and I are sitting in silence, listening to the soft rock music playing throughout the Rite Aid.

"I'm really sorry, Dad," she says, quietly.

"It's okay."

Her lip begins to tremble. "With everything going on, I just forgot."

"Tatum, sweetheart, it's really okay," I gently reassure her.

And it is.

Tatum offered to come here by herself to get the morning-after pill, and I didn't blame her after my outburst, but she was upset and I didn't want her to do this alone. I asked if I could come.

"Okay," she said, trying to hide her relief.

I didn't try to hide mine.

We spent the ten-minute drive to the Rite Aid in silence. It wasn't an awkward silence. Merely a tired, thoughtful one.

Once we arrived, I asked Tatum if she'd like me to speak to the pharmacist, but she declined and went to the counter, herself, while I took one of the two unoccupied seats next to the blood-pressure monitor. After a few words, the pharmacist gave her a clipboard with a questionnaire and a pen. Tatum sat down next to me and filled it out. I didn't ask what questions were on there.

It's not my business. The only thing Tatum asked me for was our insurance information. I got out my wallet, extracted the card, and handed it over. She finished answering the questions, returned the clipboard, and sat back down in the empty chair next to mine.

". . . I really am sorry, Dad."

"No. Tatum, listen; I'm sorry. I shouldn't have blown up like that. I absolutely do not approve that you and Aiden are having sex and that the both of you were lying to me—"

She's about to say something, but I gently put up my hand.

"Please let me finish."

She settles back.

"It was a shock for me and it's hard for any father who really cares about their daughter to hear that she's having sex. I guess I always knew it was a possibility with you and Aiden, and let's face it, I haven't always been his biggest fan. I just hoped that I had explained to you what a big responsibility sex is and no matter how much I don't like it, I'm glad you were being responsible. And, yeah, it's going to take me a little time to get used to, but I love you. And I'm proud of you."

". . . But you were so angry," she says, choking up a little.

"Yes, because even if your mom knew, you were still lying to me."

She takes it in.

I'm not going to tell her that my anger was fueled by the fact that Amy knew and didn't tell me. Somehow, it hurts more than lies about the trips to Boston.

"I'm sorry, Dad," Tatum says.

"And I appreciate that, but you're saying sorry because I found it. If you had told me sooner, things may have been different."

"Are you saying if I had told you, you wouldn't have been mad?"

I shrug. "I might have been upset for a while, but your bedroom would probably still have a door."

Despite her bloodshot eyes and runny nose, a small smile plays on her lips. I think it's the first time I've seen Tatum smile since this whole nightmare began.

"Just so you're not completely angry at Aiden, before we had . . . sex . . . for the first time, he was the one who suggested that I talk to you and Mom about going on the pill," Tatum offers. "I just felt more comfortable talking to Mom before we . . . you know . . . did it."

It makes total sense. When Tatum started her period, she went to Amy and why wouldn't she? It's not as if I would have more experience with what that's like.

"And this all happened a couple of months ago?" I ask.

Tatum nods.

I stare down at the linoleum floor. "She didn't tell me any of this."

"She said that she would tell you, but that we should wait."

"Did she say why?" I ask.

Tatum shakes her head. "She didn't say. She just said that she needed more time."

"*She* needed more time?"

"Yeah . . . but then . . ."

"Then what?"

". . . she died . . ."

My mind spins out.

Why would Amy need time? What was going on that was so important that it needed to end before she could tell me that our daughter was having sex?

"Burcham?" the pharmacist says, placing a small bag on the counter.

Chapter 27

On our way out of the Rite Aid, we purchased a bottle of water so that, per the pharmacist's instructions, Tatum could take the medication as soon as possible.

The drive back to the house is almost the same as the one earlier: silent, but again, not awkward. We're both exhausted.

"I think I'm going to take a nap," Tatum wearily declares as we walk through the front door.

"Is there anything you need?"

She pauses on the steps. "Can I call Aiden?"

"Sure."

"Can I see him?"

I take a breath. "We're gonna hit pause on that, okay? You two still lied to me and took advantage of my trust. So, the three of us are going to sit down and talk about that before anything else happens. You can tell him that when you talk to him, but it's been a long day, and I think we both can use some rest."

Tatum nods. She's about to continue upstairs but stops.

"Why did you come over to Aiden's today?" she asks.

"You weren't answering your phone."

"I know, but you suddenly called a bunch of times and then came running over. What happened?"

For a split second, I consider lying about seeing the Smoking Man, but I guess today is about coming clean.

"I saw the guy in the SUV, again. He was watching the house. I tried to go after him but he drove off. I was terrified that something had happened to you."

In the following silence, I can see her weighing Detective Harper's skepticism against my concern for her safety.

"Okay," she finally says. "I'll be upstairs."

"Okay. I love you, sweetheart."

"Love you, too, Dad."

I yank the cord and the blinds drop with a *shhhnk* over the living-room window.

After hauling a chair to the middle of the room, I have a seat and stare through the spaces between the blinds out to the street to begin my vigil.

Would the Smoking Man be so desperate to get whatever he was searching for that he would come back after I tried to confront him this afternoon?

Why not? He came back after breaking into my house and pushing me down the stairs. It's not like I'm a threat to him. How many times has he gotten away, now?

I've got to be smarter.

If he does show up, I'm not going to go running after him. I'll take a photo of the SUV, hopefully getting the license plate, like I wanted to do at the funeral, and then I'll call Detective Harper.

The hours pass into early evening, and I haven't moved from the chair, nor have I taken my eyes off the street.

Tatum comes downstairs, rubbing her eyes from her nap. She stops at the bottom of the stairs when she notices me.

"Dad? What are you doing?"

"I'm keeping an eye out."

This time, the silence is awkward.

"Do you want me to make you something for dinner?" I ask.

"No, thank you. I'm still pretty tired. I'm going to grab a snack and go back upstairs."

"Okay."

More awkward silence.

"I'm going to sleep in the guest room," she adds. "Because . . . um . . ."

"Because there's a door?"

"Yeah."

"I'll get a replacement for it tomorrow."

"Okay . . . Thanks."

It's the strangest thanks I've ever experienced but she's not being ironic or snarky. The truth is she shouldn't be thanking me. It's a strange situation.

Tatum goes to the kitchen, grabs something out of the pantry, and heads back upstairs to the guest room while I continue to stare out the window.

Over the next hour as I observe the street, I call Liz a couple times, attempting to apologize for last night. She doesn't answer. It's no surprise that she doesn't want to talk to the guy who suggested that it's her fault that her sister is dead, but at some point, we're going to have to talk.

The sun goes down, limiting what I can see but I'm not going anywhere. I'm convinced the Smoking Man is the one who broke into the house last night and the fact that he was here today is proof that he didn't get what he was after. He has to come back, and I'll be waiting. I don't care how long I have to sit here.

It's already been hours, hours of peering intently at anyone and everyone who passes by the house while turning over a thousand questions in my head.

What is this key to?

Why didn't Liz tell me sooner about what was going on with Amy and why wouldn't she tell me after Amy's death? Why did I have to pry it out of her?

And do I believe that Liz, like Detective Harper, is lying to me?

It's harder to dismiss the idea that Amy was having an affair when it comes from Liz, but the idea that Amy was having an affair makes less sense now than before.

If Amy was having an affair with this guy, why would she leave clues for me to find? Why not just tell me? If she was feeling guilty and had to get it off her conscience, why go through the business of leaving this key? And why would the Smoking Man come looking for it?

Thankfully, I can just ask them since they're standing in the front yard.

Amy is wearing the lingerie I saw her in at the morgue. The Smoking Man is standing behind her. The two of them are leering at me with twisted smiles, and even though the Smoking Man's face is obscured by shadows, I can still feel his gaze.

His head tilts down and he begins kissing Amy's neck. She sighs and leans back into him while continuing to stare at me. He reaches around and gropes her breast. Amy closes her eyes in ecstasy.

This is what you couldn't give me, Amy's mocking voice echoes in my head.

Instead of triggering anger or sadness, I almost start laughing.

This isn't what happened.

Something changes. Their images blur, like a television losing reception.

Amy's voice echoes in my head once again, but this time she sounds terrified.

What would you have done this afternoon, if Tatum had run into the house, and he was waiting for her?

Outside on the lawn, the images solidify but it's no longer Amy. It's Tatum.

The Smoking Man still has one arm wrapped around her but he's not groping her. He's restraining her with one arm while he holds a gun to her head with his other hand. Tatum tearfully struggles helplessly against his grip.

129

Mark?! Amy's voice pleads in my head. *What are you going to do?!*

I'm paralyzed at the sight of a gun pressed against my daughter's temple.

Mark! He's going to kill her!

I try to stand, but I can't move.

Mark! Amy screams. *Don't let him kill our dau—!*

The Smoking Man pulls the trigger. The gun kicks in his hand.

Tatum drops to the ground. The gunshot reverberates through the house and slowly fades.

Suddenly, I'm standing at the window, looking out onto the mist-covered lawn. The Smoking Man is gone. A body lies on the ground, but it's not Tatum's. It's Amy's. Her body is in the lingerie and lying next to a dumpster.

You couldn't protect me, Mark, Amy's voice whispers in my head while I stare at her lifeless body. *If you couldn't protect me, how are you going to protect our daughter?*

Instinctively, I look to the stairs next to the front door.

A black mist is gathering at the bottom step. It solidifies into the figure of the Smoking Man. His face is still obscured, but he's looking up the stairs. Slowly, he begins to climb.

He's going after Tatum.

What are you going to do, Mark? How are you going to protect her when he comes for her? Suddenly, it's as if Amy is whispering in my ear. *Because I promise you . . .*

I snap my head around to face her but instead of seeing Amy, the Smoking Man is looming over me.

"That day is coming," he growls, the words emanating from his shadowed face.

I jolt upright in the chair.

Early morning sunlight streams through the open blinds.

My lungs are working overtime and my heart is racing. I take a series of breaths to calm myself. Once my pulse comes down and my wits return, I yawn and stretch. Seemingly every joint in my body makes itself known with a crack.

Through the window, I scan the parked cars on the street. The black SUV is not among them.

I check my phone. I've been asleep for almost twelve hours.

Where's Tatum? I need to see her. I need to erase the image of the Smoking Man holding a gun to her head and pulling the trigger.

Hurrying up the stairs, I half expect to see the Smoking Man blocking my way.

There's a moment of sheer panic when I see the decimated remains of Tatum's bedroom door. I race into her room to find her bed empty. I'm about to call out her name when it all comes back to me.

I'm the one who kicked in this door and Tatum told me last night that she was going to sleep in the guest room.

I cross the hall near the top of the stairs, while trying to steady my nerves.

Pressing my ear against the guest-room door, I can hear her snoring inside.

I gently open the door.

She's asleep. Her phone is resting on the mattress next to her head.

I quietly close the door and begin heading downstairs.

There's a sense of relief at seeing my daughter sleeping safely, but as I continue to descend the stairs, I can still hear Amy's words in my head.

How are you going to protect her when he comes for her? Because I promise you . . .

And then the Smoking Man's voice shakes me to my core.

That day is coming . . .

Chapter 28

A night of restless sleep in a chair hasn't given me the recharge that I needed, but I can't go back to bed.

Yesterday was, to put it mildly, a shitshow, and now, as I prep the coffeemaker in the kitchen, all I want is to do something boring. Something routine. A simple task that will engage my brain without overwhelming it with thoughts of keys, my daughter having sex, a guy sitting in an SUV watching the house, or horribly vivid nightmares.

Once the coffeemaker stops hissing, I pour a cup into my favorite Dodgers mug, drop into a chair at the kitchen table, and am presented with my answer: the pile of mail I brought in before I was attacked.

It's sitting in front of me on the table untouched, save for the small padded envelope that contained Amy's ring and necklace. I weed out the junk mail, leaving only the bills.

If there was ever something dull and routine, this is it.

Bills don't bother me. Amy and I don't have any debts or creditors to hide from. It's simple busy work that I took the reins of years ago when it was clear that Amy was going to have the job and I was going to stay home with Tatum. Amy and I planned all the steps of our financial future together, but I was the one who handled the nitty-gritty of balancing the checkbook, and if I'm being honest, I love it. It gives me a sense of calm and security to see that everything is going to plan, that the bills are getting paid on time and we were making sound decisions for a comfortable, hard-earned retirement, but this is the first time I'm sitting down to do this with Amy gone.

Still. I want to do this. It feels the same as it did before this all began.

I power up my laptop next to the stack of bills, sign into our bank's home page, and begin the process of opening each envelope, checking the accuracy, and then paying it online.

There's the electric bill, which always seems ridiculously high. The gas bill is slightly lower than normal, due to the pilot light being out in the fireplace. The cable and internet bill are the same amount they've been for years.

Next up is our phone bill. All our phones are bundled together: mine, Amy's, and Tatum's. Every month, Amy submitted her portion of the bill to Fortis for reimbursement since that was her phone's primary purpose. A good chunk of her job took place over the phone: calling clients, setting up meetings, and negotiating deals. Seeing the bill reminds me that I need to cancel her phone plan.

As I start sorting out the charges, a simple question hits me. Where is Amy's phone?

Detective Harper said they didn't find it on her in the alley. He assumed that someone had taken it, along with her purse.

But where is it? Who has it?

I tried calling her from the airport parking lot and it went to voicemail. So, it was still active then.

Is it still active now? And if it is . . .

I get out my phone, dial Amy's number, and flinch as I'm greeted by those punishing tones and the automated voice letting me know that the number is either disconnected or no longer in service.

I hang up and dial the customer service number on the phone bill.

Another, much more pleasant, automated voice answers immediately, informing me that it recognizes the number I'm calling from, and asks if I would like to speak to sales, billing, or technical support.

I hit three to be transferred to technical support.

The automated voice thanks me and informs me that my wait time is eleven minutes. I spend the time staring at the bill, wondering what, if anything, I can glean from it.

An eternity later, just as the loop of god-awful hold music is about to start over, it abruptly cuts out.

"Thank you for waiting. This is Paul. How may I assist you today?"

"Hi, Paul. My name is Mark Burcham and I had a question about a phone on my account."

"Certainly, sir. What can I help you with?"

"I can't seem to locate the phone and I was wondering if you could do that thing where you track it."

There is a clicking of keys on his end.

"We can try," Paul says without much enthusiasm or confidence. "I'm seeing three lines associated with this account. Which one are you trying to find?"

I give him Amy's number.

More clicking.

"Hmmmmmmm . . ." Paul says.

"Any luck?" I ask.

"Unfortunately, no. It doesn't seem to be working."

"Why would that be?"

"It could be something as simple as the phone being turned off or the SIM card may have been removed, but it's more likely that the battery ran out."

It's not the answer I was hoping for, but I feel like I'm on the right track. Amy never turned off her phone, which means someone either turned it off after she died, or the battery ran out.

There's also the possibility that someone came across Amy's body in the alley before the cops arrived, took her phone, and then sold it to someone else who replaced the SIM card.

"Is there anything else I can help you with?" Paul asks.

I'm struck by an idea.

"Would it be possible to see the call log and text messages for that phone?"

"Sure. The best way to do that would be to log in to your account on our website. There, you can see all the calls. As far as text messages go, you can see to whom texts were sent and the numbers from where they were received, but you won't be able to see the text messages themselves."

I'm already typing the phone company's name into the search bar.

"That's great. Thank you, Paul."

"My pleasure. Was there anything else?"

"Nope."

"You have a great day, sir."

"You, too."

I hang up the phone, uninterested in the automated voice's request that I participate in a brief survey.

Sorry, Paul.

Once I'm on the phone provider website, I'm forced to go into my saved documents and open the spreadsheet I made years ago with the passwords for some of our accounts. I think the only time I've used this password was when I created it.

After logging in, it takes a few minutes for me to find the appropriate page. It asks for the line I would like to look up and has fields where I can enter a range of dates for my search.

I enter Amy's number and since I want to see everything, I leave the dates blank.

And that's exactly what I get: everything. Page after page of phone numbers, each followed by "call sent," "call received," "message sent," and "message received."

There are thousands and thousands of entries going back years. Most of them have names and numbers, but a good deal of them are listed only as "PRIVATE" with no phone number.

I've got to whittle this down. I go back to the search parameters and establish a timeframe: everything from two years ago, which is when the alleged affair was supposed to have started, and up until now.

The website recalibrates and gives me the results. There's still probably thousands of calls and messages, and many are marked as "PRIVATE," but it's a start.

I copy everything onto a document and send it to the printer in the den.

Minutes later, I return to the kitchen table with fifty-some pages of numbers. It's daunting, sure, but there's a chance that one of these numbers is the answer I'm looking for. It's just a matter of grinding through them.

The entries marked "PRIVATE" aren't going to do me any good, since there's no number I can call. There's also no reason to call numbers I already know like Malcolm's, Nadine's, and Spencer's. I'm looking for something out of the ordinary, a name that I don't recognize that appears multiple times . . . or maybe not at all. What if she was using a different phone, like a burner phone, to do whatever it was she was doing?

I stop and take a moment to breathe.

I can't do that. I can't start doubting before I even begin. I'm just going to start researching these names and hope there's something here.

There has to be.

Eyestrain sucks.

The stack of pages showing Amy's calls and texts are littered with x's after I called or looked up the name online and determined that it wasn't what I'm looking for.

It's looking more and more as if the answer might be in one

of these private numbers, which means I'm barreling toward a dead end.

I'm trying to stay positive, but a sense of hopelessness is over-taking me, accompanied by the headache caused by staring at this screen and stack of papers.

The only break I've taken was to check on Tatum, who is still asleep upstairs.

The next number on the list is for something called "Chapman's." It has a 3-1-0 area code, so whatever it is, it's here in Los Angeles. Amy called them a year ago.

My laptop, which is down to its last sliver of battery, waits as I type in "Chapman's" and "Los Angeles."

It's a restaurant in Westwood. Another dead end.

I sigh, pick up the pen, and scratch an x next to the number on the page.

According to the log in front of me, Amy called another Los Angeles–based number an hour later. The name on the page next to the number reads "L S."

I pick up my phone and dial the number, fully prepared to ask who they are, and then apologize for disturbing them.

A woman answers. "Lowes and Sons."

"Lowes and Sons?" I ask and begin lazily typing the name into Google.

"Yes," she replies. "How may I help you?"

"Hi. This is going to sound really bizarre but can you tell me what sort of business you are?"

I hit enter.

The woman on the other end lightly laughs. "We rent out security deposit boxes."

The page loads and I sit up.

"You're downtown?" I ask, reading the address on the webpage.

"Yes."

"Thank you."

I hang up the phone and grab my keys off the table.

Before stuffing them in my pocket, I hold the black key next to the screen.

It seems blindingly obvious now that I know what I'm looking at. The swooping lines and elegant swirls on the black key are an L and an S. There's no mistaking it because the logo on the key is the same as the logo on the homepage of Lowes & Sons Bank.

Chapter 29

Lowes & Sons Bank is in the Tanner Building, which is only a block away from Fortis Capital, which gives me pause.

What if I run into someone from Fortis and they ask me what I'm doing there? Do I need a cover story? A few attempts at cooking up a plausible lie causes me to realize that I'm being a paranoid idiot. I'm not going to run into anyone from Fortis. Lowes & Sons isn't some neighborhood hangout.

I debated what to say to Tatum. I briefly considered bringing her with me, but I don't know what I'm going to find here. In the end, I gently woke her up to let her know I had to run an errand.

"Where are you going?" she asked, still half asleep.

"I'm going downtown to speak with our lawyer," I lied. "I'll be back in a bit."

"When?" she asked.

"Maybe an hour or so."

"Then, we can talk to Aiden?"

"Sure. Just make sure the house stays locked up while I'm gone, okay?"

"Okay . . ." she said, drifting back to sleep.

Was that the right move? I don't know, but it's done. I hate that I left her there alone. The best thing I can do is find out what's here at Lowes & Sons and get back to the house as soon as possible.

I spent the drive to downtown trying to guess what, if anything, is in Lowes & Sons, but sitting here, parked on the street, watching the Tanner Building as Los Angeles swirls around me, I haven't come up with anything close to an answer. There's no way to know. Its darkly tinted windows give the building the appearance of a monolith.

Okay. Enough watching.

I pull away from the curb and navigate to the entrance of the underground parking garage. I take a ticket from the dispenser, maneuver past the empty accessible spaces, and find a spot two levels down.

I don't have the patience to wait for the elevator, and instead go to the stairwell. As I climb back up to street level, my hand stays in my pocket, clasping the key, my thumbnail running over the engraved logo and numbers.

What did you leave here, Amy? This key isn't some clue to the identity of a secret lover, is it? It has to be something more.

Seconds later, I'm standing in the lobby of the building.

Sunlight pours through the glass wall to my left. The tint of the windows changes it to a golden hue. Outside, people on the sidewalk pass and cars on the street stream by. There's the occasional *woosh* as someone enters through the revolving door.

According to the directory mounted on the wall, next to the elevator, Lowes & Sons is here on the ground floor, past the reception desk, near the back of the building.

I begin walking, joining the flow of traffic passing back and forth in the cavernous lobby. The sound of dress shoes and heels on the marble floor and the murmur of voices echoes overhead.

The reception desk sits in the middle of the lobby. Behind the desk is a short, frail security guard in his sixties. He's bald, wears thick glasses, and is opening envelopes with a sword-shaped letter opener.

I continue walking until I come to a large glass door upon which is etched a logo that matches the key in my pocket. I open the door and step through.

Inside, there's a young woman sitting at a desk. Behind her is a black steel door that is somehow both elegant and intimidating. A card reader is mounted on the wall next to it.

"Hello," she says, looking up from her computer at the sound of my entrance. "Welcome to Lowes and Sons. How may I help you?"

"Hi. I'm here to, uh, well—" I quit stammering and hold up the key on my key ring.

"Of course," she says. "Could I have the number?"

"Four-four-eight-seven," I reply, giving the number engraved below the logo on the key.

The woman punches in some information on her computer, nods, and then looks back up at me. "And the name on the account?"

My mind fires rapidly. Did Amy use a fake name? Possibly her maiden name? No. If she wanted me to find whatever is inside, she wouldn't have risked—

"Sir? Is there something wr—?"

"Burcham," I bite out.

A few more clicks on her computer and the nod of her head lets me know I got it right, but now, there is a little guardedness to her demeanor that wasn't there a moment ago.

"And may I see an ID?"

"Of course."

As I get out my wallet and extract my driver's license, I wonder if that's a standard question or if she came up with it on the spot because of my hesitation.

Satisfied, she hands my license back to me.

"Right this way, please," she says and motions for me to follow her over to the black steel door.

I obey and wait behind her as she holds a card up to the reader. There's a beep and then a deep buzzing sound. She opens the door and holds it for me.

"Thank you," I say as I walk past her into a short hallway.

At the end of the hallway is another, identical steel door. The only other feature in the hallway is a camera mounted in the corner of the ceiling.

"Excuse me," she says, stepping around me. She stops in front of the second door and looks up at the camera.

Seconds pass.

Finally, there's another buzzing sound and a loud *clack* as the lock disengages.

"Thanks, Robbie," she says toward the camera.

This isn't like your regular deposit box at the bank where you store your mother's pearls. This place is a fortress.

What do people keep in here?

She opens the second door and once again holds it for me.

A cold breeze greets me as I approach. I smile at her as I pass, and she follows me inside.

The vault is huge. The complete silence and frigid temperature makes it feel even more so. Small black lockers line marble walls. There are also three aisles of lockers, giving the room the appearance of a library. Each locker has a bronze plate mounted above a keyhole and a small keypad below the keyhole. In the wall to my right are three black doors.

I suddenly realize that she's waiting for me.

"I'm sorry," I say, sheepishly. "It's been a while."

"Of course," she says, that guardedness creeping upwards. "Four-four-seven-eight is this way."

She leads me toward the back of the vault. Her heels sharply *clack* against the floor. She stops at the back wall and indicates a locker that's waist high. The small bronze plate above the keyhole reads "4478."

"Here we are."

"Thank you," I say, stepping forward, and stopping in front of the locker.

Despite the chilly air, a bead of sweat slides down my back.

I slowly insert the key, trying to buy time, as I stare at the buttons on the keypad.

Amy, you didn't tell me the PIN!

I attempt to gently twist the key, but it won't budge.

Good. This might give me a couple seconds.

I turn back to the waiting woman. "Sorry. It looks like it might be broken."

She smiles. "You have to enter the PIN number first. Then, turn the key."

Shit.

"Oh, right, right, right," I say with forced embarrassment.

She lightly laughs. "It has been a while, hasn't it?"

"Yeah. It has."

I turn back to the locker.

Think, dammit. Her birthday? No. That feels too obvious. There had to have been something else, some sort of hint that she gave while telling me that the key was in the dress. Something in that odd conversation about the sundress and how I should get her another one for Christmas, even though Christmas was ten months awa—

I freeze.

I say a silent prayer as my finger reaches toward the keypad and types "1-2-2-5."

There's a beep and a click.

"There we are," the woman says behind me.

I try the key again, and it easily turns.

The sound of her heels on the marble floor alerts me that she's approaching.

"Please. Allow me."

I step to the side.

She opens the locker and extracts a black metal container about the size and shape of a shoebox.

"This way," she says, taking the box and walking back toward the entrance.

I dutifully fall in step behind her.

Back at the front of the vault, she turns left and goes to one of the three black doors. She opens it to reveal a small, pristine white room. In the center of the room is a heavy metal table and chair. She walks inside, places the box on the table, and comes back out. I step inside the room. There's a small button on the surface of the table, next to the box.

"Take all the time you need," she says. "When you're ready, simply press the button. I'll come back and we'll return the box and your key."

"Perfect. Thank you."

She closes the door, leaving me alone.

In the silence, I stare at the box, bracing myself for whatever I'm about to discover. Maybe there's a note, explaining what happened and giving me the name of the Smoking Man.

Placing my fingers on the side of the lid, I take a breath, and flip it open.

My mouth falls open.

". . . What the hell?"

Resting inside the box is a long strip of paper with torn edges.

There's writing on it.

Amy's writing.

I would recognize her deliberate script anywhere.

As I read the words Amy has written, a ringing builds in my ears and my chest tightens.

Amy, what is this? What did you do?

I read, reread, and then read the paper again, searching for something, anything, to make it make sense.

Thequeenandtherookwalktothe828treesandjump4!andturn22 !andjumpjjmp!

Chapter 30

My first impulse is to take the strip of paper and tear it into pieces.

Instead, I read it a few more times, which solves nothing.

Did Amy even play chess? Is there a hidden message here Amy wanted me to figure out? Is this just another damn puzzle?

Detective Harper would say that this is just one more way to drive myself crazy.

But Amy wanted me to find this for a reason, right?

Of course, she did, but did she really leave me riddles to find the key, which only leads to more riddles?

I clench my jaw and curse.

Whatever Amy had in mind, I don't have time to solve it here. I have to get back to Tatum.

I fold the strip of paper and stuff it in my wallet. I close the lid to the box and collect myself before pressing the button on the table.

Moments later, the woman opens the door.

"All set?" she asks, but her professional cheerfulness evaporates when she sees the expression on my face.

"Yes," I answer through gritted teeth.

I don't have to pretend to be pleasant anymore. I got what I came for, whatever the hell this slip of paper is.

*　*　*

After returning the empty box to its locker and collecting the key, I walk back through the reception room of Lowes & Son and into the cavernous lobby of the Tanner Building. As I make my way to the elevator, a black trashcan situated against the wall catches my attention. I suddenly imagine myself throwing the strip of paper away.

If this was so important, Amy, why not tell me when you were alive? Why toy with me after your death?

I'm able to subdue the urge to throw it away. My frustration was merely a knee-jerk reaction. I have to trust Amy but I'm still fuming by the time I jab the elevator button to return to the parking garage. Inadvertently, I turn my head to the filtered sunlight coming through the tinted glass wall to my right. I step over to the glass and take a moment to calm myself down and watch the people going about their everyday lives.

At least I'll be able to beat the traffic back home.

The elevator doors open behind me. I'm about to turn back to the lobby when I stop and nearly press my face to the glass.

There. The next block over.

It's barely visible from where I'm standing but on the other side of the street, just past the intersection, is a small parking lot. Parked in a spot next to the sidewalk and facing the street is a black SUV. Its front windows are down, and I can make out the silhouette of the driver inside. They're just sitting there.

I wait.

It could be anyone. They might be waiting on a friend who had to quickly run into one of the nearby buildings on an errand. It could be someone finishing a text . . . or they could be watching this building, waiting for me.

The doors of the elevator close behind me but I don't move, and my eyes never leave the SUV.

Detective Harper's words fill my head amidst the echoes of the lobby. It most likely is just one of the tens of thousands of black SUVs in Los Angeles, but I'm going to wait . . . and wait . . . until I see . . . that!

A plume of smoke escapes from the open window.

It's him. The Smoking Man. He's followed me but for the first time, I have the advantage. I can see him, but he can't see me. He doesn't know where I am or that I know he's here.

I step away from the glass and stand with my back to the marble wall, rapidly formulating a plan. Chasing him has gotten me nowhere. I have to surprise him without putting myself in danger. Then, I have to get away without him following me.

How the hell do I do that?

My eyes dart around the massive lobby, searching for answers. They come to a stop at the reception desk, where the old security guard is now working on his computer. The sword-shaped letter opener is on the desk, next to the keyboard.

I have an idea. It's an incredibly risky idea, maybe even stupid, but if I wait any longer, the Smoking Man might leave, and I'll lose this chance. Risky and stupid will have to do.

I wander back to the reception desk and stop next to the guard.

"Pardon me?" I ask in a hushed tone.

He looks up and smiles at me from behind those thick glasses. "How can I help you?"

"Where are the restrooms?"

"Right over there," he says with a nod over his shoulder.

I peer and squint in the direction he's indicated. "I'm sorry. Where?"

He stands, turns, and points to the clearly marked bathrooms only a few yards away.

"There," he says.

"Oh my gosh," I say with an embarrassed sigh. "I didn't see them. Thank you."

He turns back to me, still smiling. "And I thought my eyes were bad."

We share a laugh, even though I feel like that's a weird thing for a security guard to say.

"Thanks, again," I reply and walk off toward the restroom.

"You have a good day," he calls behind me.

"You, too."

I enter the spotless bathroom, find a stall, step inside, lock the door, and stare down at the sword-shaped letter opener in my hand, which I lifted from his desk while he was pointing out the bathrooms. I'm surprised at its weight and sturdiness. It's more like a knife, which is perfect.

What I'm contemplating is ridiculous. If it goes wrong, and there's a good chance it will, I could be in real danger.

But this won't end. He won't stop watching us and I have to know what happened to Amy.

I'm about to do something from which there's no going back.

Chapter 31

"Who the hell are you?" I ask.

The Smoking Man lurches in his seat.

"Jesus!" he gasps, dropping his smoldering cigarette out of the SUV window to the pavement. He takes a second to breathe and then turns to stare at me as I stand outside the front passenger window.

Even though he's sitting down, it's clear that he's tall and built like a house. His square jaw sports stubble that matches his salt-and-pepper hair, but all his other features are unremarkable in comparison to his unsettling, ice-blue eyes.

"Who the hell are you?" I ask, again.

"How did you get out here?" he asks in a gravelly, cigarette-scarred voice.

I have no interest in telling him that I went down into the parking garage, moved my car into one of the acessible spaces near the entrance, exited through a side door, and went all the way around the block so that I could creep up to the passenger side of his SUV while he watched the entrance to the parking garage, presumably waiting for me to drive out.

"Last time," I tell him. "Who the hell are you?"

His pale-blue eyes narrow and he regains his menacing composure. "Someone you need to take very seriously."

We stare at one another.

He nods toward the Tanner Building. "What did you find in there?"

"Not a damn thing."

He regards me with something between a snarl and a smile. "I don't believe you."

"I don't give a shit what you believe."

"Mr. Burcham, you need to—"

"Did you kill my wife?"

He continues to study me.

"Mr. Burcham—"

"Were you in my house? Were you the one who pushed me down the stairs?"

He blinks. "Is that why the police were there?"

"Yeah," I say, mocking his attempt to play dumb. "And I told them all about you."

For the first time in our brief acquaintance, there's genuine concern in his face. It's clear that my telling the police about him was not a part of his plan.

He watches the passing cars and quietly curses in frustration before turning back to me. "Get in."

"I'm fine where I am, thanks."

"I wasn't asking, Mr. Burcham."

He tries to break me down with his glare but there is no way I'm getting in this SUV.

My defiance only causes his annoyance to morph into anger.

"I want you to listen to me very carefully, Mr. Burcham; I'm going to show you something and when I do, I don't want you to panic. I don't want you to yell. I just want you to get in the car so we can talk."

As he's speaking, his hand begins to go to the inside of his jacket while his other hand holds the jacket open.

That's when I see it.

He's reaching for the gun in his shoulder holster.

And that's all I need to know.

I bolt across the sidewalk and into the intersection, sprinting for the opening to the parking garage. Tires scream and horns blare as drivers swerve around me. I somehow make it to the garage entrance unharmed and race down the incline to my car parked nearby. I fumble with my keys and eventually succeed in opening the door. I climb inside and start the engine. I throw it in reverse, take the briefest of glances behind me, and stomp on the gas. The tires squeal as they fight for traction and finally bite down on the concrete, propelling me backwards. Once I'm clear of the parking spot, I hit the brake and the smell of burning rubber fills my nostrils. I shift into drive and turn the wheel, aiming for the parking gate and the daylight beyond. I press the gas again and the car speeds forward up the ramp. Instead of stopping at the terminal to pay for parking, I drive straight through the arm of the parking gate. It hits the windshield, causing a crack to spiderweb across the glass before the arm of the parking gate snaps in two. I rocket out into the street. There are more horns and screeching tires. I yank the wheel to the right toward the 101 freeway and away from the Smoking Man.

In the rearview mirror, I can see him standing outside his SUV, staring down at the flattened back tire, which is where I propped the letter opener before we began our little chat so that it would puncture the tire as soon as he attempted to back up.

He looks up at the mayhem I caused and then turns to watch as I speed away.

Please, God, let me have bought enough time.

Chapter 32

I practically kick in the front door of the house and run inside.

"Tatum?!" I yell toward the top of the stairs. "TATUM?!"

The door of the guest room opens and Tatum pops her head out.

"Dad? What's goin—?"

"We have to leave. Right now."

We're racing across the valley, weaving in and out of traffic, and startling the hell out of the other drivers.

"Dad, you have to tell me what's going on," Tatum repeats for the umpteenth time.

At first, Tatum was too bewildered by my entrance and insistence on leaving to argue, but she's starting to demand answers but I'm too preoccupied. My eyes are cycling between the vehicles in front of us and those in the rearview mirror.

Is that a black SUV a few cars back following us? Is that him? Or is it someone possibly working with the Smoking M—

"DAD! WATCH OUT!"

I put my eyes forward just in time to see the back of the big rig we're about to slam into.

I pull the wheel to the left. If there's a car next to us, we're going to collide, but thankfully, there's a gap and we miss the big rig by fractions of an inch.

Okay. No more checking to see if we're being followed. I have to trust that my little stunt bought us enough time. If it didn't, there's not a whole lot I can do about it.

I'm forced to hit the brakes as the lane I just swerved into comes to a complete stop. The momentum pushes Tatum and me against the seatbelts before throwing us back.

"Dad, what happened?" Tatum asks, brushing the hair out of her face.

"I saw him. I saw the guy who's been watching our house. The one that was at the viewing."

"But Dad . . . Detective Harper said—"

"I spoke to him, Tatum. He had a gun. He tried to get me into the SUV, but I ran."

"You got away?"

"I popped one of his tires and then ran to my car."

"How did he find you? Where were you?"

If I tell her, she's going to have a lot more questions about keys and deposit boxes and slips of paper with gibberish in my wallet, which I can't answer.

"It's doesn't matter. Right now, I'm taking you to your aunt's and then you two are going to go somewhere."

"Where?"

"Anywhere." I get out my phone. "The important thing is that you can't tell anyone where you're going. Not even me."

"Wait. You're not coming?"

"No."

I find Liz's number and dial.

"But, Dad—"

"No arguments, Tatum," I snap.

She shrinks back in her seat.

Liz answers. "Mark?"

"Liz! I need you to listen . . ."

I pull into the open carpool lane and gun the engine.

Liz is standing on her porch with her arms folded across her chest and a concerned expression on her face as we pull into the driveway.

I park the car and Tatum and I get out.

"Mark, what are you doing?" she asks, stepping off the porch.

"I told you. I need you to take Tatum and the two of you have to get out of here. Don't tell me where you're going—"

Liz shakes her head and begins to mutter, "No, no, no . . ."

"—and I need you to stay there until you hear from me."

"Mark, I can't," she says, her voice tight and anxious.

"There's a man coming after us, Liz! He was watching the house. He was at Amy's funeral. He followed me today and threatened me with a gun!"

"I can't!"

"I'm not asking for a favor, Liz. I'm telling you, you have to take her and the two of you have to hide!"

"I can't take her, Mark!"

"What are you talking about? Why the hell not?!"

"Because they'll find us!"

Everything stops.

Liz stares at me with huge, terrified eyes.

"Who?" I ask. "Who's going to find you?"

Liz doesn't answer.

"Liz?"

She still doesn't answer. Instead, she turns to Tatum, her eyes beginning to shimmer with tears. "I'm so sorry, Tatum."

"Goddammit, Liz!" I rage. "What the fuck is going on?!"

Liz turns back to me. "I can't keep her safe, Mark. You have to get her out of here."

"Why?!"

"Because you're right; they're coming."

Chapter 33

Ringing this doorbell is the last thing I want to do, but I'm out of options.

When Aiden opens it a few seconds later to find Tatum and myself standing on the porch, his confusion is understandable. All he knows is that a few minutes ago, he received a call from Tatum's phone. Instead of Tatum's voice, he heard her insistent father, telling him that they were on their way. Now, he has none of that too-cool persona. In fact, he looks worried that I'm going to punch him. Part of me is okay with this.

"Mr. Burcham, sir," he says. "Let me start by saying that Tatum and I—"

"We're not here about that," I say and hold out the two thousand dollars that I withdrew from the bank on the way over. "You and Tatum need to go. Get to a hotel or something. Don't use your credit card unless you have to, and don't tell anyone where you're going, including me."

Aiden's fearful uncertainty quickly turns to bafflement. Twenty-four hours ago, I threatened him with physical violence if he ever tried to contact my daughter again, and now here I am, instructing him not only to run away with her, but that I'm sponsoring it.

He looks past me. "Tatum, what's going on?"

She doesn't have an answer and she's through trying to understand. She may have worried that I was losing my mind before, but Liz's reaction was proof that I'm not.

"There's trouble," I answer for her. "Someone is coming for us, and I think— No, I know he means to hurt us. I need Tatum away from here. I'm asking you to help keep her safe. I'm trusting you, even though you lied to me. Both of you did, but this is more important."

He stands there dumbfounded, which we don't have time for.

"Believe me, Aiden, if I had any other choice, I would take it, not only because of what you did, but because if you do this, you'll be in danger, too. I'm asking you because if you really care for her, if you really love my daughter, you'll do it."

Aiden takes one look at Tatum and then back at me. He's heard all he needs to hear. The resolution in his face is absolute.

He takes the money from my hand and nods.

That's that.

"Okay," I say.

Tatum walks up onto the porch and stands by his side.

"Like I said, don't tell anyone where you're going and when you get there, stay there until you hear from me but if you see something suspicious, if someone tries to talk to you, you run. Do you understand?"

They both nod.

"I'm going back to your aunt's to find out what she knows. Then, I'm going to go to the police." I take a breath. I don't know what happens next, but there's this feeling in the pit of my stomach that this could be the last time I see my daughter. "I love you, sweetheart."

"I love you, too, Dad."

I step forward and we embrace. I try to take in every detail before pulling away and look to Aiden.

"Keep her safe."

"I will," he answers.

I begin walking back toward the car but stop, unable to help myself.

"Listen, I know you both understand that this is not a vacation or a fun little getaway . . . and I know you're on the pill, Tatum, but if you're going to have sex, please, *please* get some condoms."

Before either of them can answer, I continue walking to the car.

It's stupid, I know, but I'm still her father.

Chapter 34

"What is going on, Liz? Why is this guy coming after us? Why didn't you warn us sooner? Why did you allow your sister's daughter and me to remain in danger? Why wouldn't you help us? Why all of this?! What is going on?!"

I keep speaking the words out loud as I make my way back to Pasadena. I've done what I can to keep Tatum safe. Is it enough? I have no idea. I've also put Aiden in danger, but I gave him the option, and to his credit, he didn't hesitate.

Now, I have to know what kind of danger we're in, and Liz has the answers.

Rush hour is building in the valley and the roads are filling up. I'm finally able to break free at the split between the 210 and 134 freeways, and head up the exit ramp toward Old Town Pasadena. The shops and restaurants on Colorado Boulevard fly past and I'm pretty sure I just ran two red lights. I turn right and enter the more residential area, retracing the route I took with Tatum only a short while ago.

I swing the car into Liz's driveway, slam on the brakes, and kill the engine but stop as I exit the car.

The front door to her bungalow is open.

"Liz?!"

I run up the path and leap onto the porch.

"Liz?!" I call again, stepping through the door and into the living room. There's no answer.

I turn left and head for her bedroom.

The sheets are twisted on the bed and the pillows are on the floor. Her dresser drawers are open and their contents strewn about.

Exiting her room, I cross the hall, and go into the dining room. "Liz?!"

There's still no response.

I make my way through the dining room to the kitchen.

Maybe she's in the backyard. It's the only place left where she might not have heard me call her name.

I hurry across the kitchen to the back door. It's unlocked. I throw it open and peer out across the lawn to the seating area under the oak.

"Liz?!"

"She's not here," a familiar gravelly voice says behind me.

I turn with a start.

The Smoking Man is calmly sitting at the kitchen table, watching me with those ice-blue eyes.

"She's gone, Mr. Burcham. And we need to talk."

Chapter 35

"What did you do to her?" I ask.

"Not a thing."

"Then where is she?"

He leans forward, resting his elbows on the table. "That's what you're going to tell me."

"I don't know where she went."

"You were here not long ago. Why did you come back?"

I have no idea how he knows that, but I'm not answering any of his questions.

After a few moments of heightened silence, he sits back in resignation. "All right, Mr. Burcham. This stops now. I give you full credit for escaping earlier, but that's over." He gestures to the chair across the table. "Sit down."

"No."

"Mr. Burcham—"

"Go ahead," I scoff. "Threaten me with the gun, again. It didn't get me into your SUV and it's not going to get me to sit down with you."

"I wasn't reaching for my gun," he says and nods down toward the table. "I was reaching for that."

I've been so focused on him that I didn't notice the billfold lying there.

"What is that?" I ask.

"See for yourself."

I remain by the door. I'm interested but he's nowhere near to having gained my trust.

"Put your hands on the table," I tell him.

"What?"

"You've got a gun under that jacket. I'm not moving until you put your hands on the table."

He rolls his eyes. "Mr. Burcham, we really don't have time—"

"Then put them on the table!"

"Fine," he says with a sigh and makes a dramatic show of placing his hands on the table, palms down.

"Keep them there," I add.

"You're the boss," he replies, deadpan.

I cautiously cross the kitchen floor and pick up the leather billfold while keeping an eye on him. I flip it open and am briefly blinded by a flash of sunlight off something metallic inside.

It's a badge, an eagle over a shield that reads "Federal Bureau of Investigation Department of Justice." In the other half of the billfold, visible through the plastic window, is a card upon which is printed "FBI Financial Crimes Division," accompanied by a photo of the Smoking Man, identifying him as Agent Zachary Kingston.

I look up in confusion to find myself staring down the barrel of his pistol.

I drop the billfold.

He smiles at me. "Don't worry," he says, returning the gun to the holster inside his jacket. "I'm not going to shoot you. I just wanted you to know who's in charge."

"You're with the FBI?"

"Like the ID says, I'm with the financial crimes division."

He leans over, picks up his billfold from the floor, tucks it into his pocket, and once again nods to the empty chair across the table. "Have a seat."

I lower myself into the chair.

"Where's your daughter?" he asks.

I shake my head. "No way."

He lets slip an appreciative nod. "Fair enough, and again, I give you credit for that. She's in danger. Both of you are, but not from us."

"Then from whom?"

He takes a breath. "How much do you know about your wife's 'death'?"

His implied air quotes give me pause. "She told me she was going to Boston. I dropped her off at the airport. The police said that she met someone, had sex, and then died of a drug overdose. I know that she was lying to me about going to Boston, but I don't believe them about the rest."

"Good, because none of that happened," Agent Kingston says but then checks himself. "Well, the lying about going to Boston happened, and your wife is dead. The rest is bullshit. And yes; you and your daughter are in danger."

I'm starting to lose count of the number of times my world has been turned upside down over the past few days.

"From *whom*?" I repeat, my frustration growing.

"From the people running your wife's hedge fund and the very same people who are 'investigating' her death."

It takes me a moment to process what he just said.

"So, I was right. The police have been lying to me."

"Yes."

I wait for him to go further but he only stares at me.

"You can start talking at any time," I tell him.

Agent Kingston puts up his hand. "My apologies, Mr. Burcham. I really need to start at the beginning."

"Yeah, dammit. I wish you would."

"Okay. Let's begin with Fortis Capital. How much do you know about your wife's hedge fund company?"

"Seriously?"

He nods.

"They're— They invest money. Amy was in charge of bringing in new accounts."

"What do you know of the company's history?"

I shrug. "I know they're doing well."

"Too well," he replies, his voice heavy with innuendo.

I can't do this anymore. I can't take the weird clues and the feeling that everyone knows more about Amy's life than I do.

"Listen, Agent Kingston, or whatever your name is, my sister-in-law is missing, my daughter is in hiding, you're telling me that the police are covering up my wife's death, my head hurts, and my patience is gone. Will you please tell me what the hell is going on?"

He assesses me while marshalling his thoughts.

"A few years ago," he begins, "Fortis Capital was on the rocks. Then, three years before your wife started working for them, they miraculously turned it around. In fact, it was beyond miraculous. They were posting returns on investment that were almost unheard of. So, we began an investigation . . ."

He waits as if expecting me to pick up the thread, but I'm too spent to guess what comes next.

"It was a Ponzi scheme," he finally continues. "Fortis was using money from new clients to pay older investors. They had legitimate investments, and in the beginning, it was only to make up for some bad bets, but once you start a scheme like this, you can't stop. You have to keep bringing in more and more clients to pay the old ones. It gets harder to keep up the façade and, eventually, it's unsustainable. We investigated for a year. Like all companies who do this, they have two sets of books: one that they show to the public that makes it look like they're raking it in for their investors, and another that shows what's really going on. After a few years, our investigation had gotten to the point where we needed someone inside the company who could provide us with the actual financial records."

". . . Amy?"

He nods. "She had been working there a year, long enough to know what was going on. She was the one bringing in the new clients. She didn't have direct access to Fortis's financial records, but we were sure she could get them. We approached her and gave her a choice; she could either help us with our investigation, or she could go down with Fortis."

The dark clouds in my head part. One year into her job at Fortis would have been two years ago; that was when I noticed the burnout in Amy. That's when she and Liz stopped talking and it's obvious now that Liz knew something was up.

Amy wasn't having an affair. She was caught in a trap.

"You set her up?" I ask.

"We gave her a choice. If she helped with the investigation, she would receive immunity. If not, she would most likely receive ten to fifteen years for fraud and embezzlement."

"Amy wasn't a criminal!"

"Of course, she was."

The casualness of his statement, as if he's pointing out the sky is blue, enrages me.

"You just said it! She didn't invest the money! She only recruited new accounts!"

"She knew what Fortis was up to and she knew that it was illegal. She brought in new clients by lying to them about what Fortis would do with their money, allowing the crime to continue."

I sit back. "You know what, Agent Kingston? I don't really care. You brought her into this. As far as I'm concerned, my wife is dead because of you."

"No, Mr. Burcham. She's dead because she was part of a crime."

"And yet, you needed her help."

"Yes. We did."

"If she was so important to you, then why didn't you protect her?"

"We tried. She said that she had a plan to get us the financial records. 'Mountains of documents,' she said but she wouldn't tell us what her plan was. I assume she was going to get them on a thumb drive and somehow smuggle it out of the building. The night that she was supposed to deliver it to us, she disappeared. The next morning, they found her body in the alley. She was worried that Fortis knew what she was up to. It appears she was right and they had her killed. They put her in that lingerie and dumped her in the alley in the hopes that you would think she was having an affair."

"Why? Why would they want me to think that?"

"They were hoping you would be upset and want to move on from her. That way, they could wrap up the 'investigation' quickly and quietly."

And there it is. None of it made sense and now I know why.

An indescribable feeling sweeps over me. It's anger and sadness that Amy was taken from me, but it's also relief. Amy wasn't having an affair. I put my faith in her, in us, and she proved me right. She was still the Amy I loved.

But Agent Kingston's words conjure up the memory of seeing her in the morgue.

"Is every cop in on this?" I ask.

"Not every cop, but certainly the higher-ups."

"What about Detective Harper? Sometimes I think he actually cares."

"Honestly, we don't know. He could be a part of it. He could be in the dark. It's more likely a combination of both. Because of his connection to you, they may not want to tell him everything. He may not know exactly what's going on, but someone is pulling his strings. Look how everything was handled. The speed of the autopsy. The rush to get you to accept the official story that your wife was sleeping with someone and then overdosing. They needed everything to be wrapped up quickly. They couldn't just make her disappear. It would have caused too many questions."

"But *why*?" I plead. "Why would the police help Fortis cover up Amy's murder? What could Fortis possibly have that the police would—?"

"Because Fortis Capital controls roughly two-hundred million dollars of investments from the CPSRF."

"What the hell is the CPSRF?"

"CPSRF stands for the California Public Service Retirement Fund," Agent Kingston says and leans in again, "and one of the primary functions of the CPSRF is managing and investing police pensions. If Fortis were to be taken down, a lot of policemen and women would lose their pensions. The fallout would be . . ." He tries to summon the appropriate descriptor but gives up and settles on, ". . . unimaginable."

I'm suddenly light-headed even though my body feels like it weighs a thousand pounds.

"So . . . the drugs? The affair?"

Agent Kingston shakes his head. "Never happened."

"They can just make it up?"

"Some of the most powerful people in the state are involved in this. There's not a lot they won't do, which is why you and your daughter are in very real danger."

"But . . . Liz told me that she was sleeping with someone."

"Liz was trying to protect you because she knew about the investigation. When your wife agreed to help us, she tried to keep it a secret from everyone, so that you, your daughter, and Liz wouldn't be caught up in it, but it took a huge toll on her. Liz saw the change in her. She suspected that Amy was hiding something. You know how close they were. She pressed Amy to tell her what was going on. When Amy wouldn't, Liz suspected the worst. She really thought that Amy was having an affair. She kept asking Amy to tell her what was wrong. The more Amy denied there was anything going on, the more convinced and angrier Liz got. She thought it had to be an affair. She became so enraged that she went to Fortis while Amy was at work and accused her of having an affair. She said she was going to tell you unless Amy came clean. Once Amy got her alone, she had to tell Liz about the investigation. We think that's where Fortis got the idea for the cover story for your wife's murder. Someone at Fortis overheard Liz accuse Amy of having an affair and when the time came, they took advantage of it. It wasn't a bad plan, but they were sloppy."

I sit back in my chair, trying to take it all in.

So, that's why Liz wouldn't take Tatum. She was worried that the police or Fortis knew that Amy had told her and would come after her. She was trying to keep Tatum and me ignorant to save us and now, she's on the run.

"And you weren't the one who broke into my house and pushed me down the stairs?" I ask.

"No."

"Then who was it?"

"Henry Vaughn. They couldn't send a cop in there. They sent him so that if he was caught, the police could claim deniability."

I think back and remember that I left the reception after only an hour. That's why he was still in the house. I came home way earlier than I was supposed to.

"What was he looking for?" I ask.

"Because of Fortis's actions, we think your wife was able to get the financial records. Fortis is panicking because they don't know what she did with them. It's possible he thinks your wife may have hidden them somewhere, like your house, or they might think there's a clue there as to what she did with them. Do *you* have any idea what they were looking for?"

My hesitation piques his interest.

"Mr. Burcham, you need to tell me everything. It's the only way to keep you and your daughter safe."

He's right. It's true that Agent Kingston was watching the house.

He was keeping an eye on us, but not for the reasons I suspected. He's validated almost everything Amy did.

I reach into my pocket, pull out my key ring, and show him the black key.

"Where did you get that?" he asks.

"Amy left it for me to find. It opened a safety deposit box."

"Lowes and Sons?"

"Yeah."

"What was in it?" he asks with a sudden intensity that unnerves me.

I try to look anywhere but his face.

". . . Mr. Burcham?"

I take out my wallet and extract the slip of paper written in Amy's hand.

Agent Kingston snatches it from my fingers. The movement is so quick, I don't have time to pull it back.

"Hey!" I protest, but he's not listening.

As he studies the paper, his expression grows increasingly confused. Like me, he's unable to make heads or tails of it.

"What is this?" he asks.

"I have no idea."

I reach out to take it back, but he pulls out his billfold and tucks it inside before returning it to his coat.

"She left that for me," I argue.

"I understand, Mr. Burcham. Really, I do, but your wife had been working with us for almost two years. She may have meant for you to find it, but it's safer with me. If you think it's connected to something, let me know, and we'll look into it."

I don't like it, but I'll take his word.

"Okay," I say with a sigh and look around Liz's kitchen. "It's over. I've told you everything. What happens now?"

"The only way to get you and your daughter out of danger is to find out what happened to the information your wife was trying to deliver."

"But this has nothing to do with me or my daughter."

"It does, now. You told Detective Harper about me. If he is in on it, he could put two and two together and whoever killed your wife might assume that Amy told you about the investigation and that now, you're working with us. We were at the end of the investigation. Your wife said that she had the documents but before she could get them to us, she was killed. That means that the documents are out there somewhere. They could be in her office, in your home, or who knows where else? And believe me, whoever killed your wife will have no problem killing you and your daughter if it means finding them. The only way this ends with you and your daughter safe is to finish what your wife started."

I shake my head. "Don't you think my family has sacrificed enough? Can't you find someone else in the company to get what you need?"

"This investigation has taken years. There is no 'someone else,' not when Fortis knows that something is up. We'll never get inside again."

"Look," I stammer. "I'll try to help you find out what Amy did with those documents. I don't care what happens to me, but I need to know my daughter is safe."

"If you help, you can bring Tatum to us. We'll protect her."

"And how are you going to do that? You couldn't protect Amy."

"Because she tried to do things on her own. She didn't tell us what she was going to do, so we couldn't protect her, but if you work with us, your daughter will be safe. I promise you that."

Agent Kingston extends his hand.

His words are like water in the desert. I've been on a roller coaster, just trying to hold on, and now he's let me know that Amy wasn't having an affair and he's offering to keep Tatum safe.

For that, I'll do whatever he asks.

I go to shake his hand but stop, our palms inches apart.

Reaching out to shake my hand has caused his sleeve to slide up a few inches, exposing the tattoos slinking around his forearm and wrist.

Amy's words echo in my head.

I don't trust guys with tattoos.

"Mr. Burcham?"

"No," I whisper.

He blinks. "No? What do you mean 'no'?"

"I . . . I need some time to think."

His frustration quickly morphs into smoldering anger. "What are you talking about? You and your daughter—"

"I said I need time to think," I insist, trying to keep my voice from shaking.

He glowers at me. He knows something just happened, something that caused me to pull back, but he has no idea what it was.

Finally, he stands, steps around the table, and looms over me.

"Don't think too long," he says, once again taking his billfold out of his jacket pocket, and extracts a card. "I promise that the people who killed your wife won't."

He drops the card on the table, turns, and walks out of the kitchen.

Chapter 36

It's me, sweetheart. I'm safe. Don't tell me where you are but let me know that you and Aiden are okay by sending me a thumbs-up.

Her "thumbs-up" emoji reply is almost immediate.

I'm about to put the phone away when it chimes with another text.

What's happening?

I hesitate to reply.

I wasn't planning on having a conversation. In fact, it's probably better to keep our communications short, in case she accidentally tells me where she is, but knowing that she's on the other end of this phone is a feeling I don't want to let go of.

I begin typing.

I don't have all the answers yet but I have some. We'll talk when it's safe.

When will that be?

I don't know but you and Aiden need to stay hidden.

Okay. Be careful.

I will. You, too.

Good night, Dad.

Good night, sweetheart. I love you.

Love you, too.

I want to keep talking. I want to know where she is and to tell her that everything will be okay, even if I don't know that to be true. One thing that parenting teaches you is that telling your child that everything will be okay when you're not sure that it will be is part of the job.

I stare at the phone, willing her to send me another message, but the screen goes dark.

I place the phone next to Agent Kingston's card on the passenger seat and stare out the windshield.

The view is unbelievable.

From this spot, on a lonely road in the mountains over Burbank, I can see the entire valley. I can even see over the Hollywood Hills and into the city beyond. The skyscrapers look like sparkling toys. Below them, the city is laid out like a glowing carpet.

After leaving Liz's bungalow, I got in my car and drove. I had intended to head home, but instead I exited the freeway in Burbank. Once I was satisfied that no one was following me, I went up into the mountains, passing homes that were probably worth millions just for the views, alone. Eventually, I was so high up that the steep slope made construction impractical and there's no need for streetlights.

I kept driving until out of nowhere, I came across a red fire hydrant by the side of the road. After the monotony of passing trees, bushes, and rocks, it was so random that it jolted me out of my thoughts. I pulled over and parked nearby.

If I were to roll forward a few feet, I would plunge down the side of a wooded ravine, but the steep incline offers an amazing panorama of Los Angeles.

It has never ceased to amaze me that in a city of millions, you don't have to go very far to be utterly alone, but this is what I needed. I needed a place to sit and think and, up here, I'll be able to see anyone coming from miles away. I roll down the window to let in the cool night air. Even the noise of the city can't reach this high. The only sound is that of an occasional breeze or the yapping of a coyote that must have caught a rabbit.

Okay. So what now?

Not for the first time since I got the call to go to the morgue, everything has been turned on its head. Agent Kingston was a threat when he was some mysterious figure watching us from the shadows, then he became an ally as he explained what happened to Amy, and now, thanks to Amy's clue about tattoos, he's a threat, again.

It's once again time to ask myself what I believe.

I believed in Amy, even when Detective Harper and Liz told me I shouldn't, and I was right.

Detective Harper is either lying or simply refusing to believe me. Liz was lying, as well, but it sounds like she was trying to protect Tatum and me.

Which brings me to Agent Kingston.

I believe that Agent Kingston caught Amy in a trap. I believe that Fortis was cooking the books and that the FBI enlisted Amy to help them in their investigation.

I believe that Amy had the information that Agent Kingston needs. His insistence that I help confirms that.

I also believe that Agent Kingston wasn't lying when he said the only way I can get Tatum and myself out of danger is to find what Amy did with Fortis's financial records.

So why didn't Amy trust him?

She warned me about him for a reason. I don't know what that is yet and I couldn't call him on it at Liz's place. I needed time to process what to do after seeing the tattoos.

Now that I've done that, the answer is simple; I still have to trust Amy.

I have to find what she did with those documents, and when I do, I won't give them to Agent Kingston. I'll go around him.

Until then, because Amy didn't trust Agent Kingston, neither will I.

Chapter 37

Heaven smells like bacon, eggs, toast, and coffee.

It smells like normality, like the beginning of a mundane day, when you plan all the mundane things you have to do before going back to your mundane bed; things you roll your eyes at until your wife is murdered, dumped in an alley, the people who killed her might want to kill you and your daughter, the cops are in on it, and sipping from a mug of coffee over a plate of scrambled eggs sounds like a luxury you'll never experience again.

At least in this moment, that's what I believe heaven smells like.

That's where my mind is at, sitting in this booth in the far corner of the diner while chugging coffee. Sleeping in my car last night was only mildly more rejuvenating than sleeping in that chair.

I didn't go back to the house. I can't. Not with the knowledge that the police are covering up Amy's murder. That same logic is also why I'm sitting in this particular booth.

From here, with the security of a locked exit door behind me, I can see everyone in the place.

The four guys at the counter all appear to be your run-of-the-mill workers, enjoying their breakfast before punching in at the warehouse, the factory, or their delivery job.

Do people still punch in? Is that a thing?

The waitress does a drive-by and refills my coffee.

After thanking her, I shake my head to clear the cobwebs.

I haven't felt this tired since we brought Tatum home. Those first few months are a crucible that no one can prepare you for; the endless hours spent trying to figure out what will make them sleep, the days when you suddenly realize you can't remember the last time you brushed your teeth. There were times I wasn't sure that Amy and I could make it, but we did, and came out stronger for it.

I wrap my hands around the mug with the chipped rim and bring it to my lips. The scalding hot liquid immediately causes my tongue to go fuzzy. I have to make that horrible decision of whether to swallow it down and damage my throat or do the unseemly act of spitting the coffee back into the cup. I swallow it and it feels like my throat is blistering. I reach for the ice water in the opaque plastic tumbler in front of me to chase it down, but the damage is done.

Well, I'm much more alert now, so mission accomplished, I guess.

I check the time on my phone, 7:17 a.m.

Agent Kingston is late.

He was supposed to meet me here at seven, but I only told him that an hour ago and never heard back. If he didn't want to meet me here, that's fine, but if I'm such a priority, he needs to tell me where he would be comfortable meeting.

In frustration, I pull up my last text to him and add, "*Waiting.*"

I don't know what I'm expecting. A reply like "*omw*," as if we're two friends getting together to catch up over breakfast? Are we going to show each other pictures of our kids on our phones?

Speaking of which, I back out of the text chain with Agent Kingston and bring up the exchange I had with Tatum and stare at our last message. The desire to speak to her hasn't abated.

I know I shouldn't, but it's just me here and I really need to hear her voice. I hit the call button and bring the phone to my ear.

"Dad?" she answers, her voice on edge. "Are you okay?"

"Yeah, sweetheart. I'm fine. I just wanted to check in to see that you and Aiden are safe."

"Yeah. We're safe. We're at a motel in Northridge. Are you going—?"

"Northridge?!" I blurt out, unable to contain my frustration. "Tatum, I said don't tell me where you are."

"I'm sorry! I'm sorry!"

I grunt and run my hand across my face.

"Should we go somewhere else?" she asks, meekly.

"No. If you're safe, then stay there but you can't tell anyone else, okay?"

"Okay. Where are you?"

"I'm meeting with someone who's going to tell me more about what's going on."

"Who?"

"I can't say right now but I'll call you again later, okay?"

"Okay," she says.

"And I mean it, Tatum; do not tell anyone else where you are."

"I know. I know. I'm sorry."

"It's okay. Just lie low and I'll call you later. Okay?"

"Okay."

"I love you, sweetheart."

"I love you too, Dad."

I hang up the phone and place it on the table.

I really wish she hadn't told me where she was, but Northridge isn't a bad place to hide. Like a lot of neighborhoods in Los Angeles, Northridge is a city unto itself. It's got roughly a hundred thousand people living in it and covers an area of ten square miles. They could have gotten a little farther away from Sherman Oaks, but Northridge is big enough that—

Agent Kingston slides into the booth, across the table.

For moment, I can only stare in shock.

"How did you—?" I turn my head to see the door behind me silently close and look back at him. "That door was locked."

Agent Kingston regards me as some sort of idiot. "Mr. Burcham, we're the FBI. We know everything about you. We know your routines. We know who you talk to. We can listen in on conversations from a hundred yards away if we want. Give me five minutes with your phone and I can make a clone of it and know every text message you send or receive. I can even send text messages that people will think came from you. Do you really think that a thirty-year-old deadbolt on the door of a greasy spoon is going to present a problem?"

I fumble for a comeback. All I can think to say is, "You're late."

He twists in his seat to take a mental snapshot of the rest of the diner. "I had to make sure you weren't followed." He turns back to me. "So, have you seen reason? Are you going to help us?"

"Yes."

He breathes a sigh of relief. "Good. Now, what we need—"

"On my terms."

His lips purse and he cocks his head.

". . . Beg your pardon?"

"I'm going to help you finish what Amy started, but on my terms."

"What terms? You have no terms," Agent Kingston grumbles. "These people killed your wife—"

"We're going to do this my way."

"Your way? I don't . . . What are you talking about?"

"I don't trust you, Agent Kingston."

He shakes his head. "May I ask why?"

"Because Amy didn't trust you."

He holds me in that ice-blue stare but I'm not backing down. "Your wife trusted me," he says.

"No, she didn't. Why else would she leave the clues for me to find instead of you?"

"There's more than the key and the slip of paper?"

"Yeah."

He gives me a look that tells me not only does he know that Amy didn't trust him but that he also knows why.

"Mr. Burcham," he says, trying to recover. "Your wife wouldn't tell me her plan to get the information out of her office and now she's dead. Please, don't make that same mistake. You need to think about Tatum."

"Do not mention my daughter, again," I quietly seethe. "Don't even say her name. She has nothing to do with this."

He dismisses me with a wave of his hand. "The people who killed your wife do not care and they will use her to get what they want from you. That information is worth more to them than your lives. The best way to protect her is to do what I suggest," Agent Kingston says.

"The information she had is worth more than our lives to you, too!" I spit back, fighting to control the volume of my voice from attracting the attention of the other diners. "If you really cared about my daughter and me being in danger, the second that Amy was killed, you would have stormed in to protect us. Instead, you hung back because there was still a chance to find those documents. I could have been killed when Vaughn broke into my house, but it took me hiding my daughter and Amy's sister going on the run for you to show up. You didn't reveal yourself to me because you wanted to protect us. You did it because you're desperate. So, don't act like you're better than Fortis or the police."

He tries to deflect, to find some way around my accusation, but gives up.

"What do you want me to say?" he finally asks. "Yes. This case is bigger than the lives of you, your wife, or your daughter, but here's the difference; I need you alive because I need your help. Fortis and the police don't. They need to find those documents too, but if they can't, they might decide that their best move is to silence you and your daughter, and that possibility will never go away. The two of you will never be safe."

"We're not safe with you either. Amy's death kind of proves that."

"And I told you; she died because she wouldn't work with us. She never gave us the chance to protect her."

I sit back and cross my arms. "Okay, then. Let's hear it. What's your plan?"

"You have to go back to your wife's office," he says. "There may have been something there you missed."

My mouth hangs open. "You can't be serious."

"Of course, I am."

"You must be out of your damn mind," I say, almost laughing in disbelief. "These people killed my wife and you want me to just pop back in there?"

"Say that you forgot something. Say that you weren't in the right frame of mind last time. The police had found the body of your wife only hours earlier. It would make total sense. They'll believe it."

"And what happens if they figure out what I'm really doing there?"

"Why would they suspect anything?"

"Because I told the police about you!"

"That won't matter. They won't put it together."

"They knew Amy was up to something and they killed her. It might not be that hard to figure it out and in case you haven't noticed, I don't have the best poker face. I mean, are you really that desperate to risk this?"

"Yes," he answers, unflinchingly. "You have to get back in there as soon as possible. If she hid those documents in her office and couldn't get them out because she was being watched, we have to find them before they tear the place apart."

"Isn't that what warrants are for?"

Agent Kingston sighs and pinches the bridge of his nose in frustration.

The waitress approaches the booth, clocks his expression, and does a quick pivot to another table.

"A warrant requires us to know exactly what it is and where we'll find it," he explains. "We can't go in there on a hunch. But more importantly, we don't have time for a warrant. You have to get back in there now."

"Really? Get back in there? You're telling me that I have to go back and stand face to face with Henry Vaughn, the man who killed my wife? Go back in there and talk to Malcolm, who probably gave the order to do it? And I'm supposed to pretend to casually search her office? And when I can't keep up the façade, when they see right through me, which they will, what happens then? What happens to me? More importantly, what will happen to Tatum?"

"This is our only option."

It's like he hasn't heard a word I've said, so I shake my head. "I'm not going back there, Agent Kingston. I can't."

He contemplates me from across the table in the ensuing silence. "So, if you're not going to go back to her office, what *are* you going to do to try to protect yourself and your daughter?"

"I'm going to search the house again to see if Amy left any more clues. There are some other places I'm going to look, as well."

"In other words, you're not going to tell me why you won't trust me, what your wife said to you, and you're not going to help us search her office?"

"Nope."

"And there's nothing I can do to make you see reason?"

"No, and I am being reasonable."

"Suit yourself," Agent Kingston says, standing from the booth and stepping toward the door from which he entered.

"Where are you going?" I ask.

He stops. "They're going to come after you. You and your daughter. I'm going to try to keep two more bodies from showing up in an alley."

Agent Kingston exits through the door.

"So am I," I mutter under my breath.

Chapter 38

A few hours after my arrival home, it looks like a bomb went off.

The couch cushions are on the floor in the living room. In our bedroom, the contents of our dresser are scattered across the bed, along with everything from the walk-in closet. I've rummaged through all drawers and cabinets in the kitchen, even the junk food in the pantry. The sheets from the linen closet are lying on the carpet in the hallway. I've even turned the garage inside out, although Amy rarely ever set foot in there.

I should have done this the moment I found the key. It doesn't matter that her clue was specific to the sundress, I should have searched this place top to bottom. I don't care that I haven't found anything. I would simply be that much further in my search, now.

Whatever Amy took from Fortis, it's not here. There are no more keys or secret messages.

In the two hours it takes to put the house back together, I've had plenty of time to think about what Agent Kingston said.

It's still insane to have me waltz back in to Fortis, surrounded by the people who killed Amy, and try to convince them that I'm just dropping by to see if I missed anything of sentimental value the last time I was there. When I told Agent Kingston I don't have the best poker face, I meant it. I wouldn't be able to pretend that

I didn't know I was speaking to the man who killed my wife, put her in lingerie so that I would think she was having an affair, and then dumped her in an alley. I wouldn't be able to thank Malcolm for his kind words when I now know that he's full of shit.

And, as I asked Agent Kingston, what happens when they hear the hesitation in my voice or see in my expression that I know they killed Amy to shut her up. They would have no problem killing me. Will Vaughn keep that jovial demeanor as he figures out how he's going to do it? He'll go after Tatum, too. They're not going to leave any loose ends.

The thought stops me in my tracks.

I haven't heard anything from Tatum since the diner. I suppose that no news is good news, but the idea of Vaughn going after her has me momentarily reconsidering Agent Kingston's plan.

I'm not being a coward. If Agent Kingston knew for certain the documents were in Amy's office, I'd do it in a heartbeat, but he's not. And once I'm in there, I'm afraid of what happens when I can't hide what I know from Vaughn and Malcolm, not because of what will happen to me.

It's what they'll do to Tatum.

"Dammit, Amy, what else did you want me to find?" I ask aloud, standing in the living room.

Okay. Okay. I can do this.

She was leaving me clues on the way down to the airport.

There was the pocket in the sundress. I figured that out, along with the mention of Christmas, which turned out to be the code to the safe.

There was the remark about the tattoos. Got that one, as well.

What else did we talk about? We talked about the trip that we were going to take to Italy. We talked about the four-star hotels we'd stay at, but that we would also find a . . . Fairfield Motel . . .

* * *

183

The speed limit is merely a suggestion as I drive to Universal City.

The Fairfield Motel is a dive hotel nestled between a strip mall and a small used-car lot on Lankersham Boulevard. Its one saving grace is that Universal Studios is only a fifteen-minute walk across a pedestrian bridge that spans the 101 freeway.

Three years ago, Amy and I got pretty worked up for each other at her first holiday party at Fortis. She looked absolutely incredible, and we were both intoxicated by the champagne, the opulent party, her new job, and what it meant for our future. We had to have each other right then and there. We left the party early and didn't even make it home.

Amy spotted the hotel and told me to pull over.

We checked in to room two-one-five and were like teenagers after the prom.

The next morning, we even joked that it would be the last time we ever stayed at a dive motel. Nothing but four stars from then on out.

As I stand in the parking lot, staring at the Fairfield Motel, it's clear that it's had a facelift. Before, it was that tan color that you see on buildings all over Los Angeles. Now, it's gray with green trim. The outward-facing doors to the rooms have been replaced, and there's a new sign with a revamped logo above the check-in office.

If there's anything here, I know exactly where to start.

I enter the office. It's the same cramped space that I remember from before but it's trying hard to be "boutique."

"Hello, and welcome to the Fairfield," says the attendant from behind the desk. "How can I help you?"

"I'd like a room, please."

The attendant smiles and begins typing on his computer. "Great. Would you prefer a king bed? Two queens?"

Keeping my hands hidden below the counter, I cross my fingers. "Actually, is room two-one-five available?"

* * *

184

This was our room.

Like the rest of the place, it's had a facelift. When Amy and I stayed here, there were two queen beds. Now, there's a single king bed. The carpet is gray and surprisingly thick. Three years ago, there were photos of Disneyland, Hollywood, and Universal Studios on the walls. Now, they've been replaced with some sort of abstract art.

I checked in for the night, but I have no intention of sleeping here. In fact, I'll probably stay for only an hour or two, just long enough to see if Amy left anything for me to find.

Maybe I'll find a thumb drive here, or a key to a storage unit stuffed to the ceiling with boxes of documents, and that will be the end of it.

Anything to keep me from going to Fortis.

A little over an hour later and I'm sitting on the corner of the bed, silently cursing.

I got it totally wrong.

There's nothing here. Nothing in the empty drawers. Nothing in the bathroom. Nothing hidden under the bed, in the small loveseat, or the desk. I even had the bright idea to check the air-conditioning vents.

Of course Amy didn't leave anything here, because she wasn't the one who mentioned the Fairfield Motel on the way to the airport.

I did.

I was the one who made the joke that we would find a Fairfield Motel on our theoretical trip to Italy.

It's one more dead end and one more hour wasted while Fortis and the police are probably that much closer to—

My phone lights up with an incoming call.

I hit the answer button.

"Tatum?"

"DAD! THEY FOUND US!"

Chapter 39

LAX. Parking Lot C.

I'm back to where this nightmare began.

I take a ticket from the machine and pull into the lot as the roar of a plane passing overhead causes the car to tremble.

Moments later, I'm gently bouncing over the speed bumps while buses prowl the aisles, picking up occasional passengers and their luggage from the designated stops to transport them to the terminal.

Where is Section J? That sign says that I'm in Section B. Do I go right or left? What is the logic of this lot? Is there a shortcut I can take?

I thought I understood the layout of this lot, but I guess not.

Wait. I just went from Section B to Section A. Does that mean I'm going the wrong way? It might be better to keep going. Maybe Section J is after—

"HEY!" a voice cries out as something slaps the hood of the car.

I instinctively stomp on the brake, causing the seatbelt to dig into my chest.

A couple is standing just to the side of the front of the car.

"Watch where you're going, you fuckin' moron!" the man shouts.

"I'm so sorry," I plead.

He wants a few more words but the woman pulls on his arm and they walk toward one of the nearby stops to catch an approaching bus, dragging their luggage behind them. He casts one last glance over his shoulder, muttering profanities in my direction.

I deserve those.

I've got to stay calm and not draw attention. The LAX parking police probably aren't a part of the Fortis/police conspiracy, but I can't help but wonder if my name is on some sort of list and if it or my license plate is entered into a system, it'll catch the attention of those who are.

This meet-up is potentially dangerous, but I have to see Tatum for myself. I have to talk to her in person and I figured Parking Lot C at LAX, one of the biggest parking lots in Los Angeles, would be a safe place to meet. I also stopped at an ATM and took out some more money to give them. That way, we can all pay cash to leave the lot without there being a record of a credit card. I'm probably being overly cautious. If they want to find us, they can probably find us. There are cameras all over the place, sure, but as long as we don't give them a reason to check, I'm counting on our presence here being lost among the hundreds, if not thousands, of other cars that are passing through.

I take another moment to steady myself after nearly running over that couple and continue snaking through the seemingly endless rows of parked cars. Finally, I arrive at Section J at the back of the lot.

Telling them to meet me here in this section may have been a mistake. We're as far away from the entrance as possible and if something happens, there's no chance of making a quick getaway. Should I call it off? No. I'm doing the best I can. I'm making decisions on the fly with no prior experience, but my doubts will have to wait because I recognize Aiden's Mustang. I can see Tatum's silhouette inside.

I pull into the empty spot next to them and get out.

Tatum exits the Mustang, runs over, and throws her arms around me.

"Are you okay?" I ask, gripping her tightly.

"I'm okay," she says, breathlessly. "But we have to get Aiden to a hospital."

"Tatum, I told you I'm okay," I hear Aiden say.

I break from our hug and look toward the Mustang. I can just make out Aiden lying across the back seat. The window is half-open.

I nudge Tatum back to the Mustang. "Get in."

"But Dad—"

"Get in," I repeat, pushing her a little harder.

She makes a noise of disapproval but gets in the front passenger seat.

I walk around the front of the car to get in the driver's seat but stop. The side of the car is crushed inward, and the windows are gone. Someone slammed into them.

By some miracle, the door still works and I climb inside, ignoring the bits of glass that litter the floor.

I twist to look in the back seat.

"Aiden, are you okay?"

"I'm all right," he replies, sitting up with a painful grunt.

"No, you're not," Tatum insists.

"What happened?"

"We were at a hotel in Northridge," Tatum answers. "We thought we were okay, but they found us."

"Who found you?"

"There was a car in the parking lot with these two guys just sitting inside," Aiden says. "I thought they were watching the place, so I told Tatum that we were going to leave. As we walked out of the room to the car, one of them got out and came at us. He—"

"He said my name," Tatum interrupts, unable to control herself. "He knew who I was. He mentioned something about being from Mom's work and that he needed to talk to us."

"I told Tatum to run," Aiden says. "So, we ran to the car and got in. The guy ran back to his car. I gunned the car for the parking lot exit, and the guys tried to block us in. They rammed us but I kept going."

"Did they chase you?" I ask.

Aiden shakes his head. "I don't think they could. Their car was pretty messed up."

I look down at the driver's door. It's bent in, nearly touching my arm. Aiden would have taken the worst of it in the driver's seat.

"Are you sure that you're okay?" I ask, again.

"I smacked my arm and my head pretty good when they hit us, but I'm okay."

"No, you're not," Tatum says. "You need to go to the hospital."

"Tatum—" Aiden begins to argue.

"Dad," Tatum says, cutting him off. "Tell him he needs to go to the hospital. His arm might be broken. He might have a concussion."

I take out my phone and pull up the flashlight app. "Look right here," I say, shining it back toward him.

He winces as he stares into the light. His pupils contract and after a second or two, he turns away from the bright light, which is good. I put down the phone and hold up my index finger.

"Follow my finger."

I slowly move it from side to side. There's enough illumination from the many streetlights that populate the lot for me to still see his pupils. They follow my finger without listing or jumping. I'm not a doctor but I know enough to be reassured that he doesn't have a concussion.

"Let me see your arm."

Aiden gingerly rolls up his sleeve in obvious pain.

A deep purple bruise runs from his upper arm to his elbow.

"Can you move it?"

"Yeah," he says and gives me a demonstration of bending his elbow, rotating his shoulder, and flexing his fingers. He's putting on a brave show but he's hurting.

189

"See, Dad? We have to get him to a hospital."

"I'm okay," Aiden again insists.

"Tatum, he doesn't have a concussion," I explain as calmly as possible. "He might have a hairline fracture in his arm, but it's not serious."

"Not serious?!"

"Sweetheart, listen to me—"

"He needs to go to the hospital. We need to call the police!"

"We can't call the police."

"What are you talking about?"

"Tatum, we can't."

"But, Dad—"

"The police are helping the people who murdered your mother."

All the air is sucked out of the car.

They both stare at me in shock.

It's time to do what I should have done a long time ago.

I'm going to tell them everything.

". . . And that's when I told you to meet me here."

They've been silent for the better part of twenty minutes, hanging on my every word.

"And until I can find what your mother did with the information she took from her work, you two aren't safe."

"Neither are you," Tatum argues.

"I know, but I can try to find it. Your mother left me clues."

"Can't this FBI guy help us?"

"You mother was cooperating with the investigation but she left a clue, telling me not to trust him. I don't know why."

Tatum stares out at the parking lot. "So, what do we do?"

"You have to go into hiding, again. This time, you need to go somewhere with a lot of people. A lot of hotels and a lot of people."

"What? Like Disneyland?" Tatum asks.

She was being sarcastic but it's perfect.

"That is exactly what you're going to do. You're going to find a hotel by the park and stay there. Make sure it has gated parking. No, better yet, a parking garage so that no one can see this car from the street." I turn to Aiden. "There's no way to avoid this, but do you have a credit card?"

"Yeah. Well, it's my parents'."

"Good. You're going to have to use it. They might be on the lookout for Tatum or me but I can't imagine they'd be on the lookout for your parents. Got it?"

Aiden nods.

I look to Tatum.

"Yeah," she reluctantly adds and then asks, "What are you going to do?"

After paying with the cash I brought, we pull out of Parking Lot C and onto Sepulveda Boulevard. Aiden and Tatum take a left, heading south to Anaheim, while I turn right, heading back toward the city.

I don't like that they're driving a car that can now be easily identified but, hopefully, it'll soon be buried deep in a parking garage, lost in a sea of cars and thousands of tourists.

As to Tatum's question, there is only one thing I can do.

This has to end before they find her, again.

We tried it my way and it almost got Tatum and Aiden killed. Thank God for Aiden. Who knows what would have happened if he hadn't done what he did?

Passing under the ugly yellow glow of the streetlamps, I look in the rearview mirror, hoping to get one last glimpse of them as they drive away, but they've already disappeared into the river of red taillights, heading in the opposite direction.

After driving a few blocks, I pull into a gas station and park. I scroll through my recent texts, find the number, and dial.

Despite the late hour, it's answered on the second ring.

"Mr. Burcham?" Agent Kingston asks. "Where are you? What's going on?"

"Okay."

"Okay, what?"

"We'll do it your way."

Chapter 40

"Am I going to be wearing a wire?" I ask Agent Kingston as he sits across from me in the booth of a different diner than yesterday.

"No."

"Why not?"

"There isn't time. It's like the warrant you were asking about. A wire requires lawyers, a judge, paperwork, and time we don't have."

Under the table, my palms are sweating, and I can't stop my knee from bouncing up and down. The plan is for me to be at Fortis in a few hours, but my nerves are already shredding. The only thing that's brought me some measure of comfort is that Tatum called me this morning to let me know that she and Aiden were safe.

"And what exactly am I looking for?"

"Someplace she could have hidden a thumb drive."

"Do we know it's a thumb drive?"

"No, but it's our best guess."

"That's not very reassuring."

"Tough."

"That is also not very reassuring." I look around the diner. "How do you think they found Tatum?"

"I told you; I don't know. They may have been following her this whole time." The annoyance in his voice is most likely because it's the fourth or fifth time that I've asked him. "But I need you to focus. If you can get into your wife's office and spot what we're looking for and get it out of there, you and your daughter will be safe."

"And if I blow it?"

"That's why I'm telling you to focus. The office opens in an hour. We're sending you in two hours after that."

"Why wait? Why not just get this over with?"

"I want the office in full swing when you arrive. I'm hoping they'll be distracted. You can fly under the radar and get in and out as quickly as possible."

My stomach plummets.

"Don't you think they're going to find it a little insane that the morning after they attacked my daughter, I'm going to show up to root around my wife's office? Going in there as if nothing happened last night is going to be proof that I'm up to something."

Agent Kingston sighs in frustration. "You have to trust me—"

"No. I do not."

"We think that the only ones who know what really happened to your wife are Malcolm Davis, Henry Vaughn, Nadine Trembly, and Spencer Harris. They're not going to—"

"How do Nadine and Spencer know what happened to Amy?"

"Your wife believed that Spencer and Nadine were the first ones to suspect that she was up to something after Liz confronted her at the office. They told Malcolm Davis, who most likely had Henry Vaughn take care of her, but listen to me, we can find out what really happened to your wife after we find the financial records she took. Until then, I need you to get your head straight. I'm fairly certain they're not going to do anything to you."

"Really?" I ask, pouring on the sarcasm. "You're *fairly certain* of that?"

"They won't. Not in front of everyone at Fortis. Just make sure that you stay visible at all times."

My jaw hangs open.

"That's it?! That's your advice to keep me alive. We're going to call their bluff and if it all goes wrong, all I have to do is 'stay visible'?"

"This is the best and only option that we have. If the information your wife took is somewhere in her office, we need to find it before they do."

I scan the diner in disbelief, briefly taking in all the people enjoying their breakfasts and wondering how their mornings are stacking up against mine.

"I told you that they would come after your daughter," Agent Kingston says, snapping my attention back to the table and those cold blue eyes of his. "And they did. I didn't expect them to move so soon, and I don't know how they found her, but I'm telling you right now, they'll try to finish the job. There's only one way to make sure the both of you are safe."

My knee stops bouncing.

He's right. He did tell me what would happen. He knew what Fortis's next move would be. Last night wouldn't have happened if I had listened to him, and his plan, thin as it sounds, is the only way I can see forward . . . and yet, Amy's warning rings louder than ever in my ear: *I never trust guys with tattoos.*

"Mr. Burcham?" he asks.

"Yes."

"I'm telling you, they won't hurt you in broad daylight. You have to go in there and s—"

"I said yes."

Chapter 41

There's no one riding up in the elevator with me this time. No woman in a power suit pretending not to notice me. I'm alone, attempting to steady myself and rehearsing what I'm going to say.

"Hi, Linda. Sorry I didn't give you a heads-up. I was just in the neighborhood, and I thought I would—"

I was just in the neighborhood?

That makes it sound like I do my grocery shopping in the Financial District.

"Hi, Linda. Look, last time I was here I was a little . . ."

What? Off? In shock? Slightly out of sorts because your boss had my wife murdered?

The elevator chimes and the doors part.

The level of my anxiety is matched by the surprise on Linda's face.

"Mr. Burcham?"

"Hi, Linda. I, um . . . I'm sorry I didn't give you a heads-up before I came by, but, uh, this was a spur-of-the-moment thing . . . Look, last time I was here I wasn't in the right headspace. I wanted to check Amy's office, again, to see if there was anything I missed that I would like to have."

"Oh . . . ummm . . . Of course," she stammers, trying to maintain that professional pleasantness. "Let me get Mr. Davis."

"No, no, no," I protest, holding out my hand. "I don't want to bother him."

It's too late. She's already hitting the button on the panel behind the desk.

"Linda," Malcolm answers with a threatening undertone. "I told you that I wasn't to be disturbed."

"Mr. Burcham is here."

"Oh . . ." The annoyance evaporates. "I'll be right there."

Amy had said that Malcolm's demeanor could turn on a dime, that she believed there was an angry beast lurking just below Malcolm's surface. I had never seen or heard it until now.

Linda forces a smile in my direction. "He'll be right out."

"Thanks."

There goes the first chance to catch a lucky break and fly under the radar. It was a long shot, but now we have to rely on that poker face I warned Agent Kingston about.

Seconds later, the door opens and Malcolm steps into the lobby. There's no trace of the anger he displayed only moments ago through the intercom.

"Mark?"

"Hey, Malcolm. I'm sorry. I didn't want to disturb you."

"Is everything all right?"

"Yeah. Everything is fine. Well, not fine. It's . . ."

He waits expectantly. In contrast to mine, his poker face is spot on. It's a mask of genuine concern but I know that the man standing in front of me gave the order to kill Amy and to go after Tatum.

The thought causes my spine to stiffen and I find the use of speech.

"Look, when I was here the other day, I wasn't in the right frame of mind. Amy had been found only a couple of hours earlier. I wasn't thinking straight."

"Who would be?" he asks, sympathetically.

"Right. I think it was the same at the funeral, when you asked me if I had gotten everything I needed from her office. I've had some time to process it and I'd like to check again if that's all right. Maybe I *would* like some of those pictures she had on the wall. She really was proud of what she did here. She always, uh, she always talked about how good it made her feel . . ." I stop stuttering and get to the point. "Anyway, I'd like to check her office, again."

It feels like asking permission was the right way to go.

I'm expecting him to say "sure" or "of course" with that benevolent charm of his. Instead, Malcolm hesitates.

"I see . . ." he replies, scratching his chin and casting his eyes to the floor.

"Malcolm?"

He looks up at me.

"What's wrong?" I ask.

"It's— It's sort of a bad time, right now. Maybe we can set something up for later?"

I'm not letting this chance slip away. I have no interest in accommodating the people who murdered Amy.

"Malcolm, I want to see if there's anything that I missed. Five minutes. That's all I'm asking."

He winces. "I'm afraid it's not that simple."

"Why not?"

The drywall is smashed, leaving gaping holes that expose the metal girders and air-conditioning ducts underneath. The desk is in pieces. The photos that once hung on the walls have been unceremoniously tossed in the corner.

"We've been doing a little remodeling," Malcolm says to me as we stand just inside the doorway, where a plastic tarp hangs to keep the dust from floating out onto the mini–trading room floor.

I take a few more steps into the room.

"I'm terribly sorry, Mark, but you said that you had everything you needed, and we felt it might be best for everyone to change it up. It could help everyone move on."

"No. I understand," I utter.

Thankfully, my expression can be interpreted as emotional shock. My real shock is at how blatantly Malcolm is lying.

I've done remodels. There was the time the shower in the upstairs bathroom sprung a leak. I had to replace some of the ceiling and drywall in our dining room.

This isn't a remodel.

You don't rip out the drywall like this. You don't take apart furniture. You don't throw framed photos in a corner. The only reason they would do this is because they were looking for something, just as Agent Kingston predicted.

This is a demolition.

"Believe me, Mark, if there was anything here that we thought was personal, we would have sent it to you," Malcolm adds.

"It's fine," I mumble, letting my eyes wander about the devastation.

My gaze is instantly drawn to the decimated walls. The air-conditioning ducts snake through the girders. There's one on each side of the office and each end in a vent near the ceiling. The vents stare down with slotted grins, open perfectly straight, so that from where I'm standing, I can see inside.

The one in the left wall looks slightly different than the one on the right. I can't put my finger on it at first, but then I see the difference. There's something inside it. It's small and it's only because I'm standing in the perfect spot with the grate open that I can see it.

A small camera.

At that moment, the plastic tarp crackles as it's lifted and another person enters the room.

"Was there anything in particular you were looking for?" Henry Vaughn asks.

He's slightly out of breath, but still has that rugged allure, chiseled face, and movie star smile.

Did he see me looking up at the vent? Does he know that I've seen what's in there?

Due to my stupid expression, Malcolm answers for me.

"Mark was only double-checking. He was distraught last time—"

Vaughn nods, compassionately. "Completely understandable."

"—and he was making sure there wasn't anything he missed."

Vaughn grits his teeth as he surveys the office. "I'm sorry you had to see this. It probably comes off as pretty callous."

"It's okay," I try to reassure them while fighting the spike in my heartrate.

I'm too late. They've destroyed the place. I won't find anything here.

Did they find it? No. They couldn't have. If they did, why would they go after Tatum last night? And these guys are doing a masterful job of pretending as if they know nothing about it.

Another horrifying thought hits me: What if they did find it and they went after Tatum anyway as a form of security in case Amy told either her or me about the investigation? That means they're going to go after her again, no matter what, and I'm really not safe here. I need to get out. I have to get back to Agent Kingston. Everything he said was true and there's a chance it's about to get much worse.

"Thank you both for your time," I say. "But I should get going."

Vaughn gives Malcolm a collegiate pat on the arm. "You get back to your meeting. I'll walk Mr. Burcham out."

"No," I argue. "I can see myself out."

Vaughn shoots me one of his patented smiles. "It's no trouble at all."

He heads to the tarp-covered door, but not before passing Malcolm an unfathomable message in the glance they share. He then holds the tarp open and gestures.

"Right this way, Mr. Burcham."

I'm fighting a couple different things at once.

I can't go too fast or I'll appear more suspicious than I already do, but my wife's potential killer is walking a few steps behind me.

I can't look over my shoulder. That might give me away, too, but I want to see Vaughn's face. I want to see the face of Amy's killer. I want to turn to the man who attacked my daughter and look him in the eye.

We finally reach the reception area and I hit the button, summoning the elevator, while still fighting the urge to face him.

"Thank you, Mr. Vaughn."

"Please, you can call me Henry."

Fuck you, Henry.

"Thanks, Henry."

"You're sure you got everything you need," he asks as we wait.

"Yeah."

"You weren't looking for anything specific?"

"No."

"Really?"

So many thoughts flood through my brain, I'm not sure which ones made it to my face, but he notices.

"I'm sorry," he says, smiling as if he's embarrassed. "It's just that it's a little odd that you were looking for something 'in general,' you know? Most times, it would be something specific, like something you two bought on vacation. Something so personal that you would have remembered it before you came here and saw it in her office."

His not-so-subtle accusation that I'm hiding something while he's pretending nothing happened to Tatum last night causes a ball of rage to ignite in my stomach.

"Like I said, it just seems a little odd," he adds with a shrug.

I'm through fighting the urge to look at him.

I stare at him squarely in the face, not caring what I might be giving away.

"I guess that I'm still having a hard time processing things," I answer after a momentary standoff.

He nods. "I totally get that."

The doors open.

I'm ready to erupt. I want to tell him that I know all of it, but that would accomplish nothing. I have to get out of here and back to Agent Kingston.

"Thanks again," I say, stepping inside the elevator and pressing the button for the lobby.

To my horror, Vaughn steps in with me.

"I'll ride down with you."

"No, Mr. Vaughn. It's fine."

"I told you; it's Henry," he says, stopping at my side.

The elevator doors begin to close and two words blare through my skull. *Stay visible.*

My hand twitches and I almost reach for the button to keep the doors open, but it's too late. We're descending, and I'm worried what any sudden movement from me will cause him to do.

"It really is difficult," he says, slightly turning toward me, "when someone you care about dies."

He's standing way too close, trying to make me uncomfortable, which is unnecessary. I already am, but his tone is softer. If I had any doubt that he killed Amy, I might think he doesn't understand personal space. Instead, all he's doing is confirming it. He knows that my coming here in case I missed something of sentimental value is bullshit. He's playing mind games, trying to get a reaction out of me to see what I know.

"What would you know about it?" I ask, staring straight ahead.

"In a previous life, I was with Special Forces. Seventy-fifth Ranger Regiment out of Fort Benning, Georgia. Saw action in Iraq and Afghanistan."

More mind games. He's not talking about the hardships of serving and seeing brothers in arms die. He's telling me what he's capable of.

I turn once again so that I can look him in the face.

"Thank you for your service," I say, dryly.

He smiles.

I can't tell if he's impressed with my response or amused.

202

"How is the family taking it? How's her sister? *Liz*, right?"

I shift my eyes back on the doors, which offers a distorted, burnished reflection of the two of us standing too close together.

"We don't talk that much, but I'll tell her you were thinking about her."

"And your daughter . . . Tatum?"

That's it.

The ball of rage is back. The fear of being alone in an elevator with him is gone. I don't give a shit about his intimidation tactics. All I can think about is Amy's lifeless body on that table and Tatum's frantic, terrified voice from last night.

This time, I don't just turn my head. I turn my whole body toward him.

"She's fantastic, *Henry* . . . but I'm sure you already knew that."

Vaughn's tough, intimidating exterior drops.

What just happened?

He blinked. No. He didn't merely a blink. He flinched. There's genuine confusion in his face.

He doesn't understand what I'm implying.

What the hell is going on?

"I'm sorry?" he asks.

It's my turn to study him.

He has to be lying, but who is he lying for? It's just him and me in this elevator and we both know why I came to Fortis and we both know he went after Tatum last night. Why try to play stupid when—?

"Did something happen to your daughter?"

He's got some of his composure back. His question is earnest, not out of care, but out of a need for information.

"Are you serious?" I ask in disbelief, totally forgetting what this man is capable of.

To my shock, he is serious.

He really doesn't know what I'm talking about. He doesn't know what happened to Tatum.

We're pressed into the floor as the elevator slows, preparing to stop.

Someone is about to get on.

I sense it coming a fraction of a second before it happens.

Vaughn moves to hit the stop button on the panel before the doors open.

Reflexively, my fist fires from my side and knocks his hand away.

Both of us are so stunned that we don't move as the elevator stops a split second later.

The doors open and a short, rotund, tired-looking guy steps into the elevator. He gives us only the slightest of polite nods as he enters and turns to the panel. He reaches to press the button for the lobby but sees that it's already been pressed. His hand returns to his side and the doors close.

The elevator resumes its descent.

The man must really be in his own head because he can't sense the tension between Vaughn and me filling the elevator.

I'm slowly inching away from him, positioning myself for when the doors open. Out of the corner of my eye, I can see him mentally preparing. His arm is tensing. I can only guess what he's going to do once the man exits.

My stomach goes heavy as the elevator reaches the ground floor and stops.

There's the familiar chime.

I move just as the doors open.

Stepping forward, I rudely brush past the guy standing in front of us as I force my way out of the elevator and into the lobby. I take the quickest glance over my shoulder and see Vaughn reach for my arm, but I snatch it away.

"Hey!" the man protests.

I step into the flow of people passing by, and turn back.

The short guy exits the elevator and glares at me. "We all got places to be, asshole," he says and walks away.

I don't care about him. I'm too busy staring back at Vaughn, who hasn't left the elevator.

There's nothing he can do to me here in front of all these people.

He regards me with frustration and anger as the doors close in his face, leaving me to stare at my own reflection in the elevator doors.

Vaughn didn't know that Tatum and Aiden were attacked last night. How is that possible? It had to have been him or someone acting on his orders.

It had to be.

Who else could it have been?

What would anyone else gain by threatening Tat—?

. . . Son of a bitch.

"Mark?" Agent Kingston asks through the phone. "Where are you? Are you still inside the building?"

"My car is there. You'll find it on level three in the parking garage, but I'm long gone."

"'Long gone'? What are you talking about? What happened? Did you figure out where your wife hid the records?"

"Oh, I have definitely figured some stuff out."

There's a pause. He has to be realizing that this has gone way off the rails.

"Where are you, Mark?"

His tone says that he has.

"I've got some things I need to do. I'll text you where to meet me later."

"Mark—"

I hang up.

After getting a rental car and buying some clothes and toiletries, since I'm not going back to the house any time soon, I return to the Fairfield Motel.

"Checking out?" the attendant asks from behind the desk.

"No. Actually, I'd like three more nights, please."

He's a little confused, since I don't seem too happy about extending my stay at their establishment.

Once I get back to my room, I throw the clothes on the bed, turn right back around, exit the room, and get back in my car.

I wind my way through the mountains over Burbank, back to the red fire hydrant by the side of the road. I continue on for almost half a mile and find a secluded spot. I pull over and park between two large clusters of shrubs. The car isn't invisible, but close enough.

I walk back down to the fire hydrant and find some bushes about twenty yards away. There's a perfect little area where I can sit, completely hidden, and still have a clear view of the road.

Thankfully, I still have one bar of reception on my cellphone to text Agent Kingston.

Old Telephone Road. Burbank Hills. Drive until you see the red fire hydrant and park next to it. Be there in two hours.

I hit send and return my phone to my pocket.

He's not going to surprise me this time, like he did at the diner.

I'm in control now, and he's got a lot to answer for.

Chapter 42

Agent Kingston is sitting in his SUV, which is parked next to the fire hydrant, perpendicular to the road; the steep incline of the ravine is behind it. It makes sense. If he has to move, he can pull onto the road and head in either direction. He's smart. He's also incredibly anxious, scanning the bushes and trees, searching for me, but without any streetlamps and the moon as the only source of light, he's not having any luck.

Good. Let him be anxious. Let him wait. I'm not moving until I'm satisfied that he's here alone.

The time of our appointed meeting passes by one minute. Then five. Then ten. From my spot here in the shadows, I can see him growing increasingly restless. He's swiveling his head more frequently. Finally, he looks down. A faint glow illuminates his face and a moment later, my cellphone vibrates.

"Where are you?" he asks, royally pissed.

"Right here," I answer, standing from my hiding spot a few yards away.

I walk over to the SUV, get in the passenger seat, and slam the door shut.

As the interior cabin light fades, the apprehension in his face is apparent.

"I don't know what you think you're doing, Mr. Burcham," he says, going back to scanning the darkness. "But we're not safe here. This is the worst possible place—"

"No. No, we don't need to go anywhere. You need to sit here and answer my questions."

"And we couldn't have done that over the phone? Or any place safer than this?"

"Look around you. This is as safe as it gets."

"No, it's not."

"I had to make sure you weren't followed."

"It's not me being followed that has me worried," he snaps, still trying to see into every cluster of shadows surrounding the faintly moonlit road.

"Why?" I ask, sarcastically. "Who's coming for us, now?"

"Christ," he hisses. "Who do you think? The people who tried to hurt your daughter."

"I'm not worried about them."

"Yeah?" he asks, scrutinizing a nearby grouping of cedar trees. "And why is that?"

"Because they're sitting right next to me."

He makes a face. "What the hell are you—?"

"Stop. Just stop. The performance is good, but I'm tired of being lied to. I know you set that up."

"Don't be stupid. Why would I attack your daughter?"

"To make me think it was either Fortis or the police. You were trying to scare me so that I would go back to my wife's office."

He shakes his head and takes a deep breath through his nose. "Listen to me. If you didn't find anything at your wife's office, then we need to—"

"It didn't make any sense," I continue. "Why would they say that they were from Amy's work, unless that's what they wanted Tatum to believe?"

"We've been over this, Mr. Burcham. How would I have known where to find her?"

"Easy. That was a really great speech you gave at the diner about what you could do if you had my phone for five minutes, but you didn't even need that, did you?"

"I have no idea what you're talking about and we need to leave here, now."

"Tell me, Agent Kingston, how long were you standing behind me?"

He stops scanning the road and stares down at the dashboard. It's just him and me.

"At the diner? How long were you standing there?" I ask. "You didn't just walk in and sit down. You heard me on the phone, talking to Tatum when she slipped up and said she was in Northridge. Then, after I hung up, you pushed open the door like you had just entered, when in reality, you had been standing there the whole time . . ." I wait for him to respond, but he continues staring down at the dashboard. "Come on. Just say it; you attacked my daughter and tried to make it look like it was someone from Fortis so that I would go back to Amy's office. That's why you were so sure they wouldn't be suspicious about my visit, even though my daughter had been attacked the night before. It's because they didn't know anything about it . . ." His unwillingness to respond finally causes me to explode. "Come on. I'm tired of this shit! Just admit it, you fucking coward! Admit that you attacked my daughter to get me to help you!"

He whips his face in my direction. "She would have been fine if her boyfriend hadn't tried to be a fucking hero!" He stops after his outburst and grits his teeth in frustration. "You have to understand, Mr. Burcham; justice is served not with nudges and polite requests, but with twisting arms and breaking backs. I needed you to help me. To help this case. We didn't have time for you to 'think it over.' There has never been anything like this. Other companies have committed fraud, but we're talking dirty cops, dirty politicians, the wealthiest of the wealthy, and we are inches from the finish line. We can't afford to fail, now. I took a chance. We needed to find what your wife did with those records and we needed you to do it. Your daughter was safe. It was going to be an empty threat but then her boyfriend got in the way."

"Got in the way? Got in the way of what? They didn't know it was an empty threat! They thought their lives were in danger because you convinced me they were!"

"Dammit, Mr. Burcham! Don't you get it? Your lives are in danger—"

"From who?! Because right now the only one who has threatened my daughter, the only one that has hurt her, is you!"

Agent Kingston throws up his hands. "Yes! It was a mistake. It was a gamble made in desperation on my part, but whoever killed your wife will kill you and your daughter without hesitation if they think you are a threat. The only way that ends is to finish what your wife started!"

"No," I say, shaking my head. "I'm not helping you. Not after what you did to my daughter. This is done."

My hand goes for the door.

"Mr. Burcham, please, listen to me—"

"No!" I yell, turning to him. "I'm not going to listen to you! I'm not going to trust you. You said that it was a gamble born of desperation? How desperate are you now? How bad will your judgement be next time? What other stupid chance are you willing to take? Are you going to put my daughter at risk again in another 'empty threat'? What other stupid, reckless thing will you threaten me with to get me to help you?"

Staring into his face, it hits me.

"You threatened Amy, didn't you?"

He's silent and the true horror of why Amy didn't trust this man finds me.

"No . . . You didn't threaten Amy," I say, barely above a whisper. "You threatened Amy with our daughter's safety. That's how you got her to cooperate, isn't it?"

He doesn't say a word, but those icy-blue eyes convey his confession.

"That's why she didn't trust you. You threatened to hurt our daughter to get her to cooperate. It worked on her, so you figured it would work on me . . . You son of a bitch . . . What did you tell my wife would happen to our daughter if she didn't help you?"

"Mr. Burcham—"

"Tell me!"

Suddenly, I'm literally seeing red.

Agent Kingston's eyes go wide. He grabs me by my shirt and pulls me down, causing my cheek to slam into the gearshift. My cry is stifled by a popping sound and I'm showered in bits of glass. Then, Agent Kingston's crushing weight falls on top of me.

"Get off!" I grunt.

Something warm spreads across my back.

It takes a supreme effort but I'm finally able to push him away. He flops back against the door. His eyes are slightly open, as is his mouth, but part of his head is gone. Blood, black and shiny in the moonlight, pours from the wound.

I instinctively recoil.

At the same instant, there's a loud clap from somewhere outside the SUV and the headrest next to my face is torn open.

I look out the windshield to the bushes and trees across the road, except there's no windshield. Only bits of jagged glass around the frame.

There's another clap from across the road, but this time, it's accompanied by a burst of light and a loud *thwock* as the bullet hits the hood in front of me.

I dive below the dashboard just as a rapid succession of muted blasts rings out. Bullets begin smashing into the SUV, causing it to twitch and shudder with each impact. I can hear them slamming into the engine block and blasting out the remaining windows. The SUV drops as the tires are shredded.

My screams are barely audible in my own head. Random sparks

illuminate the interior, each accompanied by the sound of bullets pummeling the frame of the vehicle.

After what feels like an eternity, the onslaught abruptly stops.

The only sound is my whimpering and a hiss coming from somewhere under the hood.

I look up at the interior of the SUV.

The front seats and Agent Kingston's body are torn to shreds. All the windows are gone, including the rear windshield. I take deep, frenzied breaths, inhaling the dust swirling in the air, which causes me to cough and wheeze.

Why did the bullets stop? Is the shooter reloading? Are they waiting for me to pop my head up?

All I know is that if I stay here, I'm dead. The bullets are coming from one direction, so I'm going in the other.

I take one last look at the bullet-riddled body of Agent Kingston and am seized by a thought. Leaning over, I quickly reach into his jacket and take his wallet.

Trying to stay below the dash, hoping the engine block will continue to shield me, I crawl between the driver and passenger seats, heading toward the back. As soon as I squeeze myself in between the passenger and driver's seat, I quickly glance over my shoulder.

Through the empty windshield, a man carrying a rifle emerges from the bushes across the road. He's inserting another magazine into the gun and there's a large cylinder attached to the end of the barrel.

He sees me and snaps the rifle to his shoulder, taking aim.

I flop over the back seat as another hail of bullets begins.

I pull myself up to the opening where the rear windshield used to be. Bits of broken glass dig into my fingers as I grip the edge. Staying as low as possible, I wriggle through the opening and fall the few feet to the ground. I try to stop myself, but the SUV was parked right up against the ravine, and suddenly, I'm rolling and twisting down the embankment. Branches and shrubs scratch at my face and hands. The sound of gunfire is disorienting as I tumble.

Finally, my back slams against the trunk of a tree, stopping my fall and knocking the wind out of me. Unable to breathe, I scramble behind the thick trunk. Lying flat on the ground, I cautiously poke my head out and look back up the embankment.

The last of the sparks and bullets fly and then, all is silent.

The man with the rifle appears, steps around the back of the SUV, and glances inside. Finding it empty, he turns to look down the embankment. He's looking in my direction, but there's no way he can see me in the darkness.

He's making a decision. The embankment is too steep to walk down. He probably doesn't want to risk falling and rolling down the hill while carrying the rifle. Even if he did, there's no way he could find me.

Enraged, he swings the rifle around and sweeps the trees and bushes with a spray of bullets.

After he empties the magazine, he lowers the rifle and waits.

My lungs are only now recovering but I won't allow them air.

At the top of the embankment, the figure abruptly turns and walks away.

It's not until he's gone that I permit my lungs the oxygen they so desperately crave.

I lean against the trunk of the tree, quietly taking in long, deep gulps of life-giving air.

Agent Kingston's wallet is still in my hand. I open it and take out the slip of paper written in Amy's hand.

I once again cautiously peer around the tree and up to the SUV.

The attacker is gone.

Agent Kingston staged the attack on Tatum, but that figure was the one who killed Amy.

I suspected before, but now, I know.

By the light of the muzzle flash when he released that last volley, I saw the enraged face of Henry Vaughn.

Chapter 43

I waited in the trees, looking back up the road, for over an hour. When I finally felt sure that Henry Vaughn had left, I worked my way back to my car, which was still hidden up the road. I drove back to the motel and parked in the lot next door. Once I determined that no one was waiting for me, I parked as close as I could to my room, since my clothes were covered in blood, and quickly went inside.

The light above the mirror in the bathroom blinks on and for the first time since the bullets started flying, I get a good look at myself.

My jacket, shirt, and scalp are covered in blood.

Resisting the urge to vomit in the sink, I quickly peel off my clothes, and wrap them in a towel from the bathroom. I then turn on the shower and stand under the scalding hot water. It pools around my feet before slipping down the drain, carrying traces of Agent Kingston with it, giving it a garish, pink tint. No amount of frantic scrubbing with the small bar of soap can make it run clear. The blood only infects the soap with the same, faint pink. Eventually, after emptying the complimentary bottle of shampoo and wearing down the bar of soap, I hang my head and stand motionless under the jet of water.

It feels like the blood will never come off.

Finally, a portion of my senses returns, and the scalding water is too much.

I shut it off, grab the remaining towel from the rack, and begin drying off. After a few moments, I hold the towel away from me.

Like what's left of the bar of soap, it has a slightly pink tint.

I put on the clothes I purchased earlier and sit on the end of the bed with my head in my hands.

Agent Kingston is dead.

Even though I didn't trust him, and I had good reason not to, at least he was working against Fortis. We were on the same side in that regard.

Now, it's just me.

I could try to get to the FBI but where would I even go? Who would believe me? I'd have to explain what happened to Agent Kingston. They would take me into custody, leaving Tatum out there on her own until they sorted it out. By then, word will have gotten to Fortis and the police, and they would go after her.

I could go to the press but that would take even longer.

The police are out. I agree with Agent Kingston that not every cop is a part of this, but if I went to one, they would go to a superior, and it would go up the ladder until it caught the attention of someone who was.

My face pops up from my hands.

There is one possibility. One who would know my case, and Agent Kingston said that he might not be in on it.

Detective Harper.

Does he know? Or is it as Agent Kingston suggested: someone could be pulling his strings. Detective Harper may know that something is up but not exactly what it is. He's been trying to get me to stop digging at every turn. Was he trying to help us, maybe even protect us?

He could be a part of it, but if he's not, he could help. He'd have to, but how can I find out? Do I sit down and bluntly ask,

Hey, Detective Harper, do you know about this thing where people at my wife's work murdered her because she was helping the FBI investigate the company and now, some of your coworkers and bosses are conducting a cover-up?

I try to replay every interaction I've had with Detective Harper in my mind. Was there anything he did that indicated that he knew?

Did he know what had happened to Amy when he called me to the morgue?

Did he know what had happened to Amy as he told me they found her in an alley while I stared through the glass at Amy as she lay on that table, wearing—?

There it is.

I really can ask him, and he doesn't have to actually answer for me to know everything.

I just need to read his poker face.

Chapter 44

Detective Harper walks down the sidewalk toward the brightly lit patio area of the café. He scans the tables, searching for me amongst the first dates, friends catching up, and casual conversations.

Confused, he peers into the window of the café, even though I told him I would be sitting at a table outside. A waitress approaches and asks him something. He shakes his head. She moves off. He does another three-sixty check, confirming I'm not there, and then gets out his phone.

A second later my phone rings.

"Mr. Burcham?" Detective Harper asks.

"Yeah."

"Where are you?"

"I'm here."

He looks around, again. "Do I have the wrong café?"

"No," I answer. "I'm not at the café, but I'm here."

He stops. His posture stiffens. Through the phone, I hear his breath catch in his chest as I watch from the shadows of an alley on the other side of the street.

"Okay, Mr. Burcham. You mind telling me what this is all about?"

"Agent Kingston is dead."

"Who?"

From my vantage point, I can't tell if he's being sincere or not.

". . . What's going on, Mr. Burcham?" he asks.

"I have one question, Detective Harper. Just one."

"Come on out and I'll answer it."

"I can't do that."

"You can't come out and talk to me?"

"No."

"Then what am I doing here?" he asks, checking in every direction.

"I need to see your face when you answer my question."

He stops checking. A few of the diners sitting around him have started to notice his awkwardness.

"Okay, Mr. Burcham," he says with a sigh. "What's your question?"

"Why was Amy still wearing her ring, her necklace, and more importantly, the lingerie?"

"What? What are you talking about?"

"In the morgue. You said that there might be evidence on her ring or her necklace or on the lingerie. Remember?"

". . . Yeah. Yeah, I remember."

"If you were really investigating my wife's death, why wouldn't you remove those things and put them into bags to preserve any evidence that might be on them?"

"So, what? Are you a detective now, Mr. Burcham? I think you've seen one too many movies."

"Why was she still wearing those things in the morgue?"

His agitation grows and his searching for me becomes more frantic. He moves a few steps to the edge of the patio in an attempt at some privacy.

"I told you, your wife's death wasn't a murder."

"You couldn't have possibly known that at the time."

"Mr. Burcham, I don't know what you think—"

"Why was she still wearing lingerie?"

"Why was she—? I don't know. You tell me, since you're suddenly the expert in police procedures," he says, drawing the attention of a couple people seated on the patio, despite his attempt to isolate himself.

"Because you wanted me to see her in it," I answer. "If you really were investigating, like you said you were, she wouldn't have still been wearing that. You left them on because you wanted me to believe that my wife was having an affair, but you couldn't have known about the necklace."

He freezes. He's about to speak but doesn't. He slowly scans the other side of the street, but there are too many shadows for him to know which one I'm in.

"Did you know what they did to my wife?" I ask. "Or did someone tell you what to say?"

There's a change in his body language. His shoulders slump. He looks down at the pavement and rubs his hand across his scalp.

Then, clear as day, I see it. He bites his lip before answering. "I don't know what you're talking about, Mr. Burcham."

It's all the evidence I need. Conflicted as he sounds, he's known this whole time.

"You have to come in," he says. "We need to talk. Just tell me where you are and maybe we can sort this out . . . Mr. Burcham? . . . Mark? . . . Are you there?"

I end the call, put my phone in my pocket, walk to the other end of the alley, and exit into the night.

My last option is gone.

Chapter 45

I should be checking my rearview mirror.

I should be watching all around me for any sign of a police car, but a sense of utter hopelessness only allows me to stare at the road.

Either the police or Vaughn are going to find me. It's just a matter of time.

To keep Tatum safe, I'm going to tell her and Aiden to start driving, to hit the road and don't stop until they reach the Atlantic Ocean. Get as far away from Los Angeles as they can.

As to what happens after that, I have no idea.

I have to find a way to stop all this, even if it means giving myself up.

Instead of parking across the street from the Fairfield Hotel and waiting until I'm sure the coast is clear, I find the spot right outside my room and make my way to the door without so much as scanning the parking lot.

The room is freezing. In the frenzied return to the hotel earlier to scrub Agent Kingston off me, I forgot to turn the heat on. I don't even bother with it. I simply return to the edge of the bed and sit in the darkness.

The muffled sounds of the television in the next room are creeping through the wall. There's the white noise of the cars on the 101 freeway. The decorative curtains are closed but not the heavy blind, so the light of dozens of streetlamps and neon signs faintly illuminate the room.

Amy's dead. Liz is gone. Agent Kingston is dead. The men who killed Amy are after me and the police are in on it. I'll probably never see my daughter again. The only thing I have is the slip of gibberish Amy left in the safety deposit box.

I've never felt this alone.

What are my options? Do I have any?

Can't go to the cops. Detective Harper was my last hope there and he's a part of it.

Can't go to the press. In addition to taking too long, how can I prove any of this? There won't be an official record of Amy's death. All I have is a receipt for Amy's funeral and this slip of paper with her handwriting. Hardly a scoop.

But I have to do something. Maybe I can write down everything and send it to someone so that if something happens to me, there's at least a record of everything that's hap—

A shadow passes in front of the window and stops outside the door.

They've already found me.

The figure tries the handle, but the door is locked.

I silently leap up and stand next to the door, being careful to stay clear of the window.

They try to open the door, again.

There's nowhere for me to run and after everything that's happened tonight, I'm filled with a primal urge to fight.

They try the door one last time.

As soon as the handle moves, I push it down and violently pull the door open.

They're still gripping the outer handle and are yanked into the room.

With my free hand, I grab their wrist and hurl them toward the bed.

They stumble inside and crash to the ground as I quickly shut the door.

I'm almost on top of them, ready to slam any part of their head that gets in the way of my fist when they speak.

"Mark!" she cries, stopping me in my tracks.

I reach back and flick the switch on the wall next to the door. The woman is lying on the floor, holding up her hand, and staring at me with wide, frantic eyes.

"Liz?!"

She pulls herself onto the bed, still holding out her hands.

"Mark, I can explain," she pleads.

"Where the hell have you been?" I ask, angrily.

"Please—"

"Do you have any idea what I've been through?!" I fume, taking a step toward her. "What Tatum's been through?!"

"Listen to me—"

"You lied! You lied to me! You lied about Amy having an affair!"

"Mark—"

"You knew what was going on, but you wouldn't help us! People have tried to kill us. People have died, Liz, and you didn't—!"

"Mark, it's me!" she yells, tears streaming down her face.

I stop my advance. "What? What are you talking about?"

"It's me . . . It's Amy."

My heart catches in my chest. ". . . What?"

"It's me, Mark."

"Liz . . . what are you doing?"

"Please. You have to listen to me," she pleads from her sitting position on the bed. "I can explain."

"Amy is dead."

"No. It was—"

"She's dead, Liz! I saw her on that table. She was wearing her ring! She was wearing Colleen's necklace! You saw her at the funeral!"

She lightly shakes her head, staring at me with wide, tearful eyes.

Liz must be having a mental break at the grief of losing her sister and to be honest, after the events of this evening, and now to be confronted with this, I'm not that far behind.

"Why are you doing this, Liz?"

"That was Liz you saw on the table. That was Liz inside the coffin at the funeral. You hadn't seen her in two years and she was trying to look like me when she was killed." She stands from the bed and takes a cautious step toward me. "Mark, I know this—"

"No . . . no . . . Amy's gone."

"Mark. It's me."

"Why are you doing this?!" I ask again. "What are you doing here?!"

"Because you mentioned this hotel in the car on the way to the airport!" she snaps.

I freeze.

"And after I ran from Liz's house, I didn't know where else to go. So, I came here . . . and then I saw you in the parking lot."

I stare at her. There's only one person in the world who knew of our conversation.

". . . Amy?" I whisper.

She comes closer and takes my shocked face in her trembling hands.

"It's me," she says.

I study her face in the dimness of the room. I want to believe that Amy is standing in front of me, but a part of me won't allow it.

She senses my hesitation and then gently pulls me toward her.

Our kiss is hesitant at first, but the feel of her lips, the movement of her tongue against mine. The way we fit together, the placement of our hands, the timing, all the things that we had practiced for decades were more proof than any driver's license or fingerprint could ever offer.

Amy and I had each other again.

Chapter 46

That kiss, which began as a hesitant test, grew out of control.

We fell to the bed and made love in a way that defies description. It was hungry, fearful, joyous, a release of grief, anxiety, and doubt. There was a lot to talk about and yes, we were still in danger, but for a precious few hours, the world outside this hotel room didn't exist. There was only us, losing ourselves in each other after believing it would never happen again.

Finally, we're lying on the bed, naked and entwined, breathless, and covered in sweat, coming down from the incalculable physical high. We could both use a glass of water but neither of us want to run the risk of getting out of this bed for fear of waking from this dream.

But the moment has passed. Amy and I are reunited. We've released our pent-up fears and emotions, and the world outside is slowly creeping back into existence.

"Amy?" I ask, quietly.

"Yeah?" she replies.

"Tell me everything."

She sighs and nods, gripping me tightly. "Okay . . . You remember how excited we were when I got the job?"

"Yes."

"I knew that it was going to be stressful. I wanted that, but I had no idea just how stressful it was going to be. Malcolm, Spencer, and Nadine were constantly leaning on me to bring in more accounts. I tried to keep up, but it never seemed to be enough. That's when I started to suspect something was wrong. I couldn't understand how we could be posting such large returns and at the same time, constantly need to bring in new accounts. It didn't make sense."

"When did you know for sure?" I ask. It's not an accusation. It's not an admonition. I simply need to understand.

"The end of that first year. I knew something was wrong, but we were making more money than ever. We had the house. We had saved enough so that Tatum's tuition would be paid off before she graduated. I guess I buried my head in the sand and looked the other way." She collects herself before continuing. "But still, they kept pressuring me to bring in more and more money. It was then that I knew. I didn't have solid proof, but I started looking elsewhere."

"You were looking for other jobs?"

"Mmm-hmm. I didn't tell you because you would ask me why and I wasn't sure I could lie to you."

"Well, you got pretty good at it."

"Babe?"

"Sorry."

"I started sending out feelers. I wanted to find something in Los Angeles so that we wouldn't have to move. A month later, I was contacted by a recruiter who said he was with a hedge fund here in the city and wanted me to come in for an interview. I thought it was perfect but when I arrived, something felt off. He was asking questions about Fortis and why I wanted to leave. On top of that, he didn't tell me a thing about the hedge fund he was recruiting for. It got to the point that I tried to end the interview. That's when he sprung the trap. It was Agent Kingston. The FBI had created a dummy company to try to recruit someone from inside Fortis and there I was. He laid it out. Everything I had suspected was true. Fortis was running a Ponzi scheme. They were paying older investors with funds from new investors. That's why they needed me to keep bringing in more accounts. Fortis had started slow, but it was like a growing cancer. The FBI had been building a case against Fortis for years and they were at the point that they needed someone who could get the real financial records."

"But you didn't have access to them, right?"

"No, but Agent Kingston didn't care. He told me that I had to get them. I tried to convince him that it wasn't possible. He asked me again why I was leaving Fortis. I tried to lie. I tried to make up some bullshit story about not being happy there, but he saw right through it. He had me. He said that Fortis was going to collapse and the fact that I knew what they were up to meant that I would go down with it, even if I left the company. My only hope to stay out of jail was to help them. If I did, I could walk away . . . I told him no."

"Are you serious?"

"When he told me about the people involved, the police and the politicians, I told him it was too dangerous. I couldn't risk those people coming at us if they found out what I would be doing."

"What did he say?"

"He said that I was right. He said that these were powerful people and if they even suspected that I was working with him, they might come after us . . . that they would come after Tatum . . . Then he said . . . he said it would be really unfortunate if they made a mistake and believed that I was working with the FBI when I actually wasn't. Then, he took out a folder full of pictures, pictures of you dropping off Tatum at school, of her with her friends at the mall . . . of her at her bedroom window."

The blood in my veins turns to ice.

"He said it was the last piece in their investigation," Amy says. "He said something about justice being served not by polite requests but by breaking backs."

"I got that same speech," I fume.

She sighs. "So, I told him that I would help if he kept you and Tatum out of it."

"You should have told me."

"I was trying to protect you and Tatum."

"I could have helped you."

"No, you couldn't have."

"Amy, it's our daughter—"

"And if something happened to me, you would be safe. You and Tatum wouldn't be a part of it."

"You still should have told me—"

She raises her head from my chest to look at me. Even in the dimly lit room, I can see the determination in her expression.

"Tell me you wouldn't have done exactly the same thing, Mark. Tell me you wouldn't have done everything in your power to protect Tatum and me from harm, even if it meant sacrificing yourself, even if it meant lying to me. Tell me that is not exactly what you would have done." She waits, daring me to answer, but I don't. "I know the answer. And I know it because I know you better than anyone in my life."

I can't let it go.

"Amy, I love you, but you should have told me."

"Dammit, Mark." She groans and buries her face in my chest.

"We could have done this together. We would have figured it out."

She looks up at me, again. "Mark?"

"What?"

"Where's Tatum?"

"What does that have to do with the investigation?"

"I'm asking you; where is Tatum?"

"I— I don't know."

"Why don't you know?"

"Be— Because—"

"Because you sent her away so that if something happens to you, she'll be safe, right?"

227

There's no use in arguing, so I nod.

"Now do you understand why I did what I did?" she asks.

I do. Everything she said is true. I would have done exactly the same thing.

God, I love this woman.

"And I'm sorry, Mark. I'm sorry I lied to you, but I was trying to protect our family."

"What happened to Liz?" I ask after a long silence.

Amy once again takes a moment to sort her memories.

"She saw the same thing you did two years ago. She saw the stress overtaking me. She knew that I was hiding something. I kept telling her that everything was fine, which only made her more suspicious. Then, she caught me in a lie when I went to meet Agent Kingston. After all my denials about hiding anything, she finally assumed the worst . . . She thought I was having an affair. I told her it wasn't an affair but couldn't tell her what was really happening. Of course, she didn't believe me. She was convinced that I was cheating and told me that I had to tell you. I kept trying to push her away until finally, she stormed into Fortis one afternoon and said that if I didn't tell you about the affair, she would. I got Liz out of the office and told her what was really happening. About the case. The FBI. She was so sorry and so scared for us. She said that she would help me but, like you and Tatum, I wanted to keep her out of it. I told her the best way to help me was to stay away, now that she knew what was really happening. That was when we first stopped talking."

"You weren't fighting?"

"I was trying to keep her safe. I didn't tell Agent Kingston that Liz knew at the time because I didn't want to give him another way to threaten me. I thought I could get the documents out of Fortis myself but after Liz's outburst, everything at Fortis changed. Nadine and Spencer began looking at me differently. Everyone became paranoid. Security suddenly became a priority. They brought in Henry Vaughn and he basically changed everything.

My part in the investigation was only a few weeks old. I still thought I could handle it. I needed to get access to the information Agent Kingston wanted, so I started making friends with more people in the records division. There was a younger guy I started flirting with. We'd go to lunch. I'd hang out in his office sometimes. Eventually, I was able to get his password and username."

"But . . . You didn't—?"

She shakes her head. "No. Just got to know him well to see over his shoulder as he typed in his password. The plan was to download all the documents on to a thumb drive and then just walk out. For a little extra protection, I put a password on the thumb drive and made it one that I would never be able to remember. That way, if I was caught with the drive, no one would be able to open it. They could never prove what I had. I took the only copy of the password and stashed it in the safety deposit box at Lowes and Sons and hid the key in the sundress."

"Well, at least I know what that gibberish was, but it took me forever to figure out what the key was for."

"I thought you'd be able to find it by the letters."

"I couldn't read them."

"Then, how did you solve it?"

"I went through your phone records. You made one call to Lowes and Sons."

She nods. "It was the first time I called them. Agent Kingston gave me a burner phone. That's how we communicated, and after that first call to Lowes and Sons on my cell, I used the burner phone. I was hoping that you would figure out the clue to the sundress, get the key, get the password, and then use it as leverage to get yourself and Tatum clear of everything."

"We almost got there."

She lets out a light laugh before continuing. "Anyway, I had everything in place. I went to the computer in my office and logged in using his username and password. It took weeks of rooting around the company's network before I finally found what I needed. I started downloading the information onto the thumb drive, but something was wrong. Suddenly, it was like someone else was trying to take over the computer remotely. I was so stupid. I was using someone else's login and password on my computer and accessing the company's most sensitive files. Of course, it would raise a red flag. They stopped trying to take over the computer and right then I knew that Vaughn was coming.

"I was able to finish downloading everything and logged off my computer. I looked up through the glass wall in my office. Vaughn was practically running toward my office across the trading floor. I did the only thing I could do; I was able to hide the thumb drive only seconds before he came in. I tried to play dumb, like I had no idea what was going on. He played along. He said that there was some sort of network error, but there had been some 'unusual activity' on my computer and he had to take it. I don't think he realized that I had downloaded everything to a thumb drive. He thought it was still on my computer, that he had a smoking gun. I told him that was fine. He could take the computer. I just wanted him out of my office but he wouldn't leave. He called in Malcolm and gave him the same bullshit story. It was like they were speaking in code, with Vaughn telling him I was up to something. Malcolm said that I should go home until everything was sorted out. I didn't want to leave without the drive but I didn't want to put up too much of a fight. I had to trust that the drive was hidden, so I agreed but when I tried to leave, Vaughn searched my purse and had me turn out my pockets. I swear, he was about to do a strip search, but eventually, he let me go. The next day, I went into the office, thinking I would grab the thumb drive and walk back out but when I got there, there was a metal detector in the lobby and two security guards. They were making employees walk through it to get in and out of the office. It was absurd but effective. I figured that I could just jam the drive into a tube of lipstick or something but then I got to my office. Malcolm and Vaughn were there, asking me all sorts of questions about how things were at home. As they were leaving, Malcolm cast a glance toward the air-conditioning vent. I waited until they were gone and I saw it."

"The camera?" I ask.

"Yeah. I knew that was why they let me back into my office. They wanted me to give away where I had hidden the drive. They couldn't risk it even existing. If at any point I tried to retrieve it from where it was hidden, they would see it and I wouldn't make it out of the building alive. From then on, whenever I was at Fortis, so was Vaughn, waiting and watching. He sat in on every meeting. I even began seeing him outside work. He would drive by the house. I'm pretty sure he even bugged my phone because he seemed to know where I would be. He constantly watched who I met and talked to, which is another reason I couldn't contact Liz."

"Did you tell Agent Kingston?"

"Yeah. I told him that there was no way to get the files out. He was livid. He felt the case was slipping away. He told me that I had to get them out. He would interrogate me for hours about what was on those files, but I hadn't seen them. Only downloaded them. That's where I was when I lied about the trips to Boston. Agent Kingston was grilling me and trying to work out a plan. I tried to get out of the deal. I said it was over, that I wasn't going to cooperate. The next day, Tatum had her accident last year. Do you remember? She said that someone cut her off and she went into the ditch?"

"It was him?"

"Yeah."

I clench my fists. It was bad enough what Agent Kingston was doing to Amy, but the fact that he had made good on his threat to Tatum to get Amy to cooperate and did the same to me softens my pity toward him that his head was blown off.

"I came back at him, screaming, telling him it was over and that I would make him pay," Amy continues. "He asked me where would I go, the cops? He said that there was only one way this

231

would end. So, I had to come up with a plan. I had to get Vaughn away from the office to get the drive. I really didn't want to, but I could see no other way. So, we came up with a plan."

"We?"

"I got another burner phone and contacted Liz. If there was some other way, I would have taken it, but Liz wanted to help. Vaughn was watching my every move. He was shadowing me, so we decided to use it. I would have a meeting somewhere with the team away from the office while Liz would go into Fortis, posing as me, and get the drive. Liz started growing out her hair and exercising so that she would look like me. We found a wedding ring that looked just like mine but felt the necklace was more convincing. Once we had the drive, we'd give it and the password to Agent Kingston, and be done with it. I told Agent Kingston that I had a plan but wouldn't tell it to him. I didn't want him to know that Liz was involved. He knew that Liz was a twin but he believed that Liz and I had stopped talking."

"But Vaughn had to know that you had a twin," I say.

"I know but it was our only chance. I stayed away so that she could finish the transformation as best as she could in the few months we had. Finally, the day came. I invited Malcolm, Nadine, and Spencer to dinner to talk about new strategies. I assumed Vaughn would be there, since he had been following my every move. Liz was going to go to the office with my work badge, and ID, posing as me, to get the drive out. We hoped that she could get in, claiming I had forgotten something, get the drive, and get out. It was important that anyone at the office would think it was me. When I got to the restaurant, I didn't go inside because I wanted to make sure they were all there. I had reserved a table near the entrance so I could see it from the street. I came late, to make sure they would be there, but when I arrived, I didn't see Vaughn . . . and I knew. I tried to reach Liz to call it off, but she wasn't answering the phone. I left without going inside the restaurant. I tried for hours to get a hold of Liz. When she didn't answer, I went to her place, hoping she would show up. Then, on Monday morning, you called and told me what happened . . . Vaughn must have suspected that I was up to something and killed Liz at the office, thinking it was me . . ." Amy once again has to pause to calm herself. "I knew that if they figured out what really happened, all hell would break loose. If I told Liz, they might think I told you. They would come after you and Tatum. The only way to keep everyone safe was to let them think that they had killed me and that Liz was still alive . . . So, I had to become her. I cut my hair. I adopted her mannerisms. Did my makeup like hers. I had to live like I was her. Shortly after you called to let me know they had found the body, Agent Kingston confronted me, asking me questions about 'Amy.' I tried to tell him, as Liz, that I hadn't spoken to Amy in two years, but he could see that something was up, so I told him that 'Amy' had told me of the investigation but didn't go into details. He believed that Liz and I hadn't spoken in two years. He thought I was Liz and, therefore, was a dead end. I spent the days after you called trying to come up with some way to get in the office but it's hopeless. Then, I started seeing Vaughn, again. He would drive past Liz's house. I think he started to suspect that something was wrong. That's why I had to stay away from you and Tatum. If one of you recognized me, if I couldn't keep up the lie and they knew I was alive, we'd all be in danger. That's why I couldn't take her when you came to me. She was going to be safer with anyone else. After you left, I grabbed some clothes and came to this motel. Like I said, I couldn't think of anywhere else to go. I couldn't leave Los Angeles, not with you and Tatum in danger. I figured I would still try to find some way to get the drive back. You can't imagine how I felt when I saw you pull into the parking lot earlier today. I couldn't believe it."

"After figuring out the sundress and the clue about men with tattoos, I thought you may have hidden something here. This was our room."

"I know."

For a long moment, I lie there holding her, just putting the pieces together, and ask the question that's been building ever since she told me who she really was.

"Amy, I understand trying to protect us from Fortis, but why did you lie to me about the affair at Liz's house after the funeral?"

"I thought for sure that you were going to recognize me."

"I hadn't seen Liz in two years. And I had seen you lying dead on a table."

"And when you said that maybe she'd be alive if I had done the right thing . . . I was angry because you were right. It was my fault."

"You tried to keep her away. Liz made her own choice and that's exactly what she would say if she were here, but Amy, why did you tell me you were having an affair?"

She takes a breath. "I'm so sorry, Mark. It was the hardest thing I've ever done but I was still trying to protect you."

"How?"

"I was trying to get you to stop. I saw the black key on your key ring at the funeral when you gave the keys to Tatum and knew that you were following the clues. I gave you the clue to the password to the thumb drive because I thought it would be safe. I never wanted you to go to Fortis. I figured Agent Kingston would do that if something happened to me, and the password would be the ticket to safety for you and Tatum. I never considered that Liz would be killed. As long as I was alive, I was going to be the one to finish it and keep you out of it, even if that meant telling you the worst lie of all. I tried to get you to believe that I was having an affair so you would stop looking, which is exactly what Fortis and the police were trying to do."

"So, if you had died, you would have let me believe for the rest of my life that you were having an affair?"

"If it meant you and Tatum would be safe, then yes. It's the worst thing I've ever done to you, Mark . . . and I'd do it again."

"I didn't believe it," I whisper, staring up at the ceiling. "Not for a second and I knew that there was no way you died of a drug overdose. Not while you were wearing Colleen's necklace."

"I know," she quietly replies, a perfect mix of relief and sadness. "I love you."

"I love you, too."

We lie there, holding each other in the darkness.

"Where is Agent Kingston?" she finally asks.

". . . He's gone."

"Gone?"

"Yeah."

"What happened?"

"He tried to make it look like Fortis went after Tatum at a hotel where she and Aiden were hiding in Northridge."

Her head snaps up. "He what?!"

"She's okay," I try to calm her. "She's with Aiden. They're hiding somewhere in Anaheim."

"What did he do?"

"Same thing he did to you. He used her to get me to do what he wanted, which was to go to your office to find the drive, but they smashed up the place. Anyway, Aiden got them out of there. He's banged up but he's okay. They both are."

Amy tenses with fury. "What did he do to them?"

"It's a long story, but I met up with him earlier tonight to call him out."

"And?"

"Henry Vaughn blew his head off."

Her wide eyes look up at me. "Jesus, Mark."

"Vaughn was trying to kill me, too. Agent Kingston pulled me out of the way, which is why he took the bullet. So, I guess he did one good thing."

Amy's mouth hangs open for a moment. Then, she groans and sinks back down. "What are we gonna do?"

"We have to get the drive. Malcolm and Vaughn haven't found it.

They wouldn't have taken the risk of trying to kill me while I was sitting right next to Agent Kingston if they had. We need to find a way back into Fortis."

She shakes her head. "It's not possible. I've spent every day since Liz's death trying to figure out how to get in there. There's no way they'll let me in, even as Liz, and you can't show your face anywhere. Besides, you said that they've destroyed the place. The drive is gone."

"Where did you hide it?"

She crawls up my body and rests her head on the pillow next to mine so that we're looking each other in the eye. "You didn't figure out that last clue I gave you, did you?"

"Which one? The remark about guys with tattoos?"

"No. It was at the airport."

My brows knit together in confusion.

She turns her head to look up at the ceiling. "It's my fault. That one *was* too vague. The others stood out. The last one didn't."

"What was it?"

She turns back to me, smiles, and then kisses me.

Our lips part.

"It was always you," she whispers.

"What?"

"I was at my desk when I spotted Vaughn running toward my office. I took out the drive and hid it in the thing closest to me, which was the photo of our wedding day. The one you had the frame made for. I popped out the photo and tucked it into the frame behind the engraving and put it back together only seconds before he arrived . . . but it's gone now. They probably found it when they destroyed . . . the . . . office— Mark? Why are you looking at me like that?"

Chapter 47

"You picked the absolute worst time to be subtle," I tell Amy over the whine of the engine as we sail down the highway to our house.

"I wasn't trying to be subtle or clever. I was trying to tell you where I hid the damn thing, but I couldn't come out and say, 'By the way, honey, for the past two years, I've been involved in an FBI investigation into my company and some of the most powerful people in the city, and just in case something happens to me, I hid a thumb drive in the frame of the photo of our wedding day on my desk.'"

This isn't a real fight. There's no malice in our barbs. We're both trying to keep up with the last few hours.

I can't believe I've had it this whole time. Only hours after they found "Amy's" body, I walked out of her office with the very thing they had "killed" her for. I've held it in my hands, not realizing that the key to our escape was inside.

It's a struggle to keep us under the speed limit, and getting pulled over by the police right now would be a disaster.

"What's the plan?" I ask.

"Plan?"

"Yeah," I reply, keeping my eyes on the road and swerving around a slow-rolling Chevy. "What happens when we get this thing? What do we do?"

Her silence is unnerving.

"Amy?"

"I don't know."

"What do you mean, you don't know?"

"I was going to give it to Agent Kingston, but now that he's gone . . ." She searches for an answer but shakes her head. "We'll cross that bridge when we have the drive."

"Okay, but first, we're going to take the drive somewhere and make a copy. Actually, a couple of copies so that Fortis won't be able to stop it from getting out."

"What about Tatum? Should I call her?"

"No. We're not contacting her until we have the thing and are away from the house. I don't care where we go."

"Okay."

That's that. It's settled.

Amy grows silent and stares out the window.

"Are you all right?" I ask, risking a sideways glance. "What are you thinking?"

"That I've been living with this for two years and in a few minutes, it could all be over."

There's our house, wrapped in shadows at the end of the block.

The only lights visible on the property are the weak solar-powered lanterns that illuminate the walkway to the front door.

Sitting here from a distance, I can't help but feel that we're staring into a trap.

"What if someone's watching the house?" Amy asks. "Should we park here and try to sneak in?"

I shake my head. "We have to have the car nearby in case we need to leave in a hurry. We're going to park in the driveway. I'll go inside and get the photo while you wait here in the driver's seat with the engine running."

"I'm not letting you go in there alone; not if there is a chance that someone is waiting inside. We'll go in together, get the photo, and get out."

"Amy, it's better if only one of us—"

"You're not going in there alone and we're not going to argue about it."

"I'm not trying to argue with you, but if there is someone inside—"

Amy throws up her hands.

"Mark, in the time that we've been sitting here, we could have gotten the photo and driven away. Let's go."

She's right. We can't waste any more time.

I switch my foot from the brake to the gas, propelling us down the block. I make the turn in front of the house, ignoring the stop sign, and pull too quickly into the driveway causing the front of the car to dip and loudly kiss the pavement.

It's a rental. Who cares?

I stop the car at the start of the walkway and put it into park. I'm tempted to leave the keys in the ignition and the engine running but decide against it.

Without a word, we leap out and hustle down the dimly lit walkway. Amy has tunnel vision while I'm watching the shadows, waiting for Henry Vaughn to emerge from the bushes with a rifle in his hands.

"Keys," Amy says, reaching behind her toward me.

I hand them to her like we're on a relay team.

We step onto the porch and the motion-sensor light next to the door suddenly comes on, freezing us in place like two escaped convicts caught in a searchlight. Amy is the first to shake it off, unlocks the door, and goes inside.

The alarm begins chirping.

Amy stops and stares at it.

"Amy?"

She turns to me.

"Let's let it go," she says. "We'll be gone by the time the cops come."

"We don't want the cops knowing we were here."

The alarm continues to chirp, counting down what's left of the thirty seconds we have to disarm it.

"Not every cop can be in on it," she argues. "It'll be another fire they'll have to put out."

I step through the door, crowd her out, and enter the code. The alarm emits two quick chirps and goes silent.

"We're not taking that chance. Let's get the drive and go."

I move down the hall and reach the kitchen doorway before I realize that Amy hasn't moved. She's still staring at the alarm panel.

"Amy? Come on."

"Okay. Okay."

She joins me at the end of the hallway, and we move through the kitchen to the living room.

The silver frame glints in the moonlight that filters through the window. I can barely make out our figures in the image. Only the vague white shape of Amy's wedding dress is recognizable.

I take the photo from the end table, flip it over, and fumble with the clasps. I'm finally able to remove the backing.

There it is, resting in the bottom of the frame behind the engraving. I toss the backing onto the couch, pull out the drive, and hold it up.

It looks like any other boring thumb drive you might find in a drawer at your desk.

"Okay," Amy says. "Let's go."

I place the photo and frame on the couch and tuck the drive into my pocket. Amy and I start moving back toward the kitchen when, to our shock, the front door opens. The light goes on in the hall. The front door closes and locks.

I grab Amy and pull her back.

A voice calls out.

"Dad?"

A shadow passes in the hallway and Tatum and Aiden emerge into the kitchen. Tatum flips on the light as she enters and freezes at the sight of Amy and me in the living room.

"Aunt Liz?" Tatum asks.

Amy steps forward. "No, sweetheart. It's me . . . It's Mom."

Tatum doesn't move. "What?"

Amy nods, causing the tears that are building in her eyes to shimmer. "It's me, Tatum. It's Mom."

Tatum's face twists, and then she sees something, something in Amy's face or hears something in her tone that is proof that what Amy has said is the truth. Tatum runs at her and throws her arms around her as she begins sobbing. Aiden hangs back, watching, still confused, but I nod to let him know that it's all right.

Amy holds Taum while trying to retain her composure.

"It's okay . . . It's okay . . ." she says, gently rocking Tatum and stroking her hair.

I'm temporarily lost in the moment of seeing them reunited. The pain of telling Tatum that her mother was dead is negated, but it's only a moment before I realize that there's something terribly wrong.

"What are you two doing here?" I ask.

Tatum separates from Amy.

"What do you mean?" she asks, wiping her nose with her sleeve. "You texted me, telling us to come to the house."

"No. I didn't."

"What?" Tatum asks and looks to Aiden, who shares in her confusion. "Yes, you did." She pulls her phone out of her pocket. "It's right here."

She unlocks the phone, pulls up her texts, and shows me the screen, which displays a message sent from my number roughly an hour ago.

Come to the house right now.

I take the phone from her hand and stare dumbfounded at the screen.

"I didn't send this."

"But . . . It's your number."

"I know, but it wasn't me."

Tatum takes her phone back and looks at Amy and me.

How? How did that text get sent from my—

Agent Kingston sitting at the diner.

"Mr. Burcham, we're the FBI. We know everything about you. We know your routines. We know who you talk to. We can listen in on conversations from a hundred yards away if we want. Give me five minutes with your phone and I can make a clone of it and know every text message you send or receive. I can even send text messages that people will think came from you. Do you really think that a thirty-year-old deadbolt on the door of a greasy spoon is going to present a problem?"

If the FBI could do it, I'm sure someone at Fortis could, but when would they—

"I'm sorry, Mr. Burcham, but we have to ask you to leave your cell phone here with Linda," Vaughn says.

Malcolm is obviously embarrassed. "We're keeping a tight lid around here."

"No. It's okay," I say and hand my phone to Linda.

I gave them my phone when I went to the office. Vaughn had to have cloned it.

They've had a copy of my phone this whole time. They've been watching and reading all my texts but Agent Kingston said they couldn't listen in to phone calls.

That's why they didn't know Tatum and Aiden were in Northridge.

242

She told me in a phone call. Same thing with our meeting in Lot C at LAX. It's how Vaughn knew where I was when I met Agent Kingston and ambushed us.

They've known almost every move I've made and now. Everything— us, the drive, and the password—is all in one place.

They're coming for us.

"Mark?" Amy asks.

"We have to get out of here."

I grab Tatum and move toward the hall, but I'm stopped by the sound of car doors closing outside.

It's too late.

They're already here.

Chapter 48

For a moment, no one moves.

Then, Amy quickly strides to the alarm by the door leading to the garage. She punches a few buttons. It emits two quick beeps, followed by another two, activating the silent alarm.

"We have to take the chance," she says.

I nod.

Amy rejoins us and glances down at my hip pocket, containing the thumb drive, and back up at me.

I've got the one thing they want. Everyone else needs to get out of here.

"Go," I say with a nod to the back door.

Amy immediately understands.

She motions to Tatum and Aiden. "Come on."

"Wait," Tatum protests. "Dad—"

"I'll be right behind you."

I hate that my last words to my daughter are probably a lie, but if it gets her away from here, so be it. I need to give them time and I don't want them to see what I'm about to do.

"Tatum, Aiden, let's go," Amy commands.

They reluctantly, but quickly, step out the back door.

Once they're gone, Amy gazes at me with a sense of helplessness.

I had missed my chance to tell her last time, when I thought I would never see her again. I'm not missing it now.

"I love you," I tell her.

"I love you, too," she replies.

Something crashes against the front door.

I nod. "Go."

She steps outside, closes the door behind her, and disappears off the deck, following Aiden and Tatum into the night.

There's another crash against the front door, accompanied by a sickening crack.

I take the drive out of my pocket. I've only got a few seconds.

I quickly kneel next to the couch, grab the center cushion, unzip the back a few inches, pull the drive from my pocket, and stuff it inside.

Two more blows fall against the front door and it gives way. There are footsteps in the hall. I'm able to shove the cushion onto the couch and back away to the middle of the room. I could try to escape out the door, but I don't want whoever is coming down the hall to follow me. I need to give Amy and the kids every second I can.

Standing here, listening to the approaching footsteps, an indescribable calm sweeps over me.

Stall them for as long as I can. That's all that matters, now.

Detective Harper emerges into the kitchen. He spots me and aims the gun in his hand at my chest.

"On your knees!" he shouts.

I oblige.

While I'm composed, he's anxious, bordering on panic.

There's another set of footsteps in the hall and a second later, he's joined by Malcolm Davis.

He steps around Detective Harper and takes control of the room without obstructing the officer's line of fire.

Malcolm walks over to me. That feral animal that Amy had told me about is on full display.

Detective Harper follows a few feet behind, keeping the gun on me.

Malcolm glares down into my neutral expression with one of rage and contempt.

"Where is she?" he asks.

I keep my eyes locked on his, trying not to look at the back door.

"Let me ask you something, Malcolm; when did you figure out that you had killed the wrong person?"

He only stares at me.

Detective Harper speaks up. "After the funeral when everyone started running."

"Don't answer his questions," Malcolm spits at him before turning back to me. "He's trying to buy time . . . So, let's get right to the point; where is the drive?"

Now, instead of avoiding looking at the back door, I avoid looking at the couch but Malcolm notices the dissembled frame that is lying on the far end, next to the armrest.

He walks over and picks it up while Detective Harper keeps his gun trained on me.

Malcolm studies it, exhales through his nose, and draws his lips back in a frustrated snarl. "This is where she hid it, huh? It was sitting on her desk this whole time?" he rhetorically asks, his tone rising. "And you just walked out with it!"

"Yeah. I just walked out with it," I reply, unable nor wanting to resist the light mocking smile that plays across my face. "And now, it's gone, as are Amy and my daughter . . . It's over."

My smirk fuels his rage and he hurls the photo and the frame against the wall next to the fireplace behind me.

He goes back to standing over me, trying to figure out what to do when Detective Harper's phone pings. He pulls it from his pocket while keeping the gun aimed at me. He checks the screen and his face goes pale. He searches the room and spots the alarm panel by the garage door.

"Oh, yeah. I forgot to tell you," I add. "The cops are on their way."

Judging from his expression, I don't think Malcolm is used to not being in control of any situation he happens to be in.

"Is he telling the truth?" he asks Detective Harper.

The detective nods.

"Call them off," Malcolm instructs him.

"And tell them what?" Detective Harper asks. "That we're already here? Someone is going to ask why."

Malcolm curses. "How much time do we have?"

"Ten minutes. Fifteen at most," Detective Harper answers. "We have to go."

"Without that drive? That's what this whole damn thing is about." Malcolm then motions to me. "And are we just going to leave him here?"

"I'm telling you, we have to get out of here," Detective Harper insists.

Malcolm steps over to him. "Don't forget what you were told; no more loose ends, understand?"

Detective Harper stares at him in bewilderment.

"Do your job," Malcolm adds.

I've just heard my own death sentence, but Detective Harper is wavering. The gun is still aimed at me, but his arm is slack. He's shaking his head.

"The loose ends have been your fault," he says. "And I've tried to clean up your mess every time—when you killed the wrong person, when your guy was almost caught breaking into this house, when you killed an FBI agent—and now you're telling me to shoot him so that my guys can come here and find the body? How is that tying up a loose end? You think that I can somehow—?"

With a deftness I wouldn't have thought possible for a man of Malcolm's age, he snatches the gun from Detective Harper's hand. It happens so fast, I don't have time to worry that he might accidentally pull the trigger while it's pointed at me.

Detective Harper is in shock.

"Fine," Malcolm snarls and steps back over to me, confidently handling the gun. He presses the opening of the barrel against my forehead. "Last chance, Mr. Burcham. That drive is here, somewhere. I'm guessing it's in this room. Tell me where it is, and your wife and daughter will be free. This time, you really can save them."

My heart is working faster with the gun pressed against my head, but there's still a sense of calm. My goal hasn't changed. I still need to give Amy and the kids every single second I can to get away.

"Why would I believe a word you say?" I ask with a sneer. "And besides, you have nothing. My wife and daughter are gone. The police will be here soon. Shoot me if you have to because you have nothing left to threaten me with. You'll never find that drive. There's nothing left you can threaten me w—"

There are voices in the backyard.

Our heads turn as the back door opens and in walks Amy, Tatum, and Aiden with their hands up, followed by Henry Vaughn, who's pointing a gun at their backs.

Malcolm turns to me with a sinister grin.

"You were saying?"

Chapter 49

"They were trying to leave out the back," Vaughn informs Malcolm.

Amy looks at me, at the gun being pressed to my head, and mouths a simple message: *I'm sorry*.

"The police are on their way," Detective Harper tells Vaughn.

"How long?"

"Minutes."

Vaughn looks at Malcolm. "All right. That's it. We have to leave."

"Not without that hard drive," Malcolm says, once again giving me his undivided attention and nodding to the shattered remains of the picture frame behind me. "It was hidden in there. It has to be nearby." He presses the gun harder against my forehead. "And now, you're going to tell us."

I clamp my mouth shut.

Amy and the kids don't know where I've hidden it. They can't give it away. All I have to do is stay quiet. If he shoots me, he'll never find it before the cops arrive and by the growing tremor in his hand and the tightening of his lips, Malcolm knows it too, but the sight of the gun against my head is too much for Tatum.

"Dad!" she cries. "Just tell him!"

Amy tries to silence her but it's too late.

Malcolm is struck by an idea. He gets lower, right in my face. "A moment ago, you said that I didn't have anything to threaten you with. Now, I do." He quickly takes the gun away from my head, steps over to Tatum, grabs her hair, pulls it back, and puts the gun under her chin.

Tatum screams as he roughly pulls her in front of me.

I'm screaming too and lunge from my knees toward his feet. He easily sidesteps and kicks me in the head. He takes another step forward past me and turns with his back to the fireplace so that no one is behind him.

The floor tilts below me and I try to blink my vision back into focus.

Amy rushes at Malcolm, but Vaughn is too quick and slams his fist into her jaw. She crumples, but her momentum causes her to stagger past Malcolm. She collapses against the wall, falls to the floor next to the fireplace behind Malcolm, and lies still.

Tatum cries and shrieks as she tries to twist against Malcolm's grip.

My vision clears just as Aiden yells something and moves toward Malcolm, who shoves the gun harder under Tatum's chin. Vaughn aims his gun at Aiden.

"Get back!" he roars.

"Aiden, stay where you are!" I yell from my kneeling position on the floor.

Aiden and Detective Harper are to my right; Vaughn, Malcolm, Tatum, and a motionless Amy on my left.

"Goddammit! Enough!" Detective Harper cries out, holding out his hands. "This is totally fucked," he says, addressing Malcolm and Vaughn. "Now, I listened to you and the chief when this thing started, but you've screwed up every step of the way and now, you're holding a gun to a girl's head while my guys will be here any minute. There's no way to cover this up. No one can."

"Detective Harper," Vaughn says in a warning tone. "You've been told what has to happen. Your boss—"

The detective shakes his head. "No. No, I'm done. We can try to work something else out but let her go."

There's a long, interminable silence.

Vaughn looks back at Malcolm, who nods. Vaughn moves his aim from Aiden to Detective Harper and fires.

Detective Harper drops.

Tatum begins screaming again, but Malcolm moves his hand from her hair to cover her mouth.

"Quiet!"

Tatum is reduced to whimpering.

Malcolm glares at me while keeping his hand wrapped around Tatum's head and mouth, causing her to struggle for breath.

"You know what we're capable of, Mark. You and your family are nothing, but you can save your daughter. Just tell us where you hid the drive." His voice is shaking. Flecks of spittle fly from his lips. "This can all be over. No one else needs to get hurt. It's in this room, right? Just tell us—"

There's an ear-shattering blast and Vaughn's face disappears in a red mist as he's spun like a top and crashes to the floor.

Malcolm flinches.

For a split second, I worry that he'll pull the trigger.

Thankfully, he doesn't and instead, looks past me.

I glance over my shoulder.

Detective Harper is lying on the ground, holding the smoking revolver he's drawn from his ankle holster. His face is determined but it's clear that he's in agony. Protruding veins map his forehead. His eyes bulge. Aiming the gun at Malcolm is taking all the effort he has, but Tatum is in the way.

Malcolm is aiming his gun at the detective while using my daughter as a human shield.

Detective Harper coughs and blood erupts from his lips. He tries to keep the gun level, but it's as if it weighs a ton. Slowly, his arm sinks to the floor and his body relaxes.

His eyes remain open, but Detective Harper is gone.

Malcolm, more desperate than ever, puts the gun back under Tatum's chin.

"Tell me, Mark! Tell me right now where the drive is or I will kill her! I will shoot your daughter right here in front of you!"

Somewhere, amidst his screaming demands, I'm aware of a smell.

My momentary distraction enrages Malcolm even further. "You don't believe me? Fine! I'm going to count to three. If you don't tell me where that drive is, I'm going to kill your daughter."

He watches me, making sure I understand.

I know this smell. I know where it's coming from. I know what's happening and what I need to do. I'm going to take the hit. I don't care about that. I just need to keep Malcolm's focus on me.

"ONE!" Malcolm shouts.

Tatum squirms, desperately trying to breathe. "Dad!" she calls out, her scream muffled by his hand over her mouth.

"TWO!"

Click.

For a second, I panic and once again think he's pulled the trigger, but the click was too soft.

Click.

"Tatum," I say.

She stops squirming for a moment to look at me, as does Malcolm, who is so distracted by my words that he's forgotten about his countdown.

"Shut your eyes," I tell her.

Click.

Malcolm hears it that time. He looks around, searching for the source.

"Sweetheart," I say. "Shut your eyes, *now.*"

Malcolm turns to check the one place he hasn't: behind him.

Amy.

With an unsteady hand, she's holding the cheap, red lighter to the opening of the fireplace.

She's turned on the gas all the way open. It's been running for minutes and now, with the pilot light out and the damper closed, the living room is filled with fumes.

Malcolm roars, releases Tatum, and begins to pivot, bringing the gun to bear on Amy when—

Click.

There's a low, concussive thud and I'm blinded by a ball of fire.

Chapter 50

My lungs don't work.

My muscles and brain are fighting for air, but my chest is on fire, trying to expel oxygen that isn't there. My face feels like it's been plunged into a furnace.

It's made worse by the fact that I can't even hear myself wheezing over the high-pitched whine that's filling my ears.

The vice around my chest presses tighter. I can't scream. I can't call for help.

These have to be the last specks of consciousness before my brain descends into darkness.

Then, like a valve being opened, my chest expands and air floods in.

My body goes from not getting enough oxygen to trying to take in too much, and I'm wracked by gasps and coughs. The ringing in my ears subsides and I can hear screaming.

There's also a faint sound intermingled with the screams. Distant police sirens.

I open my eyes to stare up at the ceiling. The smell of burnt fabric fills my nostrils, but the room doesn't appear to be on fire. I roll over onto my side, still coughing and gagging.

Where's Tatum? Where's Amy? Where's Malcolm? Where's the gun?

I forget about my torture, pull myself into a sitting position, and look around.

Tatum.

She's sitting on the floor, a few feet away. Aiden is crouched next to her. They're both looking at something past me with wide eyes.

I quickly pivot and all my questions are answered.

Malcolm is lying on his back, trembling, holding up his hands with his palms out, and staring upwards as Amy stands over him, pointing the gun at his face.

The explosion must have sent Malcolm to the ground, causing him to drop the gun. Amy had to have recovered first and grabbed it. Her hand is shaking but her face is resolute. Strands of spittle hang from her lips as she takes deep, ragged breaths.

"Please," Malcolm begs, that feral animal of a moment ago nowhere to be found.

Amy's not listening.

Lying before her is the man who killed her sister and threatened her daughter. Malcolm is responsible for all of it.

In that moment, something about that image, of Amy standing over him, holding the gun in Malcolm's face, his fear of not being in control, the realization that he may have to suffer the consequences of his actions, that he can't buy, strong arm, or cajole his way out of this, causes me to see it.

There's a way out, a horrible way that this can all be over, but it requires one thing; Amy can't kill him. The only way through is to stop her before the police arrive.

"Amy?" My voice sounds a million miles away. "Amy, look at me."

Her breath is sliding in and out of her clenched teeth in wet hisses. The spittle drops from her lips and mixes with the tears of rage falling from her cheeks.

"You killed my sister," she says, giving no indication that she's aware of anyone else in the room besides Malcolm. "You killed Liz."

"I—I—I didn't kill her. It was Henry—"

"You told him to do it!" she explodes.

Amy's grip on the gun tightens.

Malcolm sees it and tries to sink further into the floor.

I have to stop her.

"Amy, please," I say as gently as I can. "You have to listen to me."

"Mom!" Tatum cries. "Stop!"

Amy doesn't hear her. She's in another world, a world populated only by rage and grief.

I turn to Tatum.

"Go outside."

She's still focused on Amy. "Mom, please!"

"Tatum!" I say as firmly as I'll allow myself for fear of startling Amy. "Go outside!"

Both Tatum and Aiden look at me.

If this all goes wrong, I can't let her see this. I can't let her see her mother shoot someone in the head.

"Now! Both of you!" I insist.

Tatum's eyes dart between Amy and me.

I look at Aiden and silently plead with him to get Tatum out of here.

He lightly takes her arm. "Come on. Let's go."

He gently pulls her to her feet and quickly guides her out of the living room, through the kitchen, down the hall, and out the front door toward the approaching sirens.

I turn back to Amy and Malcolm.

He's looking at me, begging for help.

Amy is still seething. The gun in her hand is shaking but it's so close to his face that if she pulls the trigger, it's over.

"Amy? . . . Please . . . Listen to me," I say as quietly but as urgently as possible. "Don't kill him."

"But he killed Liz," she says, still focused on Malcolm.

"I know."

"He tried to kill you," she says, her rage growing.

"I know."

"He was going to kill our dau—"

"Amy, I know. I know all of it, but if you kill him, Tatum and I will lose you . . . We can't go through that, again . . . I can't go through that, again, but listen to me . . . I have an idea."

Amy's breath catches. For the first time, she looks at me in shock and disbelief while still aiming the gun at Malcolm's face.

I keep my arm extended, my hand outstretched, asking for the gun. "Please, Amy. Don't kill him. You have to trust me."

The gun shakes even more. She's wavering, and slowly, that world of rage and vengeance shifts, and it's just her and me.

I raise myself up and step over to her.

"Amy, I thought I had lost you. He tried to make me think you had been unfaithful. The only thing that kept me going was our daughter, my belief in us, and the life we created together . . . Amy?" I hold her eyes with mine and tell her, "It was always you."

Amy stares at me. The tension flows from her and with a sigh of resignation, she hands me the gun. She takes a few steps away and begins sobbing.

I stare down at the gun. The grip is still warm from Amy's grasp.

The sirens are getting closer.

"Thank you," Malcolm whispers.

I stare past the gun to the floor to Malcolm, whose face is a mask of relief.

"What did you say?" I ask.

"I said thank you."

"For what?"

"For . . . for saving me."

"What makes you think I'm saving you?"

Amy's sobs stop.

Malcolm's relief vanishes as quickly as it appeared and is replaced by confusion, and then a slow, horrific understanding.

I aim the gun at Malcolm's terrified face.

I want him to know. I want him to understand what's about to happen.

"You killed my wife's sister because you thought it was her. You tried to make me believe that she was unfaithful. Then, you tried to kill me. You had a man's head blown off while I was sitting next to him." I crouch next to Malcolm to get closer while still keeping the gun trained on his forehead. "And you just held a gun to my daughter's head. You hid behind her while someone aimed a gun at you. You would have killed her. You would have killed all of us to save yourself. So why on God's green earth would I save you?"

"But—but you said that you said you had a plan," he stutters. "You said she couldn't kill me!"

"I do have a plan and that plan does not include sparing your life. If this doesn't work, I don't want it coming down on my wife. It will come down on me. So, believe me when I tell you this, I'm not saving you." I nod to Amy. "I'm trying to save her."

The sirens are right outside. There are the sounds of screeching tires and shouting voices.

I stand, keeping the gun aimed at Malcolm's forehead.

My hand is not shaking.

Doubt is a stranger.

I pull the trigger.

Chapter 51

There's an old analog clock on the wall, the kind that reminds me of high school. Its metronome-like ticking fills the small room where Amy and I are sitting, side by side, in uncomfortable, generic office chairs. We hold hands as we stare at the floor. Her cheek is swollen from where Vaughn hit her. My face feels tight from Malcolm's kick and staring down a fireball.

Malcolm's blood is still on my shirt.

The agent standing guard at the door asked me if I wanted a clean one.

"No," I replied.

I wasn't about to accept comfort from anyone who had played any part in putting my family in danger.

The confused agent nodded. "Okay. The boss will be here any moment," he said and resumed his silent vigil by the door.

It was chaos after I shot Malcolm.

The police and the FBI showed up almost simultaneously.

The first police officers to arrive were responding to the silent alarm and not part of the plot to cover up Amy's death. They had no problem getting out of the FBI's way when agents started flashing their badges. However, at some point, someone must have made a phone call, because more police showed up and began demanding that the FBI hand us over. Threats of contacting powerful people were made, and Amy, Tatum, Aiden, and I were suddenly whisked away in black cars by the FBI to their field office on Wilshire Boulevard in Westwood. The place was in full swing when we arrived. There were checkpoints to enter the parking garage and armed guards who kept a careful eye on us as we were guided through the lobby to the elevators.

"Is it always like this?" I asked one of the agents who was escorting us.

"Nope. You're a special occasion."

He took us up to a small room on the tenth floor. Aiden and Tatum were led away to be checked out by a doctor. Amy was hesitant for us to split up but I convinced her it was okay.

If the FBI doesn't go for this, I don't want her to know what actually happened.

So, here we sit, watching the floor, waiting for "the boss."

Finally, after losing count of the seconds being announced by the clock, the door opens and in strides a diminutive woman in her fifties.

"Sorry to keep you waiting," she says in a commanding voice I didn't think could come from such a small figure. "I was having a pissing contest with the mayor." She looks to the agent at the door. "That will be all, thank you."

The agent steps out into the hallway and closes the door behind him.

The woman leans back against the table and crosses her arms. "I'm Special Agent Donna Chesler . . . and you two have created one hell of a mess."

I cock my head at her. "I beg your pardon?"

"We needed Malcolm Davis alive."

"You have the records," Amy says.

"We needed his testimony. We needed to know who else was a part of this. We needed to make an example of him"—she turns to me—"and you blew his head off."

"He tried to kill my wife. He tried to kill me. He held a gun to my daughter's head."

"He wasn't holding a gun to her head at the time. You told us he was lying on the floor, defenseless."

I shrug. "I don't give a shit. You hold a gun to my daughter's head once and I'll make sure you never get the chance to do it again."

She scoffs. "Is that the defense you're going to use at your trial for murder?"

Amy's jaw nearly hits the floor. "You can't be serious."

"I most definitely am, and I'll ask you again, is that the defense you're going to use at your—?"

"It damn sure is," I answer without a hint of sarcasm. "And I can paint a pretty good picture of a father who was pushed over the edge, a father who thought his wife was murdered by someone she was having an affair with, a father who was shot at, a father who saw a gun pressed against his daughter's head, and don't forget, a father whose daughter was attacked by your agent in an attempt to get him to cooperate with your investigation not once, but twice."

She blinks.

"We—." She stops and starts again. "Agent Kingston was trying to keep one of the biggest cases of fraud this country has ever seen from falling apart—"

"Once again, I don't give a shit!" I repeat.

"—not to mention the fact that Agent Kingston is dead."

"So is my sister!" Amy yells.

Agent Chesler turns on her. "Because you decided to come up with your own plan to get the documents out of Fortis. He could have helped you."

"He threatened the safety of our daughter! I was never going to trust him," Amy fires back. "And he was so desperate for my husband to help him, he did it again."

Agent Chesler shakes her head. "This case is more than—"

"How many ways can we make it clear to you that we don't care about your case!" I rage. "All we care about is our family."

"And what am I supposed to do with you?" she asks. "There are dead cops. Dead agents. Without Malcolm Davis, you and your family are going to have to testify."

I shake my head. "Not a chance."

"I wasn't giving you an option."

"Fine. Then all of it comes out: the threats, the attack on my daughter by your agents. All of it."

Agent Chesler curses and stares down at the carpet.

"You see the problem here, don't you?" I ask. "You go through with this and suddenly Malcolm Davis, Fortis Capital, and corrupt cops aren't the only bad guys. The FBI will have a lot of questions to answer. It might even cost you your precious case . . ." I wait, letting it all sink in before adding, ". . . or this all can end with Malcolm Davis."

Agent Chesler makes no effort to hide her surprise, but it's brief and her eyes narrow. I can even feel Amy turn and look at me.

"What are you talking about?" Agent Chesler asks.

"You have the documents. You get your case. Fortis Capital goes down, as do the crooked cops. Agent Kingston can die a hero and my family is never mentioned . . . It can all end with Malcolm Davis."

Everything hinges on this moment. It's why I had to be the one to kill Malcolm. If this doesn't work out, Amy will be safe. She and Tatum are out, and my life will be all but over.

Ironically, I can live with that.

Agent Chesler crosses her arms, weighing the scales in her mind.

She takes a deep breath and looks up at us.

"I'm listening . . ."

Chapter 52

"Tatum Burcham."

Aiden, Amy, and I leap up from our seats, clapping and cheering as Tatum walks across the stage in her scarlet gown and cap with the gold tassel. I tuck my fingers into my lips and let out an ear-piercing whistle. Even from the back of the arena, I can see her shaking her head and smiling with embarrassment as she takes her diploma from the principal. She turns to us and waves as we continue to call her name, not stopping until she finally descends the steps.

We promised we wouldn't embarrass her, but I don't care. A few months ago, in the middle of everything, I wouldn't have thought this day was possible.

In the end, Agent Chesler agreed to my plan. The official story is that Malcolm knew that the FBI was closing in, that Fortis was about to collapse, that he was going to spend the rest of his life in a jail cell and took the cowardly way out by shooting himself. There was even a note. The events at our house were covered up and everything was laid at his feet.

Well, nearly everything.

Spencer and Nadine still had to play along, but that wasn't a problem. After all, if they opened their mouths about what really happened, they would be admitting that they were more heavily involved in Fortis's crimes, which would add years to the relatively light sentences they had received. There was no way to avoid all the blame.

That bothered Amy, but not nearly as much as what will happen to Liz as we move forward.

For now, Amy is still living as her sister. It's the only way this can work. There was a funeral. People we know were there. Amy has to stay dead for a little while longer. Now that Tatum has graduated, we're going to move far away. It was always the plan to move when she started college, but now, it makes even more sense after the tragedy we've gone through. Liz (really Amy) is going to move, too, for the same reasons. Then, after a few months of slowly losing contact with our friends in Los Angeles, Amy will gradually come back while Liz will fade into the ether. That won't be as tough as it sounds since the FBI informed us that there is no official record of Amy's death. There is no autopsy report. No toxicology results. Only a receipt for a very nice funeral. The FBI has assured us they'll smooth everything out as far as paperwork goes. In return, we never mention Agent Kingston's strong-arm tactics or the fact that he hurt Tatum and Aiden. As promised, he gets to die a hero.

It's maddening but the payoff is that our family is never brought up in the story of the sensational fall of Fortis Capital. It's still been a scandal for the police and the mayor. It's even made the national news, but Malcolm has remained the central, tragic, Shakespearean figure. And amidst the firestorm, we've been able to quietly slip away.

Other hedge funds and investment firms stepped in to cover the losses of the CPSRF. It was a public relations goldmine to come to the rescue of California's finest.

It isn't a perfect solution but it's not a perfect world.

Some nights, I'll wake up to the sound of Amy quietly crying about Liz. Other nights, she'll wake up to the sound of my panic attacks at the memory of killing a man, remembering the weight of the gun in my hand, the feeling of pulling the trigger, the kick, the expression on Malcolm's face at the realization that I was about to take his life.

Do I regret what I did? Absolutely not.

Everything I said to Malcolm was true. He had Liz killed, thinking it was Amy. He held a gun to Tatum's head. He would have had no problem killing everyone in my family if it meant he could escape responsibility. I did what I had to do. It was the right thing and I will never apologize for it.

That doesn't mean shooting him in the head didn't have an effect on me.

The one I really worried about was Tatum. I worried that she wouldn't be able to stay quiet about what really happened to us. I worried that she would look at me differently if she suspected or even knew that I killed Malcolm.

After the FBI agreed to my plan, Amy and I sat down with Tatum and Aiden and told them that we all had to play along. They said they understood. We told Tatum that she could talk to us about it, but it was as if she stuffed what really happened into a box, put it on a shelf in a back closet of her mind, locked the door, and threw away the key. To her, the official story became the true story. I really hope it hasn't damaged her psyche and it comes out in some future session with a therapist, but if it does, we'll deal with it. She'll get whatever help she needs but for the past few weeks, she's been getting ready for college.

This has been our life ever since that terrible night.

Amy has been living at Liz's place. I'll go over there sometimes in the guise of a grieving brother-in-law but more often, she'll come over to our place. It's almost like old times but there's a cloud in our home. I feel it every time I stand at the top of the stairs and remember the sensation of being pushed, or when I catch the faint smell of singed carpet from the fireball I took to the face, or when I stare at the spot on the floor where I shot Malcolm.

Tatum and Amy feel it, too. Everyone is eager to move on.

And this, Tatum's graduation, is the last milestone.

Amy, Aiden, and I return to our seats as Tatum walks back to hers among her fellow classmates.

Once everyone is settled, Aiden nervously leans over to Amy and me.

"Can I talk to you?" he asks.

Amy and I exchange a glance. I'm trying to act surprised.

"Sure," Amy says. "What's up?"

"Can we maybe go somewhere a little more private?"

"Yeah. Of course," I answer.

Amy and I have always secretly loved that due to our last name, Tatum's participation at school functions usually happens early in the program. It might appear rude to bolt right after Tatum received her diploma, but this is important. Well, I know it is. Amy, who is still posing as Liz when we're in public, has no idea.

The three of us rise and maneuver past the rest of the parents sitting in the row to the steps that will take us to the walkway under the stands. Once we're below, Aiden leads us away from the few people near the restrooms so that we can be alone. The names of students still echo through the corridor over the PA system.

"What's going on?" I ask as we come to a stop, still trying to sell, but not oversell, my faux confusion.

Aiden anxiously runs a hand through his hair. "Well, Mr. and Mrs. Burcham . . . I'm in love with your daughter. I have been for a long time and, uh . . ."

We both know it and he's done more than enough to prove it by going along with the plan, even keeping it from his parents and making up a story about getting in an accident while they were away to explain the damage to his Mustang.

It's odd seeing him like this, nervous and unsure, especially when I remember the first few months of our acquaintance. I try to give him an encouraging nod without Amy noticing.

266

"Aiden?" Amy asks.

Aiden reaches into his pocket and pulls out a small box. He opens it to reveal a gold ring studded with small diamonds.

"I want to ask Tatum to marry me and I'd like your blessing."

Amy gasps. I try to mimic her shock.

It's not as if Amy and I haven't talked about this possibility, but to have the moment finally here is something else. We're confident that Aiden loves her but there were issues that Amy and I discussed, which is why I once again try to give Aiden a covert nod to keep going.

"I know that—uh, I know that she's only seventeen and I'm only nineteen and that she's just graduating high school, which is why— Well, I want to ask her to marry me but we won't get married until after she graduates college."

I steal a sideways glance at Amy. I can see her shock lessen a little. That was one of the big obstacles we had talked about. We both wanted Tatum to graduate college before getting married and that's what I told Aiden when he secretly came to me a few weeks ago.

"And I'm going to be going to college, too," Aiden quickly adds.

Amy's eyebrows go up. "Really?"

"Yeah," Aiden says, sheepishly. "I'm going to start taking some business classes. I think I might want to start my own auto repair shop."

"Aiden, that's great!" Amy says.

"It really is," I add.

"So . . . do I have your blessing?" he asks, apprehensively.

Amy looks at me, tears starting to build.

"Honey?" I ask.

"Yes!" she says, clapping her hands. "Of course!"

She throws her arms around Aiden and clutches him tightly.

"Thank you, Mrs. Burcham," he says.

She squeezes once more and lets him go.

Aiden turns to me and holds out his hand. Even he's got

some tears going. Instead of shaking his hand, I pull him in for an embrace.

"Thank you, Mr. Burcham," he says quietly.

"Thank you, Aiden."

He pulls away and wipes his eyes with the back of his sleeve, clearly embarrassed.

Amy laughs and hugs him, again.

"Okay," he says, tucking the ring back into his pocket. "Okay. I was holding it in because I was nervous, but I really need to go to the bathroom."

We laugh as he heads toward the bathroom, leaving Amy and me alone.

"You did good," Amy says as we watch him walk away.

"What are you talking about?"

"Oh, come on. You told him to say those things."

"I have no idea what you mean."

"Mark, stop it," she admonishes with a light laugh.

I desperately want to kiss her right now but have to remember that to everyone here who knows us, she's Liz.

"So, when did he come to you to talk about all of this?"

"A few weeks ago," I answer, dropping the charade.

She shakes her head. "You should have told me."

I smile at her. "I can have secrets, too."

About an hour later, after the caps have been tossed and everyone filed out of the auditorium, we find Tatum with her friends gathered outside in the warm California afternoon.

We all hug and pose for photos as everyone passes around their phones.

Tatum turns to one of her friends and holds out her phone. "Meghan! Meghan, take our photo."

Meghan takes the phone while Tatum reaches for Amy and me.

I put up my hand. "Hold on. Let's get Aiden in here, too."

Tatum lights up.

She has gotten photos with Amy and me, and she's taken photos with Aiden this afternoon, but not all of us together. In fact, now that I think about it, I think this is our first photo together, ever.

Tatum quickly gestures to Aiden. "Come on! Get in here."

The four of us pose, arms around each other with Tatum in the middle.

"Thank you!" Tatum says, taking her phone back from Meghan.

Aiden looks at me and Amy.

Now, I mouth to him.

Aiden takes a breath. "Tatum?"

She turns to him.

Aiden lowers himself onto one knee and takes the box out of his pocket. He looks up at Tatum's stunned expression.

My hand finds Amy's at my side and our fingers entwine.

"Here we go," Amy quietly says.

I lean toward her and whisper, "Hey."

"Yeah?" she asks.

"It was always you."

A Letter from Steve Frech

Thank you so much for choosing to read *The Good Husband*. I hope you enjoyed it! If you did and would like to be the first to know about my new releases, please follow me on X and Instagram:

X: https://twitter.com/stevefrech

Instagram: @stevewritesstuff

I hope you loved *The Good Husband* and if you did, I would be so grateful if you would leave a review. I always love to hear what readers thought, and it helps new readers discover my books too.

Thanks,
Steve

Secrets to the Grave

The girl was lying face-down, the soles of her socks covered in fresh grass stains. Her wavy, chestnut hair fanned out across the pavement, as if across a pillow. She almost looked as if she was asleep . . .

When a teenage girl is found dead on a quiet suburban street, Detective Meredith Somerset is called to the scene. The victim is shoeless, the only clue to her identity a silver heart-shaped charm hidden in her grass-stained sock. Did she run from her killer across the smooth lawns of Willow Lane? And if so, how did no one in the surrounding houses see or hear a thing?

As Meredith investigates, she's haunted by flashbacks. Years ago her little sister disappeared in broad daylight, and no one saw a thing then either. It's the reason Meredith became a detective—to get the justice her sister never did—and she won't stop until she gets the truth.

Meredith needs answers. But Willow Lane has more than one mystery behind its doors—and to find the killer, she must venture into a community that's determined to take its secrets to the grave . . .

A nail-biting crime thriller with a shocking twist, perfect for fans of Kendra Elliot, Robert Dugoni and Lisa Regan.

Want You Dead

The backyard is full of balloons and streamers, and a piñata hangs from a tree branch, circling lazily in the breeze. But beneath the table of party food, a body lies half-covered by a brightly coloured tablecloth, blood seeping onto the floor . . .

A child's birthday party ends in chaos when one of the parents is found brutally beaten to death. With no way for anyone to leave unnoticed, it's clear the killer must be another guest, but with twenty high-spirited children as a distraction, anyone might have had the opportunity to slip away from the rest of the party.

Detective Meredith Somerset soon discovers the victim had no shortage of enemies, and everyone has a potential motive. Fractured marriages, jealousy and betrayals all come to light but Meredith can't seem to cut through the lies and find the truth.

When another party-goer disappears Meredith knows the clock is ticking before the killer strikes again. But when everyone has a motive, how can she be sure who was the one who struck the fatal blow? Who is innocent—and who is out for blood?

A gripping thriller you won't be able to put down, this is perfect for fans of Robert Dugoni, Rachel Caine and Melinda Leigh.

Acknowledgements

The more I do this, the more I believe that there should be more names on the cover than mine because this book doesn't happen without the contributions of a lot of people.

A huge thank you to my HQ family; the editors, the graphic designers, the marketing team, and especially Abigail Fenton and Audrey Linton for shaping this book every step of the way.

Thank you to my parents for letting me pick your brains regarding your almost fifty years of marriage.

And, as always, thank you, reader, for giving it a read. One of my favourite parts in this whole process is getting the chance to connect, hearing your thoughts, and hoping that you had just as much fun reading it as I had writing it.

Sincerely,

Steve

Dear Reader,

We hope you enjoyed reading this book. If you did, we'd be so appreciative if you left a review. It really helps us and the author to bring more books like this to you.

Here at HQ Digital we are dedicated to publishing fiction that will keep you turning the pages into the early hours. Don't want to miss a thing? To find out more about our books, promotions, discover exclusive content and enter competitions you can keep in touch in the following ways:

JOIN OUR COMMUNITY:
Sign up to our new email newsletter: http://smarturl.it/SignUpHQ
Read our new blog www.hqstories.co.uk

https://twitter.com/HQStories
www.facebook.com/HQStories

BUDDING WRITER?
We're also looking for authors to join the HQ Digital family!
Find out more here:

https://www.hqstories.co.uk/want-to-write-for-us/

Thanks for reading, from the HQ Digital team